Wrong Side of a Workingman

Wrong Side of a Workingman

Written and illustrated by
Justin DiPego

To, Mom.

My special thanks to: Jeni Brill, my wife and partner, whose limitless support helped lift me through both writing and production. Zoe Quinton, my editor, whose insight through the editorial process helped reveal to me the story I was telling. Rebecca Barnes, my book designer, whose fonts and formatting and design helped turn the pictures in my head into the book you are holding.

Contents

CONTENTS

TO HORSES
STONEHURST
TO WINE COUNTRY
HOME
THE COLLECTIVE
SYCAMORE TREE
FARMLAND
ENCINO
THE VALLEY'S EDGE
LA RIVER
SANTA MONICA MOUNTAINS
HOLLYWOOD
MT OLYMPUS
DOWNTOWN
THE TOWERS
BOTANICA
THE TEMPLE
SOUTH CENTRAL
QUEEN CALIFIA
VERNON
PACIFIC OCEAN
CITY OF LOS ANGELES

You see the world for what it is, and you know we are in trouble. Ills beyond the reach of bankers and cops, soldiers and presidents and even kings threaten the fabric of our lives. What we need is a hero.

Chapter 1
The Workingman is here.

He was in darkness. You couldn't see much of him if you were there. A gray rubber respirator cupped over his nose and mouth. His beard prevented it from forming a complete seal, but it worked well enough that all he could smell was his own breath. The only real source of light was his headlamp, causing the bright pink caps on the mask's air filters to create a fluorescent frame to his field of vision. Sweat glowed on the fit and muscular arms in front of him. They drug through rough fiberglass insulation, leaving tiny, pink tendrils to bore into his tattoos.

The space between the floor of the attic and the underside of the roof above was only about a foot and a half. Constellations of wicked points glinted above him in the light of the headlamp—roofing nails, holding the shingles and tarpaper to the other side of the plywood he crawled beneath. He balanced himself on ceiling joists and a narrow plank that ran across them. Pushing himself along the plank, his gloved hands patted on the two-by-six framing, kneepads thumping forward to the next joist, like carefully climbing a dirty ladder laid flat across the ground. He slid a small toolbox as far ahead of him as his arm would reach, scraping it along the plank. As he moved, his back rose up to bump the underside of the roof, creating a rhythmic pat-thump-pat-thump-bump-scrape, with the bass counterpoint of his breathing amplified by the mask. Each measure propelled him forward about sixteen inches.

Pat-Thump-Pat-Thump-Bump-Scrape. Reaching his goal, he settled in place and listened to his respirations for a moment, calculating his plan of attack. He cracked open his toolbox and selected a screwdriver. In the cramped space, the headlamp wouldn't shine directly on his task, so he aimed the light for a moment to get his bearings. Illuminating the top side of a light fixture, he set the screwdriver to the screw holding the cover onto the junction box and held his breath, because sometimes it's easier to work that way in the dark. To get the leverage he needed, he had to turn his head to use the tool and the headlamp shined uselessly into a corner.

POP! An arc of electricity lit the attic for an instant. A surge like hot carbonation jolted up his arm. He jumped and crashed hard into the roof. A roofing nail pierced his back. Muffled by the respirator, he cursed God.

Pulling the mask from his face he shouted at full volume, "I turned the breaker off!"

A voice—muted by insulation, distance and class—came from the floor below. "You still need it off?"

The smells of the attic attacked him: fiberglass, dust, rot, and rat urine. He'd been in attics in the best and worst neighborhoods, and they all smelled the same. Everybody has rats. The thought sometimes made him smile, but now he grit his teeth and made an effort to sound polite. "Yes!"

He lay frozen in the dark, waiting for a response. He couldn't work, couldn't quit, without one. He slipped the mask back on and inhaled deeply, trying to clear his sinuses and lungs of the ammonia. As if lying on the top rail of a fence, he let his arms and legs relax, easing his weight onto the plank. This piece of carpentry was a courtesy nailed in place by a framer decades ago. It served no structural purpose, but that carpenter-now-dead knew that a colleague-not-yet-born might have an easier time maneuvering and working in the confined quarters. The Workingman sank and closed his eyes. The enclosing heat was hypnotic. Without his task to perform, he could easily fall asleep. Sometimes, when the Santa Ana winds blew in hot from the desert, he relished the peace of his truck cab. In there it was even hotter, but the air was still and silent. Like a big cat dozing atop an acacia limb in the savanna sun, he let the still and silent heat soak him and unspool some of the chronic tension between his shoulder blades. The tips of the fingers tingled on his right hand, and he unconsciously performed a silent guitar solo, working blood back into the fizzing nerve endings. Finally, the voice returned.

"I think something shorted out. You have to look at it."

Equal portions of frustration and resignation surged through him like the electricity had.

He forced himself up a bit. He was not on the clock, but on the job. The more time this took, the less money he took home. As best he could, he looked over his shoulder, back the way he came. A thirty-foot crawl faced him. The trapdoor down from the attic glowed with light from below like a beacon. He began the awkward maneuver of turning around. Pat-Thump-Pat-Thump-Bump-Scrape.

Hours later, the Workingman was outside in the sun, breathing air as deeply as a thirsty kid drinks at a water fountain. It was a hot day, but a chill shivered his broad shoulders as the sweat evaporated from his blue work shirt. That shirt was streaked with dirt and dust, and tiny tears pocked the fabric. Nail holes.

On the back of the shirt, one of the little holes was stained with blood, but he had no idea. On the front, over the right pocket was his title, "Electric Man." Over the left pocket was his name, "Alex."

Alex walked to his pickup truck waiting in front of a large, old house in the upscale neighborhood of large, old houses. Everything on the block looked manicured but him. The black pickup also bore the "Electric Man" logo and also was not manicured. It was scratched and dented and had one side-view mirror held on by an artful web of plumber's tape, a repair Alex was secretly proud of. The driver's door screeched like a ten-year-old with a saxophone when he opened it to toss his clipboard of invoices on the seat.

Alex hefted a fiberglass ladder like it was made of paper and stretched black rubber straps around it, securing it to the cargo rack on the back of the truck. Muscles in his forearms flexed and rippled under his skin, making a jagged, heart-ish tattoo undulate like a raft in a boat wake.

A man who was not in bad shape but who couldn't help feeling fleshy in Alex's presence had come out of the house with a bottle of water in his hand. He watched Alex loading his gear. His name was something Martinez—it was on the work order Alex remembered—but he looked and sounded as Anglo as a man can.

Martinez watched his workman step back from the pickup and unconsciously rub at the perpetual

Alex hefted a fiberglass ladder like it was made of paper.

ache in his neck, making a hard apple out of his bicep. There was some kind of tattoo there too, but it was half-hidden by the shirt.

Martinez feared any chance he might appear gay, so he protected himself by saying, "My wife thought you'd want this for the road." Alex took the ice-cold bottle and held it to his neck as he thanked the man, who appeared to be sucking in his gut. As Alex turned toward the waiting truck, Martinez spoke up again. "Tough day. Couldn't use my computer for hours."

The Workingman turned back to Martinez. Martinez was indeed on a mission from his wife, and suddenly wondered if she found this olive-skinned, rugged man handsome. Alex nodded at him. "Well, it was on the same circuit. I guess that's why you turned it back on."

Martinez was unsure if this was an admonition or not. After all, Alex was just an electrician. Uncertain how to respond, Martinez settled on his personal catchphrase. "Who knew?" He added, "Sorry you had to go up there twice," and regretted it immediately. He held out something else to Alex. The water was from his wife, but this was an extra impulse. A folded bill. Alex froze for a second. If he couldn't identify the spirit behind them, he never liked tips. He took the bill.

On its way out of the neighborhood, the truck complained with an unhealthy whine, but warmed to its task and soon settled into a mostly smooth patter. After only a few turns, Alex drove out of the shaded, exclusive avenues and onto a San Fernando Valley boulevard, dusty with road grime, and tried not to take it personally as the truck pumped, "Baby, You Fucked Up" from three of its four speakers. With an appropriate distance between him and his client, he fished the bill out of his shirt pocket. One-handed, he unfolded it and discovered…five dollars. A sarcastic laugh burst out of him. He crumpled the bill and tossed it down in the passenger seat.

Playing with the bill made him realize he was still wearing his scuffed, fingerless work gloves. He pulled them off as he drove, bits of grit spilling out, and let the air conditioner play over his joints and between his fingers. His left hand was tattooed across the knuckles: "T-H-I-S." On his right: "T-H-A-T."

The water bottle rattled in a cup holder. Alex grabbed it, twisted the cap off its neck with a crack and took a long drink, draining it. Without looking, pretending he wasn't even doing it, he picked up the five bucks and slipped it back into his shirt pocket. Absently he rubbed his chin where the respirator had pressed into his beard.

That evening, Alex walked in the front door of an apartment decorated with a frugal mix of children's art, thrift store finds and framed posters purchased at local shows. He intentionally ignored his reflection in the glass over "Smell the Magic," and refused to make eye contact with either himself or Iggy Pop. He cradled a cheap grocery store bouquet of flowers in one hand. Even that had cost more than five dollars. He set the flowers on a table by the door, covering a stack of bills, every one of them past due. The simple act of coming home drained his energy. He sagged toward his couch, but the phone in his pocket buzzed at him. He checked the screen. It read, "Mom!"

Hovering his thumb over the virtual buttons, Alex felt the device vibrate again and again in his hand, almost in time with the throb in his neck. At the last possible moment, he sighed and accepted the call without sitting down.

"Hi, Mom."

Luna Cides, Alex's mother and self-described "tough cookie," swung at him with "You screened my call?"

"If I was screening," Alex slipped and jabbed, "I wouldn't have picked up."

"Usually, you don't," Luna shot back.

Instead of ducking, Alex absorbed that by just saying, "Uh-huh."

"When are you coming to fix my air conditioner?"

From where he stood, Alex could just see the mostly empty wall calendar hanging in the kitchen. "Not tomorrow. Work."

"Then what the hell am I going to do with all this lentil soup?"

"It's too hot for lentil soup. That's why I have to fix your A/C."

"I'll freeze it."

Alex tried to sound like an idea she'd love just came to him, setting up a combination. "Hey, why don't I call you back when the girls are here?" led it off. "They'd like to talk to their grandma" closed it.

But Luna absorbed the one-two and shot back an unexpected, "Don't call me a grandma."

"Well," Alex riposted, "all your friends are." He gave a second to see if she'd jab, but she was rocked back long enough for him to follow up with, "I really have to go, Mom."

She tried to sting him with "Go where?" but this round was his—and though no outsider could have heard it in her voice, they both knew it.

"Very funny," he finished her off. "Talk to you later."

Nothing really settled, they rang off. Alex lurched to the old couch and collapsed there. The cushions folded around him as he sank deeper than he should, but he was expecting that. He relaxed. His eyes closed. For a moment, he contemplated cutting some one-by planks to shore up the couch and keep it from sagging. Maybe some plywood.

He pushed yet another project aside and cautiously reached for the remote control on the arm of the couch. He took a deep breath, let it half out, aimed at the TV and pushed the power button. The TV whined on and flickered. Static. He changed channels. All static. Picturing the envelope from the cable company, pink paper showing through the address window, he wondered what else he'd expected. He turned off the TV.

For a moment, he sat doing nothing, but there was too much in his head and that throbbing pain arced in his neck. He felt the spasm coming but could do nothing to evade it. The frequent image of a bullfighter with no cape invaded his mind. The impotent toreador stood with his feet rooted in the hard sand and could only cringe in the face of the charging bull.

The nerve seized and the neck and shoulder contracted in opposition. His deltoid crushed up to his ear and Alex grit his teeth. As if hitting the button on a morphine drip, Alex flipped the TV back on. The white hiss flickered again and he watched the static like a camper looking into a fire. The fire held the bull temporarily at bay. Drawn into the manic waterfall of light and sound, his mind went gladly blank. He relaxed and let his head loll right up to, but not actually touching, the point of permanent pain.

The muscle that runs from the back of your jaw to the sternal extremity of your collarbone is called the sternocleidomastoid, because it connects the sternum, clavicle and jaw. On the right side of Alex's neck, it felt like a copper pipe under the skin. He massaged the aching muscle, but the source of the pain was a singularity deep in the shoulder, inaccessible to his strong fingers. Nerves radiated from the point like the sharp legs of a spider. Muscles swelled around the spot, as if a wound there needed pressure to control bleeding. Medical jargon is intentionally dense and technical, but in this case this process is plainly and so accurately called "inflammation." Of course, inflamed does not mean swollen; it means "on fire." The untouchable point of pain threw hot nerves and muscles into spasm around it. Alex—or his wife— chased the spasms with massage and heat and ice, and even a combination of amethyst, angelite, and black obsidian, without ever managing to crush the body of the spider.

White noise bathed the room to the point that it was almost silence. Exhaustion crept up on him. He relaxed as much as he could, repeatedly punched away from sleep by jolts that shot from the invisible wound up to his ear and down to his fingers. In time with the throbs, the bull feinted and charged, trying to trigger another spasm. But the hypnotic strobe of the television quelled the spike of pain in Alex's shoulder.

BANG! The front door swung open. The quiet exploded. Two girls ran through the door and bounded through the room, chased by a barking dog. The girls ignored their father, but the dog saw Alex and slid to a stop. It forgot the girls and sprung up on Alex's lap. Alex tried to greet the dog with the same enthusiasm it had for him, but he couldn't compete. After a second, Alex maxed out and gave up. As is too often true when you're a parent, his first words to his kids were not a greeting, but a command. "Girls, please entertain Yucky."

The thirteen-year-old had been experimenting with a stern adult voice, and she was glad for an opportunity to use it without getting in trouble. "Yucky, come!" Yucky—a black and white, mostly white border collie mix—ran to the girl.

"Thank you, Thea," droned Alex, turning off the TV. "Where's your mother?"

The girl announced simply that she didn't know and marched out of the room with the dog trotting after. Alex turned to his younger daughter, Niki, who was eight and thus still sweet, and asked her, "She doesn't know?"

Helpfully, Niki filled in for her sister. "Mom's down at the car. We went to the store."

But that sparked a new question from her father. "You left her with all the bags?"

"Yeah," she answered sweetly, and followed her sister out of the room.

A woman appeared in the open doorway. Dara was pretty in the hardened way of a country girl who escaped to the city. Though it made her roll her eyes, Alex couldn't help admiring her figure and telling her so. Somehow, the country girl met a city boy, a Greek one at that, and she knew he was the one. She had once—and only once—been grudgingly described by Alex's mother as "also a tough cookie." Obviously, she was the source of the kids' redheaded good looks.

She spied her husband on the couch over an armful of bags. "Don't get up," she said without sarcasm, but Alex rose from his seat and took the bags from his wife.

"I'm up," he said. She tried to protest, but he told her he didn't understand what she was saying and took the bags into the kitchen. Though she hated doing it, she assessed her husband. He was maybe the most levelheaded man she ever met. In fact, that's what drew her eye to him on the night they met. The club exploded into an impromptu mosh pit, as happens every time "Party at Ground Zero" is played live. A first-wave punk who must have been sixty was knocked off his feet as he surged with the scrum. An imposing figure, big but not tall, olive-skinned and inked, appeared out of the crowd. He reached into the pit and yoiked the man off the ground before his old knees hit the concrete. With one strong arm, he'd hefted the man back to his feet and turned them both back into the flow without missing a beat. As the two skanked and slammed, Dara caught flashes of the love/anarchy tattoo on the muscular forearm. Before the song was over, she went and bought a twelve-dollar club beer and floated a lime in it, ready to hand to him when he came off the floor.

Now she looked at that same tattoo on that muscular arm wrapped around their groceries and hoped his level head would stay that way. She didn't know exactly when it had started, but the piercing, debilitating pain she could do nothing to help was crushing him. And that crush wasn't just in his muscles and nerves. His heart and head were hurting, and flares of temper fired unexpectedly from places that had once been safe. That's when she noticed the flowers. That meant he'd had a bad day, but he was handling it like old Alex. With pleasure and relief, she asked, "Are these for me?"

"Oh. Yeah," he said dismissively. Sometimes, he was embarrassed by the romance in his Mediterranean blood. Alex started putting groceries away. Dara came into the kitchen with the flowers, and gave him a little kiss as she hunted for a vase. She looked her tired husband over and smiled.

"There's blood on your back," she said.

"Is there?" He tried to look, but of course could not.

"Take your shirt off."

Dutifully, Alex unbuttoned his dirty shirt and pulled it off. Work had made his chest and back strong and well-muscled. And there were more tattoos. The one on the inside of his right arm was of

Atlas. Instead of straining to hold up a globe, he was poised to support the weight of Alex's bicep.

Dara looked at Alex's little wound. "Right in the eye," she said. Alex's broad back was covered from shoulders to belt with the intricately inked, ferocious face of a roaring lion, like an image from an ancient amphora. A roofing nail had stabbed a puncture in the lion's eye. Taking off the shirt had opened the scab. The lion wept blood.

"Right in the eye," she said.

Chapter 2

The Workingman walks a narrow path between getting by and getting nothing.

In a room that was once a walk-in closet, Dara glazed over the spreadsheet on her display. With a sigh, she swiveled to take in the view. Behind a half-open sash, acres of vineyard rolled through California hills under a blue sky studded with puffs of cloud. Of course, there was no actual window in her closet office. Alex built her the window box out of a discarded casing at a renovation site, lit the inside with dimmable LEDs, and even wired in a little fan to stir the gauzy curtains with a gentle breeze. The only expensive part of the build had been printing the large format image from a photo Dara had taken of what was once her father's ranch.

The subtle, sweet smell of silage washed over her, and she saw her younger self dashing through those hills, stomach burning from underripe grapes.

"You get that delivery away?" Morton leaned into her office with no preamble and popped her reverie with patriarchal energy.

"I did," Dara confirmed. "I was thinking…"

"Uh oh," kidded the manager, as if he were a favorite uncle.

"Ha. No." She restarted. "We could attract some higher-end clients if we highlight where we fit into the winemaking process."

"No one cares where cream of tartar comes from," Morton explained.

"Maybe not in the pantry. But in cosmetics. Women…"

"I know. Ladies like their wine. We've been doing this for decades without bragging we're in the wine business."

"Maybe. But wine, sustainability, people think differently now…"

"Not that differently. Things don't change overnight," expounded the older man.

Without looking out the window, Dara pictured the rolling hills. Her father, a rough, hard-drinking cowboy, had switched from cattle to grapes over a single season when California wine became a thing.

Morton put his friendly manager hat back on. "You want to write up a proposal? Do that. I'll have the wife look it over."

Dara smiled at the man. "Thanks, Morton."

"Good work," he winked as he disappeared from her doorway.

Fixating on the empty space, Dara pictured a different man. She'd loved her father, but as soon as she'd been able, she ran away to find her mother in San Fernando. That did not go well, but she'd never really gone back. At this moment, she regretted it. This little, windowless room wasn't helping. It was supposed to be a stopgap, a stepping stone to her larger world.

Two years ago, a cordless drill and charger had been stolen out of Alex's truck at a job site. Of course he'd been upset, but that same day he bought a replacement without wondering if the card would clear. Now, his calendar was empty, her extra income wasn't extra, and they were shedding necessities as if dumping ballast to keep a hot air balloon afloat. Dara swiveled back to face the odorless breeze.

The client had gray hair and blue eyes and wore a blue denim shirt that matched his hair and eyes. Though he was English, he'd lived in this nicer part of the San Fernando Valley for twenty-five years. But not in this house. This house was his step up—an old home with a quaint exterior and a full acre of land, and he'd had the interior gutted and rebuilt.

Now it was modern, clean angular and white white. It matched his hair and eyes. He sat in his breakfast nook, listening to "O Lucky Man!" and eating the egg his wife had scrambled for him before she left for work.

With a terrible crash, a hole blasted through the ceiling above him. The client jumped back from his ruined egg and stared at the foot jammed through the hole. From the attic, he heard Alex's muffled voice: "Fuck!"

The tidy office wasn't quite small enough to touch all four walls while standing in one spot. The desk was organized according to the five points for executive success. At ten o'clock and two o'clock were a small plant and a family photo. The productive space was clearly sectioned off for computer work and non-computer work. Nothing that wasn't actually in use cluttered the surface. There was no cup of pens and scissors. All of that was hidden in drawers except for a single ballpoint in a stand, ready in case a guest needed it in a meeting. The pen bore the company logo and phone number. Sometimes there was a cup of green tea, but today it was a glass of lemon water and a small bowl of keto-friendly candies that looked and tasted like M&Ms. There was no clock. Don't push yourself into overwhelm by regularly checking the time. With such a system, productivity can double or even triple overnight.

Behind the desk sat a youngish man with clean hands and big ideas. He ran The Collective, which handled the advertising, booking, and billing for electricians like Alex "Electric Man" Cides and handymen like Mark "Handyman Mark" Conchelos. If you called Mark's number, or Alex's, Sam's phone rang. He took a percentage from the workingmen, and they didn't have to worry about business—which they weren't good at—but Sam was.

He wore a suit and tie every day, but he hung the jacket on a wooden stand when he was at his desk, because he was getting down to work. On the wall behind the desk hung a framed inspirational poster with a photo of a charging bull. The caption read: "Bull headed, and that's no Bull." Sam liked it because whoever faced him at his desk also stood in the path of the bull's charge.

He thought of this as the head office, although it was still his only one. Someday, he'd have branches on the Westside and Hollywood, maybe the South Bay too. Today though, he had to deal with Alex.

From his in-box he drew an email he'd printed out especially so Alex could see he wasn't responsible for the number he read off. "Three hundred and seventy-five dollars."

Alex stopped pacing to take the offered work order. "That's ridiculous. The hole isn't two feet across."

Patiently, Sam explained that it was a quote from the client's contractor. Still, Alex protested. "Well, I'll fix it. I can do drywall. It'll cost fifty bucks." He let the estimate flutter back down to the desk.

Sam put the page into his out-box and explained again that they wanted their own contractor to do the work. This conversation was already taking longer than Sam had intended it to. "Is it up to them?" Alex wanted to know. And that was a good question. Technically, it was Alex's responsibility to repair the damage to the ceiling, and if they wanted to go elsewhere for the work, they had to pay the additional cost. Sam knew this, and thought Alex might know it too. Which meant he could no longer avoid the real problem.

"Alex, they don't want you back in their house."

Alex was clearly shocked. "What? I did the work. I did a good job. Anyone can have a stupid accident like that."

"It's not the accident." Sam wanted to be finished with this line. He was ready to move on to new business, but Alex prodded him.

"So?"

Frustrated, Sam decided to let the man have it. "It's you, Alex. They said you were dirty. And you... you smell."

"I smell?" Alex was suddenly livid. "It's a hundred and twenty degrees in that attic. I was in there for two hours. I smell?!" Alex began to pace again.

Sam knew it was unfair, but what could he do? "I'm sorry," he said in a tone he felt conveyed comradery. To really cement his connection with this fellow workingman, he decided to give Alex a break. "I can just add it into the advance."

Alex did not appreciate the gesture. "You're taking it out of my money?"

This was exactly why The Collective existed. Some people just weren't up for the rules of finance and business administration. It seemed so simple to Sam, but he knew he must make allowances for the men who had to go into the trades. So he explained, "It was your mistake." He paused just long enough to illustrate the distinction. "Not a Collective mistake."

"I work for The Collective!"

Sam knew Alex wasn't a Mexican but couldn't put a finger on what he was. The man was pacing and gesturing like an Italian. Sam had to talk the man down, so he reminded him "You're an independent contractor."

But Alex wouldn't listen. "So, I get no benefits and no support from you?"

Now Sam knew he was on firm footing. "I gave you that advance." Alex stopped pacing. His feet were planted. His hands hung at his sides. He faced the desk squarely. His eyes fixed on Sam's. Sam finally felt he was getting somewhere.

But Alex did not thank him. "Because you haven't been booking me."

Sam smiled a partner smile, and though he didn't mean to, he whined a bit. Somewhere in the reptile portion of his brain, an alarm was going off. "It's tough here for me too."

"It's tough?" Alex seethed. "The A/C is tough? The leather chair is tough?!"

Another conciliatory smile from Sam would settle everything, he was sure. "Alex…"

But Alex didn't explode. He explained. "You see this collar, Sam?" He grabbed his own work shirt. "It's blue! You see this one?!" He reached out and pinched Sam's white collar. "It's…"

Sam saw that big hand coming. He couldn't tell you what he actually thought was happening. The hand was going for his throat? It would gouge out his eyes? Although it was wrong now, Sam finally listened to his reptile brain. He flinched back hard in his chair and barked out, "You're fired!"

Alex was stunned. "Fired?"

Still speaking from his recoiled position at the back of his chair, Sam answered, "That's assault."

After the unfairness of the clients in the white white house, the months and months of spotty bookings, the insult of the cash advance, and now the inability of this stupid coward to understand a simple analogy, Alex's fury boiled over. He cocked back his powerful fist. Sam cringed. Alex fired off the punch.

"That's assault!"

Alex's fist blasted through the air conditioner in the window. The faceplate collapsed in on itself, folding around his knuckles like a Japanese fan. Next door, people jumped at the crash. The machine whined and bled water into the office.

Alex pulled his fist from the wreck and held it up for Sam to see. Tiny, terrifying cuts started to bleed as Sam watched, marring the T-H-A-T tattooed across the knuckles. Alex read the tattoo aloud for him. "That's assault!"

He straightened himself up and didn't look down at the man in the chair. He marched out of the office and did not slam the door behind him. The outside air ruffled and turned the papers on Sam's desk. The in-box mingled with the out-box and obscured the family photo. Sam was frozen as he watched the work order drift to the floor.

The bleeding fist gripped the steering wheel hard as the truck whisked Alex down the freeway. Wind buzzed through the bad gasket in the closed passenger side window, ladders squeaked in their rack, and tools rattled. Cars moved around him in the lanes, some slower, some faster. He saw and heard only enough of this to keep from getting killed. A talk station droned on the radio.

"So, you are a voodoo priest?" asked the interviewer. This was going to be a puff, life-in-the-big-city kind of piece, so he had a chuckle in his voice. The second voice was rich and deep, had a Mexican accent and no chuckle.

"Not voodoo," he answered. "I don't know about voodoo, but I know that in your church, if you have a problem, you get a generic answer. There is a list of answers, and you get the one they think suits you best."

The interviewer was both leading and dismissive. "That's not what you do?"

"I am a righter of wrongs. If I could, I would do this for everyone. If you come to me, we consult with God," the priest said plainly. "He does not care who you are or where you come from. He does not have a list of answers. He gives an answer to you."

"And you sacrifice a chicken." The interviewer tried to come back around to the funny headline of the story, but the other man resisted.

"Sometimes it is necessary." Now he was dismissive. "Don't be distracted by that. The universe demands balance. When you are out of balance, sacrifices must be made. Work must be done to get back to your proper place, so you can move forward. If you are stuck, if you are cursed, the balance tips against you."

Alex drove on.

On his front door he found a note flapping. He pulled it down and read it as he opened the door. With an excited use of all caps and bold words, it announced: "PAST DUE NOTICE. PAY RENT IN FULL AMOUNT PLUS $75 PENALTY."

C H A P T E R 3

When one door closes, another opens. But what if that door leads to a pit from which you cannot climb?

For an apartment this size, the master bathroom was pretty big. There was room in the built-in vanity for his and hers sinks in front of the mirror, though there was only one sink now. Alex often thought of how easy it would be to drop in a second sink or redo the whole counter out of something interesting like sealed hardwood.

Doggedly he planned the remodel to distract himself from the day, which was hard to forget because his right hand was aching and slightly swollen. Leave the cabinets and tear out the counter and sink. That would take less than a day. With the kind of construction in this place, he could do it in a few minutes with no tools, if he didn't care about breaking anything. Maybe gang up a bunch of two-

30

by-fours on the flat to make the new counter. It would look like a pier or the deck of a ship. Maybe that was too nautical. Something else. He'd do it if they owned.

Dara cleaned and bandaged his damaged hand over that single sink. Officially unschooled in such things, she'd been around enough for Alex to trust her opinion when she said she didn't think it was broken.

"What difference does it make?" he asked. "I didn't even hit him. Assault, my ass."

Dara agreed and even nodded, but she knew that griping about how right you are won't help you learn anything. Instead, what she said was, "I can't believe you didn't see this coming." Alex looked at her in the mirror with flaring eyes. She soothed him with her tone, but continued speaking. "He's hardly booked you in months. Are the other guys hurting for work?"

Alex shrugged. "I don't know. Sure," he said. "Everybody's hurting."

She agreed with that too. But there was something else going on. Not something he was keeping from her, but something that might not have gotten through to him as he focused on just doing the work. She had to try and understand. Help him understand. He was a good man and good at his job. So why was he now out of that job? If they couldn't figure that out, then even if a new job was easy to come by—which it would not be—would he be able to keep it? She prompted him. "But is he booking them over you?"

The answer Alex gave shocked her. "Maybe they smell better."

Dara's anger simmered up. "He said you smell?"

Her man smelled of hard work and olive oil, of welding slag and electricity and wood, of the lavender soap he secretly liked, of earned sweat and laboring in other people's homes, but he never stank. He was not dirty or low.

Alex felt the heat come off her and fed on it. "I stink, I'm broke, I can't pay the rent or even keep the cable on so my girls can watch TV." He was rolling, building. "Now, this goddamn Collective that's supposed to make my life easier fires me, because I smell bad!"

Dara wanted to rail with him, to curse Sam and every goddamned snob who never worked with their hands and the fucking corporate middle-managers who gladly let the CEOs piss on labor. She wanted to, but she needed to bring them back to plan-making mode. Though she tempered her anger, the best she could manage was, "Why doesn't he like you?"

But Alex was beyond that. "I don't know!" It was nearly a roar.

Dara's power to quell this man was becoming overmatched. She tried, "Well, maybe you can call him, and..."

This time, it was a roar. "Call him?!" Alex raged, losing it. "I assaulted him!" He lashed out and threw a punch. His fist crashed into his own reflected face in the mirror. The glass buckled and fractured. A spiderweb of cracks lightninged across the mirror, but it didn't collapse. Dara jumped back, shocked and scared. There was a scream. It wasn't Dara.

Thea and Niki stood in the bathroom door. Thea's eyes were wide, shocked. Niki began to cry. "Mommy, he hit you!"

Dara whirled on them, her eyes bright with anger. "No he did not!" The girls shrank from her. Instantly, she was horrified by herself, and she snapped out of it. She knelt in front of their daughters, gathering her wits.

"I'm sorry," she began. "He didn't hit me. He's never done that. This is a very hard day. It's been a bad year. Okay?" She waited for them to nod their heads. "Thea, take Niki to your room."

Thea was paralyzed for a moment. Dara gazed into her eyes. Woman to woman. Thea nodded again and led her crying sister away.

Dara turned back to her husband and rose up. "Jesus, Alex."

Alex hadn't moved since his punch rebounded off the glass. He was frozen with his arm cocked for another blow, but his fist unclenched. He held his breath, embarrassed and afraid. "I'm sorry. My temper."

"Got you fired."

Alex couldn't argue with her. He was lost. He felt like a sick man with no diagnosis. His shoulder throbbed as if stabbed by an invisible railroad spike, the muscles sucking shut around the wound. The weight of it crushed him a bit, making him stand shorter.

"Which came first, Dara? The temper, or the money problems?"

She sighed, reassuring, "The problems."

And that was the truth. He had always been passionate, even volatile. In the early days, it took her a long time to get used to. She learned to identify the difference between yelling and yelling. They had laughed once when he said, "If you think that's yelling, you've never had a friendly dinner with my mother." He had been loud and fiery, or simply Greek, as he called it, but he didn't have a violent temper. He didn't use to. This was different, and her heart raced.

"You'll get another job," she said, calming him further. "Tomorrow."

Alex's shoulders dropped and his abdomen relaxed. He let the counter take up some of his weight and leaned on his wife. He nodded, looking into the sink. There were flecks of his blood in it. If the planned sink were redwood, he might cut himself while he made it, and the stain would last for a hundred years. Dara pulled him back.

"You need a haircut," she said.

Alex tried to look at himself in the mirror but could not. "I do?"

Simply and with authority, she said, "Yes."

So Alex sat in a chair from the dinner table in front of the broken mirror. Dara stood behind him with a pair of electric clippers, trimming his hair. She gathered most of the clippings before they hit the floor. Alex gave himself over to the gentle hands that manipulated his head this way or that for a better angle. He closed his eyes. The humming and buzzing droned into a sustained riff that cleared his mind.

Dara set the clippers aside and massaged his shoulders. Her hands were strong, and the heat of his flesh felt good to her cool palms. She kneaded the muscles and felt the strength there that lifted her off the ground. That strength carried her and Thea and Niki. That strength brought flowers home from a hot, sweaty day at work and touched her with such care and love that she could weep. Alex groaned, "Damn neck," and broke the spell.

Dara stepped back and started the shower. "You get in the shower," she told him. "Relax."

Alex got up to do as he was told. He held up his bandaged hand, making it a question.

"Take it off. It was just to make you feel better."

He smiled at her and asked, "You joining me?"

She smiled back, but said, "No." Starting for the door, she said, "I'm gonna talk to the girls. But I'll get you a beer."

Steam rose around him. The spray splashing down on his head was as hot as he could take it, each scalding drop the tap of a finger that thrummed his flesh to flushed enervation. Streamers roiled over his ears and cascaded across his shoulders, back and chest. The flowing water made hot pools in the pits above his collar bones and the creases between his groin and thighs.

He sat at the base of the narrow shaft, his feet braced against one fiberglass wall and his back against the other, his knees tucked up to make a steeple he could rest his head on. He didn't feel cramped. He felt embraced. The wet heat enwrapped him and eased him. The slick walls flexed and gave a bit against his pressure, holding him that much tighter. The hot moisture breathed into him, making his blood rush. His heart pounded and the pulse waved through his entire length, relaxing and contracting in time.

The day coursed away from him as Alex thought how Dara was right about everything. In slow motion he lifted his hand to his mouth, removing his thumb at the last second from the lip of the bottle. Shocking coolness ran through him as he swallowed a sip of the beer she had spiked with a slice of lime. Effervescence

Shocking coolness ran through him as he swallowed a
sip of the beer Dara had spiked with a slice of lime.

spread through him, delivering thoughts of her to every part of his body. She was the best thing about him. She brought him the girls, and together they made him the man he wanted to be.

Alex stayed inside her shower until the bottle was empty and the water just started to turn cold. He emerged and dried himself in the steamy bathroom. Wrapping the towel around his waist, he opened the door to let balloons of steam escape into the bedroom and called out, "Hey, I needed that." There was no answer.

The bedroom was empty. Tightening the towel, Alex stepped into the strangely quiet hall. "Dara?" He called his daughters in turn and got no answer from them either. "Where are my ladies?"

When he found himself in the living room, he started to worry. The silence gored into him. "Yucky?" he called. If the dog had been there, he would have heard a tiny tremble of despair in his master's voice, but the dog wasn't there.

There was a handwritten note hanging on the inside of the front door. He could have read it from where he stood. Instead, he walked to it and took it down so he could feel the weight of the page in his hand.

Written in black marker on the back of the late notice:

Alex,
The temper didn't come first, but it's here. It scares
me. I'm taking the girls away. Don't look for us. I'll
call. We love you,
Dara
P.S. Niki wouldn't leave without Yucky.

It weighed more than anything Alex ever lifted.

He lasted three days. On the third day, Alex shuffled his way through the aisles to the electrical department. His new orange apron weighed on him like a backpack full of boulders, but he would make the best of this, dammit. He was starting at zero, but that's what he'd do if he had to. He told himself it was because of the work. The work dried up, then the money ran thin, then came the temper and the pain. And so, work must be the answer. He'd prove it and Dara would see. Dara would come back with the girls, and they would be stronger for it. But that would be then. First, he had to start at zero. And this was zero. His shift started at midday, so most of the pros had already picked up their tools and materials and the store was filling up with DIYers.

On the way to his area, he stumbled upon a young woman, maybe ten years older than Thea. She was wearing grease monkey coveralls with the sleeves cut off and the legs cut into shorts. Her hair was teal and she had one Doc Martin poised on the lowest shelf. She froze when she saw him.

"Can I help you?" he asked dutifully, trying not to sound like a parent catching a child red-handed.

"I need a box of floor flanges, but the only one is up on the third shelf."

They both looked up at the box, enticingly out of reach. They both knew what she needed.

"This isn't my department," Alex offered, "but I can page someone to come with one of those step ladders." He looked pointedly at her boot, poised on the sturdy shelf. "Or I can go. I'll go and find someone who can help you."

"Thank you," she said performatively, as if she intended to wait.

Alex nodded, turned his back, and left the aisle.

Still making his way to Electrical, he found it a bit less of a trudge because of this positive customer service experience. But now he was in Hardware and Fasteners, overhearing his supervisor pronounce with supercilious smugness, "Um, I think you mean wing nuts."

The confused customer answered, "But I'm sure they said T-nuts."

Alex sighed and sagged, not wanting to get involved. His supervisor was about the same age as the grease monkey, but he was sure she would know the difference between a wing nut and a T-nut. He walked on, the continuing conversation between customer and supervisor pulling on him like elastic. He forced himself past its tug. But as he cleared the mouth of the aisle, he caught the hard corner of another conversation.

"Well, obviously. That's what I need you for." Alex couldn't ignore that voice. He peeked into the adjacent corridor of looming shelves and then didn't retreat fast enough. "Oh. My. God. You work here?"

"Hi, Mom," Alex said, ready to throw in the towel.

"This man won't help me with the air conditioners," she informed. The accused stood sheepishly in his tidy blue polo.

"He doesn't work here. He's a rep."

"I was trying to tell her…" started the rep. Alex let him know it was okay and that he would take it from here. The rep didn't linger a second longer than he had to.

This place, the empty apartment, the stack of bills, that note. That Note. And now this. The spike augered into his nerves, spiraling flesh and muscle and temper. Alex turned on Luna.

"You don't need a new A/C."

"You never came to fix it, and it's covered with ice," she riposted.

Alex was trying. "You're right. I never came. I'm sorry."

"Oh, you're sorry?"

He let the sarcasm slip past him and tried not to jab too hard. "But it's because your A/C isn't broken."

"It's…"

"No, it's not!" he reflexively snapped. "It ices up because you turn the cold all the way up and the fan all the way down."

"The fan is too loud, and I don't like it blowing on me."

"I know. But it doesn't matter what you like. If you set it that way, it can't circulate the cold air, and it freezes."

"Then it's broken."

"No, it's not!"

And now the supervisor appeared. "Hey, Alex," he said as if to a dog, "you want me to help this lady?"

"My air conditioner is covered with ice," said Luna to the nice young man.

"Sounds like you need a new one," he smiled.

"She does not need a new one!" He did not quite rage at his supervisor.

"Alex, if it's icing up, it's not working properly," explained the supervisor, trying to de-escalate.

"Thank you," Luna responded with satisfaction.

But that was too much. "Him? You believe him?!" The rage spurted around the edges of his spike like hot blood. "He doesn't even know what a fucking T-nut is!"

"I don't know what a T-nut is," Luna defended the supervisor.

"You don't work here!"

"Alex," the supervisor warned, "if you continue to talk to talk to customers that way, you won't work here either."

"Jesus Christ! Stop using my name every time. Did you learn that in some junior manager seminar?"

Sternly, the supervisor put his foot down. "Alex, I'm going to have to fire you."

"You can't fire me, you little shit. You have to go find Brenda so she can fire me before I kill you!"

"Your prison tats don't scare me, Alex," lied the supervisor, trying to stand his ground.

Luna flared, "Prison tats?!" She advanced on the supervisor. "My son was never in prison!" The supervisor gave ground, his eyes going wide. "But he will kill you if you don't go find Brenda!" The supervisor fled, taking his first steps backward so as not to be attacked from behind. "Little shit!"

Everyone in the store jumped as Alex roared, "FUCK!" Everyone but Luna.

"Oh, you're too good for this place," Luna mollified her son, ready to go on with her day.

It was a hot day. Alex sat in his truck, parked past an orange line in the lot that kept employee vehicles away from the store. The windows were up and he sweated in the still heat. The envelope holding his final check—for two and a half days' work—grew damp in his hand, but he couldn't set it down. In his mind, it wasn't the check he was holding at all. It was That Note. That Note. He'd failed again. He felt the weight of That Note in one hand growing heavier, as Dara slipped away from the other hand, growing lighter. That other hand held his phone, the screen open to her contact page. But he wouldn't press the call button and violate her further. As the terrible balance shifted around him, something he'd heard right here in this seat came back to him. Something he'd heard, but not listened to. Something about balance.

Miles away, colorfully painted three- and four-story brick buildings lined the block of a very old LA neighborhood. Murals decorated almost every appropriate wall, some of them by artists who were once famous. Graffiti marred a few of them, but not as many as you'd think.

Los Angeles was a city before Spain lost its hold on Mexico, and the forty-four founders of the pueblo brought their Mestizo, Mulatto, Indio, Negro, Criollo, and Peninsularo languages and names to the territory. Whatever region of the city you're in now, from Los Feliz to San Pedro, the streets and neighborhoods may have Spanish names—though you should pronounce them like a local, not like a Spaniard.

In this particular neighborhood, not only were the street signs in Spanish, but the store signs too. The ones that weren't were in Korean. Only the No Parking signs were in English.

As they always had, people walked here. A stooped old woman with bags in a wheeled basket trundled the broken sidewalk, navigating around the other pedestrians. Some were headed to work, some to shop, and some merely loitered with nowhere to go. There were sleepers on the concrete here and there, and a small number of hunters who moved only their eyes, looking for a fix or for something they could steal with the smallest amount of effort.

Barely taller than the handle on her cart, the old woman took in every passerby, assessing how badly they might hurt her and how likely they would try. Still, even among the most rangy and hungry-eyed loafers, she felt unthreatened. She had buried two husbands, one of them literally, and seen a war ebb and flow around her. When the black beater pickup with ladders in the back jammed to a halt nearby and squeezed into in a space too small for it, she didn't even flinch. But when the driver's door screeched like an owl, and the serious-faced man who stepped down turned out to be white, she quickened her pace.

The man slammed the truck's door behind him. The old woman was surprised to see him walk with determination into the small shop with a red, white and green sign painted on the window that spelled out "BOTANICA."

A phalanx of votive candles guarded the door, flanked on one side by a spinning rack of cheerful greeting cards and on the other by a statuette three-quarters the size of a man. Dressed in the robes of a cardinal or a pope, his vestments practically vibrated in livid parakeet green with white trim and sparkling gold filigree. The saint's neck ended in a crimson stump. Painted blood ran down the front of the flowing casula. In its hands it held a silver tray bearing its own severed head. The eyes gazed piously to heaven, and the miter sat perfectly on the brow, pristine white. Gore gouted from the remnant of the throat, filling the tray and brimming over its lip. Sculpted drops of blood hung frozen in the act of spilling over the side to spatter the skirts of the cassock.

Alex paused at the feet of the statue, reconsidering. When he decided to proceed deeper into the store, the soles of his shoes audibly crackled where they had bonded to something sticky on the floor. "Probably just an old pool of blood," Alex dismissed.

The air grew thicker with frankincense and cinnamon and cardamom, as Alex waded through chest-high shelves displaying zip-topped bags of herbs, multicolored rosaries, wooden, clay and crystal cups, and a catalog's worth of items Alex couldn't hope to identify. He stopped at a dead end and retraced his steps to pick a different path through the confusion of displays. There was either faint music playing, or a ringing in his ears.

Finally, the labyrinth relented, and he saw the clear passage to the counter at the back. Behind the counter, a skinny old man stood on a stool to reach a high shelf. His hair was thick and rich and black, his skin the color of tobacco. Skinny arms like twine of knotted hemp ended in big hands with long, deft fingers. An overgrown and apparently forgotten mustache hid his mouth but displayed expressions of its own. He ignored his customer, busy with a terracotta bowl shaped like a pregnant woman lying on her back. Concave instead of convex, her deep belly was filled with a vegetal concoction. The man sniffed it and announced in a rich, deep, Mexican accent, "Two more days. Three? Needs to ferment." He replaced the bowl on the shelf and said "Now," as he turned to his customer.

When he saw Alex he almost dropped from his perch. "Oh my God!" he blurted. He hurried down from the stool and around the counter.

Alex looked into the eyes—which were darker than his own—and spoke cautiously. "I heard you on the radio."

"Good," said the priest emphatically.

Alex hadn't known who to call. He'd tried to do it alone, but with That Note in his hands, everything started to spin. If he fell, there was no one to catch him. If she was right to leave—and she was right to leave—he couldn't go complain to a buddy. He couldn't call his mother. He had no workmates. No siblings. He wished he had a sister so he could get drunk and call her and she'd be the only one he'd show his pain. If only he were an alcoholic, he could worry about none of this, not even losing his family. He'd go home to the bottle, and so what if he never made it right? But he was not an alcoholic, and making things right was his job. Then he remembered the resonant voice on the radio, and desperately grabbed at that lifeline.

The priest asked seriously, "Is it too late?"

"For what?"

The man looked at him with gravity. "Have you killed a man?"

Alex wasn't sure about coming here in the first place. Now he was sure he'd made a mistake. He answered anyway. "No."

"Come here," the man said, almost parentally. "Oh, it hurts very much."

Alex did not come, but he did ask, "How can you tell?"

The man was not kidding when he said, "You're the first Anglo to come to my Botanica in seven years." He squinted at Alex, as if trying to focus. "What is your name?"

"Alex. Alex Cides."

The man seemed pleased. "That is a Greek name."

"Yes, it is," Alex said, a little surprised the old man knew that. "So?" he challenged.

"When the Greeks came to their gods," the man instructed, "they brought offerings. Sacrifices in exchange for their help."

"You're not a god."

"I am an oracle," said the man. The matter-of-fact magic in his tone, in his eyes, drew Alex in. "What have you brought me?"

Alex told the truth. "I have nothing."

The thick mustache curled up in a smile. "That is what you think." The old man said, "My name is Baba. I think I've been waiting for you. Come into the back." And without waiting for Alex, Baba disappeared through a curtained door at the back of the shop. Already having come this far, Alex decided to follow.

The entire back room was an altar and shrine. Candles lit the space. The air was close and still. The smells were even stronger. A funk of sweet and pungent spice rasped in Alex's nostrils and at the back of his throat. He blinked the sting from his eyes. Primary, secondary and tertiary colors kaleidoscoped in his tears, then coalesced into figurines of saints and gods and demigods standing on every surface and in every nook. A tabletop covered in white linen stood against one wall, crowded with twelve stemmed glasses filled with water. Framed photographs fought for space with small painted images, a glass pitcher filled with flowers, a crystal skull, and another skull that may or may not have been from an actual person. A baldachin canopy of carved teak stood above it all, framing a large, livid crucifix hung high on the wall. Alex looked up at the bleeding Christ and said, "I never go to church."

"Of course not." Baba understood. "You don't think about such things."

"No," agreed Alex. "But now"—speaking the next words aloud was almost too much of an admission—"I'm...out of balance."

Baba turned on Alex and eyed him seriously. "Sit down."

Standing this close to the edge, Alex suddenly felt like a fool, and he was ready to go. "Look..."

"I have bad news. Sit." Baba's intensity stopped him. Wary, Alex sat in a chair by the altar. Baba was solemn. "There is a curse on you."

The altar, the smoke and candles, the old man's earnest eyes and terrible words all worked fear into Alex. He almost sounded like a child when he said, "A curse?"

Baba squinted at him again. "I can see it like a spike in your neck." That hit Alex like a slap. Inside his head, the grating sound of cast iron pans smashing together jarred through his nerves. His shoulder jumped in a tiny, painful tick. Automatically, his hand reached for the sore spot deep in his muscle. Baba nodded, "Right."

Why? The question was not a woeful, *why me,* but a confused, *who would bother?* Alex voiced his objection. "I'm just… nobody."

"Maybe. Maybe you are not." Baba assessed Alex's tired eyes. "How do you sleep with that pain in you?"

"Sleep? I barely remember it."

"No sleep, no balance."

Alex fixed Baba with a questing look. "The pain. It came before the money problems."

Baba knew already. "Before the wife problems. The temper."

Alex was struck again. He tried to hide it in order to maintain some distance, but his voice cracked when he said, "Yes."

"It's been a bad year." Baba was not sympathetic, just observing.

So Alex reported, "Very."

Baba leaned in close—Alex could smell the fennel, parsley and thyme on his breath—and said, "It isn't over."

Alex felt his temper mount. Not over?

He surprised Baba by breaking the tie and accepting his fate. "Great. Okay. I'm gonna go now." Alex rose and headed for the door.

Baba threw a new line out. "This is not your neighborhood."

Alex stopped. "No, it isn't."

"You drove a long way to get here."

"I get it. It's a metaphor."

"Yes and no," Baba conceded. "You are worried that everything I've told you is too spiritual, too fantastic. Too hippy-dippy."

"Well, yeah."

Baba assessed the man before him, choosing his next sally with tactical care. "Years ago, two scientists with a giant antenna heard a hiss that should not be there. They repaired their equipment, checked their settings. They even chased all the pigeons off the tower."

"So, this is the metaphor?"

Baba wouldn't let Alex slow the progress of the story. "The hiss wouldn't go away. It came from all directions. If they were detecting something real, what was it?" He paused just long enough for Alex to wonder. "It was the ripples at the very edge of the pond. A stone thrown in the middle made waves that dissipated, but did not disappear. The blast of the Big Bang created a shockwave that propelled the universe into existence. Over eons, the shockwave reverberated smaller and smaller, but it did not go away. It didn't even become invisible. It became the hiss and static you hear and see when your TV is tuned to no station at all."

Again, Alex was struck by Baba hitting so close. This time it wasn't a hard slap, but a slow, icy tingling that spread from the smallest part of his brain to the tips of his fingers and made his face feel hot. "My TV?"

"It's all how you look at things. It doesn't matter if you call it spirituality or call it God or call it science. It's the universe."

Alex was frozen, motionless with wonder, but looking back he'd tell you he had nodded knowingly.

"You watch it like a camper watches a campfire. And the universe speaks to you."

"What does it say?" Alex hadn't meant to whisper.

Baba knew he had Alex now. He drew him in further. "You can lift this curse." Acrid magic leaked out of Baba like cigarette smoke. Alex tried to ignore it, but the magic was too strong.

Defeated, Alex sighed and asked, "How?"

Gently, Baba prodded. "Who has done this to you?"

Alex was perplexed. "It's not...the gods?"

"No," answered Baba, in the tone of someone teasing out "now you're warm, now you're cold" clues.

"You know, but you won't tell me?"

Baba rushed to his own defense. "No, no. That's not what I said. I will help you find out. But are you ready?"

Impatient and desperate, Alex blurted, "Just tell me."

"I can't," Baba apologized. "You have to sacrifice."

Alex's frustration mounted. "I told you. I don't have anything."

"You have a strong back," Baba corrected. "You have arms and hands. You have a tradesman's wit."

"A what?"
"You are a workingman."
"You're damn right," Alex bristled.
Baba smiled again. "Work for me."

Baba smiled again. "Work for me."

Chapter 4

He's accepted the offer that will change his life, but will holding up his end get him killed?

There's a cool stillness on certain Southland early mornings that tells you the summer afternoon will be murderously hot. On such a day, it's best to do what you need to do as close to dawn as you can.

Scrub oaks and mustard greens and sagebrush grew in the dry dirt. The smells of fennel and castor bean mixed to a bittersweet perfume. A hawk circled above a brushy, dry hillside, the morning dew having lingered only seconds after the sunrise. There wasn't a cloud in this sky, so blue it was almost white. It might have been a thousand years ago, or ten years, or yesterday.

Jogging shoes churned up dust and dry leaves. A torn and bloody running suit barely hung on to the pumping limbs. A man—once a jogger, but now a fleeing, terrified animal—crashed through the high brush as hard and fast as he could. His face and body were streaked with blood. In his terror, he was almost blind. He didn't even have a name anymore, only a goal. Escape. He stumbled and splayed into the hard earth, skidding downhill. His right thumb jammed into the ground and broke at the first joint. The palm of his other hand abraded open and one knee split a second gash as his chin bounced off the game trail. He scrambled to his feet, unaware of his new wounds.

He bashed forward through clawing branches like a bull in full panic, not daring to slow. In a messy, desperate sprint, the bull crashed into something as firm as a wall and bounced back. He landed sitting in the dirt. The jolt was so sudden it snapped him back to human consciousness. He looked up to see what he had hit. A bearded man with broad shoulders and determined eyes loomed over the jogger, looking up the hillside.

The jogger spoke aloud the sentence that was repeating in his head. "He's got her!"

The bearded man scanned the hillside. "Where?"

Adrenaline shook the jogger all over. He thought he pointed back the way he came, but he didn't move. "Up there. I tried to pull her away."

Focused on the brush and trees, the man still didn't look at him, but the firmness of his voice was a rock to hide behind. "It's okay."

"He did this to me," the jogger explained. "I ran."

But the man was already walking away, up where the jogger had come from. He spoke over his shoulder as the jogger tried to get to his feet. "Never run."

Alex followed a clear path through the brush. Broken branches and smears of blood all pointed out the path the jogger had torn through the hillside. It was not easy going. In places the slope was so steep he sometimes came up through the underside of a scrub oak, grabbing its short trunk at the base to haul himself forward through its branches. He wondered what he was doing here, if he was ready for this, if he was crazy. Something caught his eye in the chaotic chaparral up ahead. He decided that he was here for Dara. That he was crazy, but that he was also ready. Standing out as unnatural for its straight lines and regular angles, discarded and half-concealed in a bush of poison oak, there was a bright blue mountain bike. Alex quickened his pace.

The scrub opened up and Alex stepped onto a narrow trail. Up ahead, a shape moved that was not being pushed by the slight breeze. A big shape. Alex rounded a stand of mustard flowers. Suddenly, blood was everywhere. It dripped from branches and made the ground muddy. In the midst of the carnage was a woman.

She was dressed in a tight, biking outfit, colorful for her safety. Her clothes and flesh were torn. Her eyes were wide with a terrible mix of horror and submission. She was alive.

A tawny mass squatted over her legs. It saw Alex and rose up, unstartled. The mountain lion held the woman's calf in its fangs. With its eyes fixed on Alex, in a gesture that said, "You mean nothing to me," the lion jerked its head to one side. The calf muscle tore free.

The woman shivered. She felt only a tug. She was so deeply in shock she could not move or even scream.

The big cat looked the intruder in the eye with its fiercest gaze. It knew it couldn't be challenged. Coyotes, bobcats, dogs, and men: they always backed down. The cat's brain, shrunken and damaged by hunger and rodenticides, could not fathom an enemy that wouldn't flee, that wasn't food.

Alex had been thinking about how to do this. About what his first move would be. About his options. He forgot all that now.

In the clearing of chaparral, Alex was free of his greatest fear. His seething temper hadn't physically hurt anyone yet, but his daughters had seen it, and his wife was gone because of it. The more he fought to suppress it, the greater the pain that pulsed in his cursed neck. And the greater his pain, the closer to the surface of his throbbing flesh the explosion of temper pushed. Soon, the eruption would catch Dara in its wash.

In his mind's eye, that splintering mirror echoed like thunder, and a flying shard snicked her under the eye. A single drop of blood ran down her face like a tear. It hadn't happened. He knew it hadn't. But fear and memory combined, and now that was the only way he could recall the moment. It could so easily have happened. And if he could not change, then inevitability said it would happen. He would lose everything, if he hadn't already.

But here, with acres of wild ground to buffer his rage, he could turn his temper like a turret and let it fire without fear. Deep inside his shoulder, muscles knotted around the embattled nerve. But Dara's eye, weeping blood, gazed red on him. Under its watch, like the Trinity detonation at Alamogordo, Alex exploded the pain into rage.

Filling his chest and rising up to his full height, Alex took a deep breath. A deep, guttural rumble filled the air. It could have been the lion or Alex. In the same instant, they both sprang.

With an audible crash, man and beast came together. With dagger teeth, the lion went for Alex's throat. Alex fought in the only way he knew. He fired a powerful fist into the cat's ribs. The lion had never experienced a blow like that. It was staggered.

Alex followed up with an uppercut that snapped the lion's head back. He shot his knee into the lion's gut. If he were fighting a man, this battle would be over.

The lion was not a man. It refocused on the intruder with more caution but no less ferocity. A paw that weighed as much as a baseball bat swiped at Alex's neck. Alex ducked, but not enough. Claws tore into his ear and jaw.

The force of the blow drove him down. The cat was on him. It opened its mouth wide and dove at Alex's throat, sucking wind as it came. Alex possessed a huge strength, but if he had a real gift, it was this: he was lucid. When a ladder started to slip, or an old brick wall gave way, or a bully came at him with a bottle in a bar, he could see it coming, make decisions, and act on them. Grab the vine from the trellis and lash the ladder down. Overturn the wheelbarrow and take cover. Ignore the bottle and hit first and hard.

Alex reached up and shoved his hand in the lion's mouth. The lion was shocked. With his hand deep enough to avoid the fangs, Alex held the lion's lower jaw open.

The lion thrashed. Alex held tight, folding the lion's own lip over the back teeth, pinning the mandible back against its chest. Confused, the lion backed away, trying to close its mouth. It keened a high and terrible roar. Alex got his feet back under him.

Now he was above the cat. If he let up an ounce of pressure on that jaw, the cat would kill him. With all his strength, Alex kept its head low to the ground.

*Alex kept his chest against its spine and got his free
arm around the cat's bristling neck. He squeezed.*

The lion's chin jammed back and saliva boiled over the teeth, making Alex's eyes water. Enraged, the lion snapped its head back and forth, but Alex would not let go. He wrenched himself around without losing his grip and got behind the animal. The lion reared up, trying to spin on its enemy.

Alex kept his chest against its spine and got his free arm around the cat's bristling neck. He squeezed. The lion felt fear explode through its blood. It knew. All thoughts left its brain but "kill" and "escape."

Alex's muscles strained against the thrashing. With all his strength, he tightened his grip like a vice on the animal's throat. "Kill" faded away from the lion's mind. Only "escape" remained. The lion struggled and weakened. Its eyes stared out at the sky. Instinct told it this was the end. It stopped. Alex didn't stop. The cat went limp. Still, Alex didn't stop.

There was a popping, crushing sound. All the tension bled away.

For the first time, Alex noticed how rough the cat's hide was. He had thought it would be smoother. Alex released his grip. The lion collapsed to the ground, dead.

Alex stood over the now-empty body and did not crow in victory.

With the body of the lion draped across his shoulders in a fireman's carry, Alex broke through the brush, taking an easier path down than he had on the way up. The day was growing hot, and he sweated under his burden. The pelt stabbed through his shirt and flesh, pricking up red welts and making him sting. As he came out onto a paved road, he was making a mental list of the wounds his opponent had delivered. He almost didn't see his truck waiting at the asphalt curb. As gently as he could, he lowered the body into the bed.

Sirens screamed. A paramedic, an ambulance and a squad car raced up past him, responding to an anonymous call for help. As they faded out, Alex's truck made a U-turn to take him out of the hills. Something huge towered above the hillside: the HOLLYWOOD sign.

Baba had cleared off a large space on the altar in the back room. Surrounded by candles, a dish of mezcal at its lips, the lion lay in a place of honor. It bore the scars of clashes that began the day it was born, all of them healed badges of its victories, of its survival. It was unmarred by any visible, fresh wounds. In death, it rested pristine and regal, as if waiting for its next encounter.

Alex stood staring at the lion. A thousand tiny wounds pocked his own flesh. Streaks of reddening sweat caked a fine film of mud on his skin and clothes. He'd vomited out the open door of his truck as the pickup idled patiently, letting him gather his wits. Before he drove here to the Botanica, he'd had to let his eyes unblur from the sweat, the lion spit, and the tears. And the blood. Three deep gashes and one shallow one clawed from his right ear to his jaw and down to his neck. The shallow one missed his eye by an eighth of an inch; the deepest one missed his pulsing jugular by even less. Blood crusted on the side of his head and stiffened his filthy, torn work shirt. So much adrenaline ebbed from his body, you could smell it. His hands were barely shaking now, but exhaustion crept in. Baba looked on, approvingly.

Alex quavered, but he was relieved. It didn't all make sense, but he understood the concept of balance, of a life for a life. A curse might be ridiculous, and he'd never tell Dara about it, but a curse was also comforting, because it was something you could fix. And he'd done it.

"He was right where you said he'd be," Alex said.

Baba was a little wistful. "I wish I could have seen it."

"Couldn't you?"

"It's not the same." Baba looked over the body with reverence. "King of the jungle."

"Of the beasts," Alex corrected.

"Eh?"

"Not the jungle."

"Well, the king is dead. Long live the king."

"What?"

"It's a saying."

Alex shook his head, testing how he felt about all this. "I've never killed anything before."

"Of course you have," Baba insisted.

"No, I..."

"We all have. You've set a mouse trap. Swatted a fly. Walked on the grass. Death is everywhere in life." Baba relented a bit. "You feel bad about it."

Alex faltered, "I saw what he did to that mountain biker."

"And before this," Baba told him, "he killed a hiker. He had the taste. There would have been more."

"I know. Doesn't seem fair though. He was here first. There aren't a lot of them left. And that mountain was his turf."

"The universe cares about balance," Baba instructed, "not fairness. Not even justice."

Alex wasn't interested in philosophy. "Well, if that's what I had to do to get balanced..."

Baba scoffed, surprised. "You? You are not balanced."

Alex protested, "But you said..."

"You have work to do."

"Work? I just did the work! I saved that woman. I put it all out there. Risked my life. Turned myself completely loose. I don't know...I used my temper for good! How is that not balance?"

"How is your neck?"

Alex felt his wounds. "Cut up. I don't think it's as bad as it looks."

But Baba scoffed again. "No, stupid. Your neck. Your spike."

Alex sank a bit. The old ache stabbed deep in his shoulder. "Still there."

Baba tried to be patient. He wanted Alex to understand. "You have nine more tasks to perform."

"Nine?! This one almost got me killed."

"Then don't do them." Baba threw up his big hands. "Go back to your life as it is. Go! I have to take care of him." Baba turned to the lion.

Alex pointed to his torn ear and bloody face. "What about this?"

Baba dismissed him. "I'm a witch doctor, not a doctor doctor. Go get stitches."

Baba was done with Alex. Frustrated, Alex turned and headed out.

In lieu of sleep, Alex sat on the sagging couch. Bandages tugged at his ear and the side of his face. He tried to forget another day. A strange day. A disturbing day.

He barely remembered the terrified jogger. But the cyclist, the prey—her blank eyes, beyond panic, not even pleading for help—she would never leave his brain, just as surely as he would never appear in hers. She did not lose the memories of the worst day of her life; she had never formed them. If Alex had known that, he'd have envied her. And the golden eyes of the lion, devoid of hate, deep with ancient soul, guilty only of being a lion and shut forever by his hand—those eyes would stare at him forever. Not accusing, but judging.

He played but did not listen to the voicemail on his phone. "Thank you so much, Mr. Cides. We reviewed your application and really think you're overqualified for the position. I'm sorry this isn't a great fit, but no doubt you'll find someone who can use you to your full potential."

He pulled a bottle from the fridge. Dara had pushed the cork back in after drinking only one glass. He carried the cold Roussanne back to the living room, stopping in his tracks midway as he tried and failed to fill a bistro glass and walk at the same time.

Alex drank his wine and watched TV. No channels were available to him, but he found what he was looking for. Alex watched the echoes of the universe's labor pains and for a moment, forgot.

There was a knock on the door. Alex started and jumped to his feet.

"Dara?" He rushed to the door and opened it. No one there. Another note was pinned to the door. Its bold heading read: "OFFICIAL NOTICE TO PAY RENT OR QUIT."

Cold and poisonous as a jellyfish, the note made his fingers tingle. The toxin spread from the page through his hands. He felt it wash up his arms and hit his heart. From there it exploded through his body. His knees sagged. His feet ached. The back of his head heated, and his face was like ice. The spike drilled deeper into his flesh.

He couldn't read it. The letters in the notice, the bold and the small print, were a jumble of angry voices shouting over each other. The din mashed itself into the roar of a single word. FAIL.

Fail to keep your home. Fail to keep your family. Fail to make it right.

Make it right.

Alex knew he was out of balance, because he almost crumbled to the floor.

Make it right.

There was only one way. He did not throw the note, or even drop it. He just let it go because he knew what he had to do.

Make it right.

He picked up the phone.

"Baba?"

Temptation drapes itself in the path of the Workingman. How far will he go to find his balance?

The trunk of a sycamore tree is slick and branchless and as big around as a trash barrel. The rough bark flakes off in sheets, exposing smooth skin that is almost white. It is not a climbing tree because there's nothing to grab on to 'til you're ten or twenty feet off the ground.

Alex got lucky. This tree canted at just enough of an angle for him to shimmy up the trunk. Clinging like a child to his mother's leg, he finally ascended into the lower branches and fuzzy, hand-shaped leaves. He had his tool belt on, and it tugged against the trunk, slowing him like a drag anchor. Swearing to himself, he forced his body higher.

He had no fear of heights, but no phobia is necessary when you're so high off the ground that a slip could kill you. People die falling ten feet, or even three feet. The breeze up here would have been pleasant on this already hot morning, if Alex had not been on another bizarre errand for Baba. If he died doing this one, the headline would be nowhere near as good as: Workingman Mauled to Death by Mountain Lion. Imagining his daughters keeping clippings of his weird and pathetic obituary, he gripped a limb as thick as a beer can and heaved himself forward.

The limb was dead. It shattered into chopsticks, eaten through by gall wasps. Tiny insects swarmed through his knuckles. Alex lurched around the trunk, spinning with the force of gravity and the inertia he'd delivered when he pulled at the branch.

His whole body became a hand. Chest, belly, and forehead gripped the tree. The slap his palms made on opposite sides of the trunk was audible in the breakfast nook of the house the tree stood in front of. Desperately, his thighs flexed and squeezed, astride the barrel.

He froze like that, moving only his eyes. Thirty feet of air and then the sidewalk. His eyes darted away from the drop and back to the task. The broken branch left a stub he could grab. It was too short to break. With the will of a statue forcing itself to life, Alex reached for the stub. He dragged himself up. His weight evenly distributed, he climbed to the next level.

A thicket of narrow branches guarded his goal like a rampart. Alex moved in slow motion to ease his way through and maintain his balance. There it was. A messy spiral of twigs the size and shape of a half-inflated volleyball. Alex propped himself up to look down into the nest. Three eggs.

Now it was time for the egg carton, tucked into his tool belt and torn in half to make it easier to handle. He needed two hands for this part. He balanced, using his knees and the top of his head to wedge himself between the branches and the trunk. Gingerly, he took two eggs from the nest and left one behind. The eggs went into the carton. They were smaller than chicken eggs by about half, so they rattled in the thick-walled paper cups. There was a scream.

Something bright emerald darted at Alex's face. Alex ducked. The sharp, green fist shrieked again and dove at his head. It razored a new line into Alex's scalp. Alex shouted back at it, "I know! I know! I left you one!"

As fast as he could, Alex put the carton in his belt and scrambled down the tree. He wasn't being stealthy now. Branches crashed and splintered. All the way down the parrot swooped and dove at Alex. He slipped and almost fell each time he steadied the carton with the hard-got eggs. Gravity was on his side now, as he slid by inches down the giant fire pole. Another parrot joined the attack, then a third and a fourth and more.

By the time Alex was on the ground, a swarm of green and red and yellow screeching birds opposed him. They pecked at his head and clawed at his flesh. Under the bandages, blood sprang from his stitches with the pounding of his heart. With his feet on the earth, Alex sprinted down the sidewalk of this otherwise quiet residential street. The birds chased him all the way to his truck.

Alex creaked the door open and jumped inside. He slammed the door behind him. Furious parrots flapped at the window. The golden eye of the sun gazed down on him in castigation. Compared to yesterday, he did not cut a heroic figure. "Never run," Alex chided himself.

"Never run."

Baba carefully transferred the parrot eggs to a terra cotta bowl lined with straw. Alex watched him, trying to figure out the rules of this new life. "That better not be for your breakfast."

Baba sought out a special jar on the shelf without even looking at Alex. "Parrot eggs can be a valuable tool."

Alex knew something about tools. "Whatever you say."

With the jar in one hand and the bowl of eggs in the other, Baba turned and addressed Alex like a professor. "Thirty years ago, the parrots escaped from a pet store. Now, there are flocks all over the city. The fresher the eggs, the better."

"Are all these jobs gonna be about animals?"

Baba ignored him. "These will be pickled. You know, parrots are called the dragon bird in some parts of the world. The dragon is a conduit between this world and the next."

Alex was clearly focused on this world. "Those birds chased me all the way to the freeway."

Baba nodded. He had indeed heard Alex's last question. "You will be happy about your next task."

Alex was not generally happy about tasks. They came up, and he did them. That was his job. "Sure I will," he said.

"A girdle," Baba said, seriously.

Alex was serious too. "Do I have to wear it?"

"No," Baba announced, "only steal it."

Montana Avenue in Santa Monica is about a ten-block strip of upscale eateries, boutique clothing stores and gourmet markets. On either side of the strip is street after street of homes. Montana stands as a crease of retail, hidden from outsiders, serving the mostly wealthy residents of the area. Their spiritual needs are tended to here as well. There are yoga studios, a progressive church, a Reform synagogue, and a Zen garden.

At this time of night, only dim, enticing glows illuminated the storefronts. Alex's truck parked in front of a corner property where a high wall surrounded an open patio on three sides. There were lights in the second story windows.

Alex got down from the pickup and inspected the etched brass sign on the glass door. It read: "Temple of the Goddess Most High, Inc."

This close to the ocean, the air was almost cool, and Alex was comfortable without the aid of A/C or fans for the first time in weeks. He was the only one on the sidewalk. He smirked at the sign, wondering where the hell his life had gotten to. He tried the door. Locked. He peered through the window.

An orderly and spacious version of Baba's shop, the dark store was filled with Babylonian-style statuettes, crystals, books, potions, tinctures, concoctions, decoctions, lubes, lotions, and women's clothes. At the back of the store was a staircase, leading up.

Alex backed away from the storefront and moved to the wall, which was laden with manicured ivy. The top of the wall was almost even with the sill of a second story window. Alex looked from the wall to the window, to his truck. A plan was forming, but the edges of it were fuzzy.

Upstairs, shimmering, tone-on-tone satins—hand culled from the garment district—adorned the walls in alternating falls of warm golds and burgundies and saffrons. They undulated as the Santa Ana breeze meandered through the rooms and blew through doorways framed with Middle Eastern arches. Vaguely Eastern music with lyrics in no language at all lent a sensuous tone to the breeze, caressing the low, filigreed furniture and inviting you into the abundant pillows.

Will Wick sat on a divan and waited. His family name had once been VanWicke, but they'd trimmed and Americanized it during World War II in order to avoid the kind of people who kicked dachshunds to death in the streets. He wished they hadn't. He was forty-three now, and no one had called him "Will Lick" for decades, but he still heard it in his head. William VanWicke had such a better ring to it. A noble ring. He had no siblings and his parents were dead, but he never changed the name.

Instead he sat, white and soft as dough, wearing a short, silver lamé robe, in the Temple of the Goddess Most High. The robe didn't look very good on him, but it was as near as he'd come to his nobility. He could maintain it as long as he ignored the other man in the room.

More than ten years younger than Will Wick, this other man had seen a lot more of the world. He'd changed his name too. He was called Gate, because that was his job, and he was good at it. It's what he did in the Marine Corps, where no one and nothing ever got past him without permission. That included a truck bomb, two colonels, and a Toyota Celica Supra with five armed Sunni women firing at him with AK-103s. He was big and he liked being big. He wore a black T-shirt tight across his body and loose fit black Levis. His skin was almost as dark as his clothes, like wet espresso grounds. Will Wick barely existed on Gate's radar.

Both men perked up at a sound. A doorbell. A languid woman's voice called out from another room. "Gate," she cooed, "see who that is."

Will looked nervously at Gate. He didn't like to think the evening program might change. Will wondered if the big, Black man thought he was soft for not being the one selected to go to the temple doors. Gate headed out without thinking about Will at all.

Gate walked downstairs into the store. He flipped a light switch. It stayed dark inside, but a light came on over the front door. A workman appeared in the light—a white guy in a blue work shirt with a lightning bolt logo and a tool belt. He held up his clipboard and waved at Gate with it.

Gate frowned and scanned the street outside. The workman was alone. There was no chain on the glass door, so Gate unlocked it and opened it about six inches, stopping it with the instep of his left foot. That would be stronger than any night chain anyway. The workman smiled at him and said, "Evening, bro."

"Bro?" Gate's eyes crinkled as he quickly tried to zero in on the man's greeting. You don't have to carry a big racial chip on your shoulder to recognize coded white-speak; you just have to grow up Black. Still, he thought the workman might simply be a fool.

The man went on, seeming unaware of Gate's instant calculations. "Hey," he said, "I got a call you blew a spike on the solenoid panel." Gate had no idea what that meant. He was about to say so, but the workman continued. "I know. Your lights aren't out. But I don't put a fast cap on that copper nipple and you'll be in the dark."

That all came at Gate too fast, but he wasn't stupid. "We didn't call you."

The workman nodded, on the same page. "The landlord, bro."

A clipboard is as good as a skeleton key or a backstage pass. Wave it and say you've got work to do, and people will get out of your way, let you through security, and help you carry their safe down to your truck. But only if they're harried, unprepared, and unobservant.

Gate was none of those things. He was immune to clipboards, hand trucks, Armani suits, Blackberries, and "Do you want to be the one to tell him I couldn't get in?" Gate would gladly report to his boss he'd refused passage to a blustering asshole. But only a harmless fool would call Gate "bro" twice in one night. Gate nodded and stepped aside.

Alex walked into the store. "Thanks," he said. "Upstairs?" He was already heading that way.

Gate trailed after him. "I guess."

At the top of the stairs, Alex stopped in his tracks. A shimmering, sheer curtain hung in a double doorway. The wall was thin and had been quickly made. It reached the ceiling, but only grazed it. Not up to code. Probably no electrical behind the sheetrock. But someone had done a good job of cutting the door in the shape of a minaret. Alex took all this in without thought.

The wall at the top of the stairs divided what had been a large atrium into a hall and a throne room. Through the slick curtain, Alex saw a woman sitting in a low-backed, cushioned throne. Two massive stone statues flanked her: slate black, fierce-looking bulls sitting on their haunches. She was Inanna, Priestess of the Goddess Most High.

Her skin was fair as fair can be. Her hair was dark dark. The pillowed throne conformed to the soft camber of her hips. Her breasts, confined by a low-cut gown, swelled with promise. Long legs, crossed so demurely as to be lascivious, slid from under the gown, which was slit almost all the way to her waist. Her toes curled and pointed as she spoke. The lamé gown, much more beautiful than any other Alex had ever seen, was gathered at the waist by a wide, crystal-encrusted, golden belt.

Inanna gazed into a video camera that stood on a tripod. "From the earliest times, the Goddess has taught that sex is the pathway to the Divine. My religion is thought of as new or progressive or even dangerous. But it is an ancient truth that, as the Priestess, to have sex with me is to cleanse yourself of..." Inanna saw Alex standing behind the camera. He had stepped through the curtain without realizing it. She turned her hypnotic eyes on Alex but spoke to someone else. "Will, stop the tape."

A soft man in an outfit to match that of the priestess moved into the room. He followed her command, but muttered to himself. "It's digital, but I'll stop it."

Inanna and Alex didn't see him. "Step closer, strong man."

Alex stepped in front of the camera, within lunging distance of the woman on the throne. He could see now that she was somewhere in her late fifties, age doing nothing to dampen her impact. In fact, her maturity lent her a deeper dose of magnetism. When Alex was near, she spoke again. "What brings you to me?"

Alex was intrigued, but his strength didn't ebb. "Electricity."

Gate came up behind Alex and disrupted the cord that stretched between the man and woman. "He says he's got to fix the solenoid nipple cap, or something."

Now that the spell was broken, Will spoke the question he held behind gritted teeth. "Who is this?"

"Alex, bro." Alex turned to Will to say it.

Inanna bristled when she lost his eyes. "What are you all doing in here?! Gate, Will, go away."

They did as they were told. Inanna turned back to Alex. "Now," she addressed him, "solenoid what?"

Alex smiled at her, ignoring the question. "Is that a golden girdle?"

"The ancient Greeks called it a zoster. Anglified translators call it a girdle." She arched her back and

"Step closer, strong man."

the gems caught the light as her hips swung. "It can only be removed for a single purpose."

Alex guessed, "Bathing?"

"No."

"Am I out of guesses?"

"Yes." Inanna reached behind her and undid a catch. The belt fell open. The slit in the gown exposed the soft dimple of her pelvis.

"You don't look like you need a girdle."

Inanna stood up and the zoster dropped to a pillow. "Thank you." The gown slipped open revealing supple flesh. She sized up the man before her. "You don't look like the average acolyte."

Alex held his ground and agreed, "I'm not."

Inanna moved in on Alex. "I am Priestess to the Goddess Most High."

"Is that right?"

"Do you know what that means?" She moved in closer still.

Alex knew. "You serve her. Will and Gate serve you."

"Will and Gate and others," she told him. "To serve me is to cleanse your soul."

"To serve you, or to service you?"

"They are the same thing." She covered the logo on his shirt with her hand. "You are a service man."

He couldn't argue. "I guess I am, at that."

Inanna touched the bandage on his neck. "A wound."

"It's nothing," Alex dismissed. "I was fighting a..."

Her hand brushed the bare flesh of his neck and the charm popped like a soap bubble. Inanna flinched back with an involuntary gasp and a flash of vision. "Chronus!"

Alex was shocked and so was she. Before either could react, Gate and Will rushed into the room. Inanna flared, "What?!"

It was finally here, Will's moment to be a hero. He was not an electrician, but he was an engineer. "Inanna, there's no such thing as a solenoid panel."

Alex had underestimated the room. He looked deep into Inanna's eyes. "I gotta go."

He dashed past her. Inanna gasped. Alex snatched the zoster off the pillow.

Will shrieked, "No!" Gate moved to block the stairs.

Alex turned on him. "What are you doing here, Gate? You're not the average acolyte."

Gate told his adversary the score. "I'm a bad ass Baptist bodyguard."

Alex understood. "You're about to earn your fee." He threw the belt over one arm.

"Stop him!" Inanna commanded.

Gate wasn't listening. He focused on the man before him. "You're not gettin' past me."

Will ached to act, but said instead, "He might be armed."

Alex looked at the supplicant and held up his tattooed left fist. "All I've got is, 'This.'" He held up his right. "And 'That.'"

Will took a step back. Alex advanced on Gate, who held his ground.

"Will"—Inanna's tone was penetrating—"take my Belt of Power from him."

Will wavered on the edge of a door he never stepped through, "But, Inanna…"

"I command it!"

That was the push he needed. Will took a deep breath and charged, surprising both Gate and Alex.

Will closed in on his enemy and balled his hands into fists. He wanted to let out a war cry, but his jaw was clamped shut. He hummed angrily. Years of rage seethed, and William VanWicke felt himself grow taller. The robe stretched across his back as his muscles flexed. Wind whistled in his ears from the speed of his charge.

Alex buried his left fist in William's solar plexus. In a single motion he had spun and brought up the balled mace of flesh and bone. He didn't really even have to throw the punch, as William impaled himself on the ready arm.

Will didn't see any of this. All he knew was he was doubled up, his charge was over, he might never breathe again, and the workman was whispering a sort of apology in his ear. "Just a bit of 'This,' Will."

Will was out, but Gate saw his opening. He exploded across the room like a charging bull and shouldered Alex in the chest. Alex crumpled backward. He stumbled through the curtains behind the throne and into an anteroom. Gate was right with him.

Alex fought for his balance. Gate's right hand had been broken so many times that the bones had healed into a form forged for the perfect fist. Alex flailed to keep his footing and block the punch. Just in time, he caught it on his forearm. The fist impacted on the bone and made his fingers tingle with hot needles. It felt like getting hit by a baseball. The ricochet of the punch threw off Gate's timing just enough for Alex to get his feet back under him.

Gate used his own momentum to follow up with a looping left cross that Alex saw coming like a bus. He moved his head just a quarter inch to let the bus graze harmlessly past him. Alex would never know if that cross was a feint or not, but slipping that punch put him right in the crosshairs for the killer blow of Gate's combination.

No time to duck. No time to block. Only time to eat. Alex lunged toward the incoming fist. Trains on the same track exploded toward each other. Gate's perfect fist collided with Alex's clenched jaw, loosening teeth and rattling eardrums like a sonic boom. But Alex closed the distance before Gate could fully uncoil his attack, and it didn't deliver a quarter of its potential energy.

Alex knew his brain would fritz out for a split second after the collision, so he cocked and fired his counterpunch at the same moment he started his lunge. A long, left uppercut snapped out under Gate's extended arm and stabbed into his unready chin, making him bite his tongue and snap his head back. He didn't drop his guard, but he stood up straight.

Every one of Gate's punches was designed to be a knockout, and every one was aimed at Alex's head. A blow to the head can scramble your brain, blur your eyes, knock you out, or even kill you. But unless you get it in the nose or mouth, a punch in the head doesn't hurt.

Alex twisted his hips like a torsion spring unspooling. The force surged from his hips through his spine, spinning his shoulders and unleashing a right hook that crashed into the soft tissue under Gate's extended ribcage.

Pain shot out from the nerve cluster so hard Gate felt like his nipples were bleeding. He buckled in on himself. Air exploded from his lungs, forcing him to nonsensically and involuntarily exclaim, "FUN!"

The torque of Alex's spring was now spun the other way like a knotted rubber band straining to fire off a propeller. He unleashed the energy with a left hook that made a sick and meaty sound as it impacted Gate's liver.

Gate's knee hit the floor. Instinctively he instantly sprang back to his feet and came back on guard. Gate was a warrior. Pain forced him to keep his elbows to his ribs. He rose to only half his height. But still, he blocked the door.

But Alex wasn't here to beat Gate in a fight. "You were right, Gate." Gate brought his hands up, ready for it. "I'm not gettin' past you." Alex turned to run the other way, toward the open window.

This wasn't what Gate was ready for at all. Caught off guard, he reached for Alex, but only snagged the blue work shirt. The fabric ripped as Alex tried to shrug free.

Suddenly, Inanna appeared in his path.

She raised her hand like a hammer and looked him in the eye. Before he could break her gaze, she slammed the hammer down on his shoulder as if driving the spike deeper into his body. BANG!

Alex cried out and crumbled to the ground.

All the men in the room were in pain.

Propped on pillows at the base of Inanna's throne, Alex sat as contorted as Quasimodo. Freezing tendrils of lightning cracked in and out from the invisible spike, enervating his neck and shoulders, tugging the muscles into impossible contraction. His torn shirt hung loosely from his shoulders like limp banners, juddering with the tiny heaves of his body.

Will and Gate stood by the opposite exits to the room. They were bound now by a brotherhood of pain, each suffering from the same injury delivered by the same man. Every second or so, Will took a tiny breath. His eyes had stopped tearing, but thin snot threatened to stream from his nose. He feared if he relaxed and took in a full breath, he would shit himself. He didn't hurt at the point of impact; instead pain wrapped around him like a too-small vest made of wire. He made an unhinged, squeaking sound that he was aware of, but could not stop.

Gate wore the same vest, but willed his breath into his liver, re-inflating it in his mind. Focusing on the agony took its power away. He knew his last punch connected, but couldn't figure out what happened after that. He hadn't blacked out. The exact sequence of combinations ran over and over, his and then Alex's. Why was it Gate that hit the floor?

Neither man could stand to his full height, but each guarded his door, ready for action if he had to be.

Inanna stood by her throne, her Belt of Power back in place. She took in the puddle of men before her and she did not feel contempt. She did dismiss them. There was a sensation she had never felt before, but recognized—inherited from the sister-mother priestess before her, or perhaps the one before that. The ebbing surge of adrenaline left over from the melee made her vibrate slightly out of phase with the room. With decades of practice, she focused her vibrations on that sensation. Something was happening. Something that was not just a thief in the night. Looking down over Alex, she pronounced a single command. "Speak."

Through gritted teeth and throbs of pain, Alex unfolded the story of why he was there. He started with, "Are all these jobs gonna be about animals?" and filled in from there. Though he hadn't used the name yet, Inanna knew exactly who he was talking about. "Baba," she spat.

"He said he needs your girdle…"

"Belt of Power."

"Belt of Power to find the form of…whatever it is. My next task."

Inanna was incredulous. Alex had finally said something she didn't follow. "To find your task?"

Alex would have shrugged, but his shoulders were already pinned as high as they could go and wouldn't move further. "My tasks. Or errands or jobs I need to do to get balanced. This was one. I have seven more."

Inanna shook her head. "And the little man can't see it."

"The little man? No. He can't see it without the belt."

"The belt is a symbol of my power, not the source of it. He just won't admit it."

"I'm not here to get in a domestic dispute."

She laughed at that. "That's what I felt when I touched you, Electric Man. You're not just cursed, you're special."

"You see the curse too?"

"And the special." She stooped behind Alex and put her hands on him. "Don't forget the special." With hands both soft and strong, Inanna rubbed his sore shoulder, bringing her body very close. "I can ease your pain, but even I can't budge your spike."

The pain did ease, and his shoulders did relax. "Oh, you see my spike, but not that I'm a married man."

Inanna shrugged that off and continued her massage. "I see what's relevant to me," she dismissed. "I bet Baba saw it right away."

"He did at that."

Like the pendulum swing of a hypnotist's watch, Inanna's hands stroked in time, each beat burrowing deeper into him. She didn't touch the point of Alex's pain. One hand held him where the shaft of his neck met the mass of his shoulder. The other hand worked into the tip of his shoulder where it entered the crease at the top of the deltoid. In opposition, she squeezed with one hand and then the other, pumping energy through nerves and flesh and muscle. The flow surged like fluid around an obstruction, sending blood into tissue that had been blocked off by the contractions of his invisible wound. Heat moved to places he hadn't felt in years. His skin reddened. His lips tingled. His eyes closed.

Inanna felt the warmth even through the ruined shirt and smiled a bit, knowing exactly what she was doing. When Alex was ready, she continued. "I also see that we are off our axis."

Alex nodded in rhythm with her hands. "I'm out of balance."

"Oh, darling," Inanna admonished gently, "it's not about you. The universe. The universe is off its axis.

It must right itself, or it will swing too far to came back."

Alex followed the story like a sleepy child. "Then what happens?"

Matter-of-factly she informed him, "The end of the age of man."

"Oh."

"Do you know the god Chronus?"

Not wanting to stray away from the heady drone of his ebbing pain, Alex forced himself to search through myths his mother had told him. "Father of Zeus? Chronus ate him and Zeus fought back."

"Good, but no. That's Kronos, the titan." She rewarded him for being close with an extra deep grind into his muscle. He groaned, and she explained. "Chronus is an elder god, the personification of time itself. A primordial being, as old as creation. With his consort, Ananke, they twined themselves around the world egg and in their passion, cracked it open, spilling out the Earth, the sky, and the seas."

Entranced, Alex followed where he was led. "Ananke?"

It pleased Inanna that Alex gave good questions. "Inevitability."

"Of course."

"Time is a three-headed serpent, stretched through all eternity."

"Three-headed snake?" Alex said with muffled surprise, picturing the thick beast undulating to the same cadence as Inanna's rhythmic caress. "So

Chronus slithers and the heads swing back and forth. Like a pendulum."

That delighted Inanna. She could feel him being drawn in and in turn it drew her deeper. "Exactly."

Alex took in the lesson and repeated it to the rhythm of her massage. "I'm not out of balance. Chronus is out of balance."

"Sweetheart, no. You are terribly out of balance. But the path you're on isn't about righting you, it's about righting the three heads."

"Three heads."

"Chronus is a winged serpent, with the heads of a lion, a bull and a man. The man is in the center but..."

But Alex was hit with the cold water of realization. "A lion? A lion and a bull?"

Inanna was caught up now, not catching Alex's tone, wanting to continue her lesson. "Yes. The lion fights the bull. They are equally powerful and could fight to a standstill. But if some little thing happens, one could slip and the other will dominate."

Alex started to tense under the soothing caress. "This isn't about my curse."

"No," she answered, misunderstanding the flexing of his muscles. "It's about Inevitability and the undulations of Time. It happens again and again every several generations. Then a hero needs to be sacrificed to take the side of the wavering head and set things right. Gilgamesh was a lion. Nüwa was a bull. Heracles was a lion. Hunahpu and Xbalanque were a lion and a bull."

"And it's happening again. Now?"

"Yes," she answered, getting closer to the end of the tale. "Something's made the lion slip. The bull knows it's wounded. It will track the lion down."

"The bull is hunting the lion?" His intensity turned to anger.

Inanna matched his growing heat. "Exactly!"

"And Baba knows this? The lion has to be sacrificed?"

"Of course he knows it."

That's not what he told me, said Alex, but not out loud.

"Your quests aren't to balance yourself, or even to fight the bull." She leaned around his shoulder to try to look into his eyes. "You have to find the lion."

Alex abruptly shot to his feet, his torn shirt falling away and staying in Inanna's hands. She gasped, speechless.

Seated on the step leading up to her throne, Inanna gazed up at Alex. The ferocious face of the roaring lion peered down at her, covering his entire back. As if in the presence of the divine, she trembled under its gaze.

Alex seethed, not sure what to do next.

Inanna quelled her quaking and took in a deep breath. Her storytelling had reached a conclusion she never expected. Baba had not sent this man to find the lion at all. Slowly, she stood. On the step of her throne, she now loomed over Alex. She put a hand on his arm and gently turned him to her. Silently, she reached behind her back and undid the catch.

Will Wick looked on in awe as she offered her Belt of Power to the Workingman.

Alex pushed open the glass door and stepped out of the priestess' shop. He had what he came for, but it didn't feel like a victory. The turgid body of the serpent snaked its heads back and forth in his mind, tick-tocking relentlessly through the cosmos. All six eyes sneered at him.

He walked to his ladder, still set up against the high wall surrounding the temple's patio. He barely looked up to the window he could have jumped from to land on top of the wall to scramble down the ladder. With practiced thoughtlessness, he collapsed the extension.

The wall was stuccoed cinder block, eight inches across. Without shuffling or even being very careful, he could have run along the top for a few yards. His balance was good. Did that count for anything?

With his ladder over one arm and the Belt of Power over the other, Alex headed to his truck. Maybe that's why he was the lion—if he was the lion. Because he was out of balance, but he had good balance. He did not notice Inanna in that open window, watching him go. He strapped the ladder to the rack and climbed up into the cab.

Minutes later, the pickup motored down the dark streets. Alex balanced the God of Time against his invisible curse, against "the end of the age of man," and against a tattoo he'd been inspired to get decades ago during a hypnotic, nine-and-a-half-minute Paul Gilbert guitar jam at a concert he hadn't even wanted to go to. Streetlights struck a spark from the zoster's crystals.

Baba was right: this was a task he might have enjoyed. And Baba was awake right now, in the Botanica, waiting for Alex and the zoster. Alex pictured the man, long fingers tapping each other impatiently, mustache twitching. Baba never wore a watch—Alex was pretty sure—but there must be a clock somewhere in that cluttered shop, and Baba would be checking it. Impatient to sacrifice Alex to the universe? The truck droned toward the barrio, away from where Alex wanted to be. He gritted his teeth and turned the truck hard around.

Chapter 6

The Workingman cannot work alone. Who will be his true guide?

A two-lane, straight-as-an-arrow highway cuts through the scrubby California high desert. The terrain is so featureless, you could fall asleep behind the wheel and not know it when you wake up ten minutes later.

Before dawn, desert animals come to life. Morning dew is the only direct moisture some of them will ever know. By the thousands, caterpillars migrate across the highway, not aware of where they are going or why. Compelled to move by a need beyond their understanding, guided by energies they don't even know they are sensing, they inch as fast as they can across tarmac that in a few hours will be hot enough to cook them.

A lone vehicle sped through the night, humming as wind leaked in through closed windows and sang through ladder rungs like oboe reeds. Alex's F-150, racing down a lane, killed hundreds of caterpillars—collectively, an insignificant number. He couldn't even feel their deaths through the vibrations of the steering wheel.

The truck rolled up the gravel drive of a very old ranch house set in the middle of acres of alfalfa fields and pipe corrals. The gray-shingled place sagged a bit, but it was taken care of lovingly and well. The electricity had been upgraded and rewired from top to bottom; there wasn't a short in the whole house.

An old windmill once pumped water from the dried-up well. Alex planned to get it running again to generate wind power for the house and barn. He pictured the cam in his mind and wondered about gearing ratios. It distracted him from Chronus' chaotic clockwork, which he could see only well enough to know he couldn't understand it.

Steam wisped from under the hood in thermal eddies as the heated moisture deconcentrated into the cold, dry desert air. Alex shut down the engine. The truck hissed and creaked, metal parts straining against equilibrium. Opening the door slowly to mute the metallic squeal, Alex stepped down from his seat. He stretched his back and rubbed his aching neck, keeping the driver's door open so as not to repeat the awful noise. He drew a deep breath to take in the country quiet and stillness.

Something darted out at Alex from behind the house. Alex didn't see it coming. It hit him hard and knocked him back into a fender. Black ears, black mask, white snout, black nose. Alex tried to whisper and shout at the same time. "Yucky! Down!" The excited dog porpoised up to lick Alex's face. "Okay. Okay. Down. Quiet."

Yucky did as he was told. He wriggled down at Alex's feet and rolled on his back, offering up his belly. Alex couldn't resist reaching down to rub his overjoyed dog.

The east glowed as the sun burgeoned below the ragged horizon. A light came on inside the house. "Dammit, dog. I told you to shut up."

Yucky didn't care. He burrowed his head between Alex's knees.

The front door of the house opened, and a figure drifted out onto the screened-in porch. The screens filtered the light like gauze. A woman appeared in the artificial mist, hazy and ethereal—Dara. From the creaking dais, she considered her man, weighing her conflicts, and almost said nothing. Then she spoke softly, her voice carrying across the morning stillness as if she were by Alex's side. "How did you find me?"

Alex stepped away from the dog and turned to the woman. "I know you," he answered. He did not approach. He did not whisper but he kept his tone low enough for only her to hear. His words thrummed with bass across the space between them. "I love you."

Dara looked down at him from three steps up. She frowned. "You're not supposed to be here."

Alex was in the wrong and he knew it. He could explain. "Dara, I was with this woman last night, and…" That didn't sound right at all. "Let me start that over."

"Maybe you better."

Alex stepped up to the porch. Her eyes cast down upon him. Moving only her hand, Dara reached out and set the hook lock on the screen door.

Alex understood. "Okay, I'm staying down here." Dara on the porch seemed to float even higher in clouds above him. She gazed down, heavenly and mysterious through the filtered light. Alex smiled to himself, knowing why the Goddess had reminded him of his wife.

"She made me think of you. I'm always thinking of you," he clarified, "but she talked about cleansing your soul…my soul, and I realized you didn't know."

Wary and suspicious, she asked him, "What don't I know?"

"I'm gonna make it right," he promised. "All of it. It was my fault. I'm out of balance and I'm gonna set it right."

"And she's helping you do this how?"

"She?" This was getting away from him. "No. She just reminded me of you. She doesn't look like you. Actually," he said finally, "it wasn't her."

"She didn't remind you of me?"

The Goddess had reminded him of his wife.

Alex wished he could start this all over. "Forget her. She was just at a job I was doing."

That sounded promising. Dara asked, "You're working?"

"Yes. Sort of. I have to restore balance to…It's hard to explain." Alex stumbled.

"No, Alex. This all makes perfect sense." Her promising impression of him, fleeting at best to begin with, was all gone now.

Alex started from scratch. "Dara…I'm sorry. I just wanted you to know I'm working to get us back."

"Good." She meant it—this was the best thing she'd heard in days. She looked more closely at him. "What happened to your face?"

But that was nothing to him. "How are the girls?"

"They're fine," she gave him. But though he'd said he would, he hadn't set it right yet. "You have to go."

"I know." Alex stepped back, satisfied. "I just wanted you to know. I'm not just sitting on the couch waiting for you to come back."

This was getting harder. "Thank you."

"I'm going," and he was. "I'll sit in the truck for ten minutes so it can cool off."

"Okay."

"Tell your Uncle Scotty, so he doesn't shoot when he sees me."

Dara almost smiled, but any crack of emotion would end her right now. She called out and stopped him.

"Take Yucky with you. Thea and Niki have the horses to play with."

Alex looked at the dog, already sitting expectantly in the driver's seat of the pickup. "Thank you." He was at the truck now.

The sun cracked over the far hills and gold streaked across the high desert. The coming of the light made Dara invisible behind her screen.

She whispered across the yard, knowing he could not hear, but hoping the dawn breeze would carry her words across the yard and he would absorb them through his skin. "Put some ice on your face."

Alex climbed in after his dog and closed the door behind them.

A tall, white-haired cowboy stepped onto the porch behind Dara. "How'd he find you?" he asked.

She answered simply, "He loves me." She watched Alex petting the dog in the cab of the truck. She started to smile, and—as she knew they would—tears filled her eyes. Her uncle stood as still and supportive as a fencepost. She leaned on him and cried.

Around midday, Alex opened the door to his apartment and Yucky bounded inside. With a certain mild contentment, Alex pulled the cord that parted the curtains and allowed in the sun for the first time in days. He droned to the kitchen, selected one of Dara's Viogniers from the fridge, returned to the living room, flopped into the cushions, and turned on the TV. The static hissed on the screen. Alex didn't hit mute. Yucky jumped up on the couch and put his head in his master's lap. Alex took a single sip from his thick-bottomed glass and gazed into the celestial snow. The cosmic hiss worked into him like the fingers of the priestess and the voice of his wife. The Clockwork unwound the tension just a tick and his shoulders dropped. He fell asleep.

The windows were dark. Only the strobing television illuminated the room. Alex still slept, slumped up on the couch with Yucky curled next to him. The jumping static from the screen threw a craze of lights through the space.

On the wall behind Alex, shadows jerked and shrank and grew. In Alex's own flickering silhouette, there was something different. If you blinked, you'd miss it—or rather, if you blinked in the wrong sequence, you wouldn't see the juddering profile of a spike in his neck, cast in the reflected light of the Big Bang.

Yucky did not blink at all. Some deep stirring in the ancient, instinctive brain woke the loyal animal. The dog gazed in awe as the flickering form of the shadow strobed and changed and loomed over Alex. It flared across the wall. Powerful. Fierce. Solemn. A lion. The great maned head of Alex's shadow lorded over them, diligent, as the man slept.

Suddenly, Yucky leapt off the couch and dashed to the door, barking furiously. Alex jumped in his seat and the glass spilled in his lap. There was a knock at the door. Alex got to his feet, mopping white wine from his pants and telling the dog to shut up. He tried to adjust to what was for him sudden darkness.

The knocking continued. "Just a minute!" He looked at the barking dog with irritated authority. "Yucky, go!"

The dog moved away from the entrance but continued to growl quietly, a ridge of standing hairs along his spine. He stared at the door. Alex pulled it open. There was Baba, looking impatient. The mustache frowned. "Where is the girdle?" He started to move past Alex into the apartment. Yucky growled more intensely, fur flaring on his shoulders like a mane. Baba decided to stay in the doorway.

"Hello, Baba," challenged Alex. "Come in."

Baba stared at Yucky. "Are you going to shoo him away?"

Alex said simply, "No."

Baba edged into the room and sidestepped a bit further from the dog. "Did you get it?"

*The jumping static from the screen threw
a craze of lights through the space.*

"I did." Alex closed the door.

Baba was both relieved and annoyed. "I thought you got caught."

"I didn't." He had felt eased since his moment with Dara, since revisiting his purpose. But he hadn't forgotten what the priestess had said. Face to face with Baba, Alex was suddenly tired of being a tool in all this. He turned on the lights. "You know, Baba, I'm not a thief. I got the eggs, I killed the lion, I get it—explain again why you'd want me to steal that lady's girdle."

Baba was particularly venomous when speaking of Inanna. "Not a lady," he spat. Anger made the mustache tick and jump in an involuntary sneer. "Not a priestess."

"Not a priestess?" Alex protested. "You've never seen her place." But he suspected Baba had.

"I have seen her supplicants. They go to her for help. She takes their money."

"That's what you do."

Baba answered the charge indirectly. "She saw you, yes?"

"Yes."

"What did she think?" Baba quizzed, smugly.

"Of me?" Alex thought about it. "She called me 'strong man.'"

"And your neck. Did she mention your neck?"

Alex considered his answer carefully. "No."

Baba opened his palms and spread his fingers as if

to say, "See?" Alex took in the man's satisfaction, and his eagerness. "Then what happened?"

"I was in the throne room," Alex recalled. "She undid her girdle." Alex watched Baba's eyes widen, already knowing the implication. "And she told me there was only one reason she would do that." Baba nodded, rapt. "Well, I resisted that, and I snatched the belt right out of her hands."

"Yes," Baba encouraged.

As the story unfolded, Alex gauged its effect on Baba. "So, she has these two guys, 'Will' and 'Gate.' Will's like an acolyte. He comes at me."

"A big man?"

"Well, you know how she is, right?"

"I do."

"So, yeah. Big Will charges in. And I've got the girdle in one hand. What am I gonna do?"

"One-handed."

"Right. I feint with the girdle, like it's a whip. He buys it. So, I sneak a left hook right up under his ribs."

"You hit him?"

Alex held up his left fist. "Just a little bit of 'THIS."

"And he…"

"And he's out."

"One punch?"

"Okay, I have to admit, Will's big—but he's not a fighter, so that was it for Will."

"Oh my God."

"Right." Baba had sent him on this mission, and Alex could see the man relishing the telling, as if Baba had been the one in the fight. "Will was out, but Gate sees his opening. Now, Gate is a big man too, but he's some kind of bodyguard, so he knows what he's doing."

"He's a fighter."

"Exactly. He explodes across the room like a bull."

"A bull?"

"And BANG! He shoulders me in the chest. I go flying through these curtains behind the throne, into the next room."

"You fell?"

"I catch my balance and bring my guard up just in time. Gate's right on me. He throws a combo to my body and face. I block one, slip one and take one on the jaw."

"Oh!"

Alex pointed to the bruise blooming through his beard. "I roll with it and counter with a hard right. He's on his heels. I follow up with a fist to the gut. He starts to crumble. I shove him back, but he jumps up right away and blocks the door. I say, 'You were right, Gate. I'm not gettin' past you.' Because he already said no one ever got past him."

"Ah," Baba relished the quip.

"So, I turn and run the other way."

"You ran?"

"I'm there for the belt, not for a fight, right?"

"Right."

"Gate doesn't know what's happening. I jump out the window."

"Out the window?"

"I set up my ladder under the window when I got there."

"You knew?"

"I guessed. So, the priestess runs in too late and orders me to stop, but I run across the top of a wall, scramble down my ladder and collapse the extension before Gate can follow me."

"Yes!"

"So, with the ladder over one arm and the girdle over the other, I run for my truck. Your priestess leans out the window and shouts, 'You bastard!' But I drive away."

"This is amazing! And you have the girdle?"

"It's right here."

Baba didn't actually rub his palms together with anticipation, but his glee in his victory was impossible to miss. He had the upper hand, and he knew it. Alex pressed him. "But you didn't answer my question. Why did I steal a woman's girdle?"

"The Belt of Power is a conduit."

"Belt of Power?"

Baba nodded without stopping. "It can focus the energies of the universe."

"Like crystal therapy."

"Good," Baba complimented, a little surprised this workingman might know what that was. "Different crystals vibrate at different frequencies. The belt helps me filter the frequencies to better read the scales."

"Like music scales? To see where I am out of balance?"

"Right."

"And to see what I have to do next. For balance."

"Exactly."

"So, taking it helps you, but it was also one of the things I have to do for me?"

Quickly, Baba explained. "There's more than one reason the universe needs something done."

"Good. Because I really feel like taking it helped me."

That caught Baba off guard, but he said, "Good."

"Yeah. I mean I know I'm not done. But I do feel more balanced since I went there."

"You do?"

"I know it's weird. But up to now, I've felt like, I don't know…" He searched for the words and then looked Baba right in the eye when he found them. "Like a lion fighting a bull."

Baba was startled, but he smothered it. His mustache cringed back as he asked, "A lion and a bull?"

"Yeah," Alex answered casually. "Evenly matched. Neither one can get the upper hand. You know what I mean?"

Baba wasn't sure how to answer. "A lion and a bull. I think…I think you are more a poet than I realized."

"But you get my image, right?" Alex clasped his hands together and made them wrestle. In the steeple of his forearms, muscles rippled under the skin, animating a triptych tattoo that stretched almost from elbow to wrist. He made sure Baba could see it, and Baba pretended he didn't. "You can picture it?"

"I can picture it." His mustache shifted quickly from side to side, as if detecting a noxious odor. He pointedly bounced his eyes away from the blue-ink rattlesnake wrapped around Alex's arm to end not with a snakehead, but with three grinning sugar skulls. The flexors rippled and the snake writhed. "But…but you feel more balanced now. That the lion is winning?"

"Well, at least that it can win. But you're being more literal than me. It's just an image I thought of."

Baba stared back at Alex with suspicion. Alex pretended not to notice, as if the awkward silence was a natural pause in the conversation. He took Inanna's bejeweled zoster from the kitchen table and handed it to Baba.

"So, can you see what I have to do next?"

"Next? Now?"

"Well, I have to get back in balance to get my family back, right?"

"Right."

"There another job for me?"

Baba considered this. He looked out the window, into the night. "You are ready now?"

"I just got nine straight hours sleep for the first time in years. Time to go to work." Backed into a corner, literally, Baba's fingers flexed the zoster, squeezing it from an oval to an O and back. "Do you have to put it on?"

Baba looked down at the Belt of Power, not wanting to share its use with the Workingman. "No," he said, as the snarling dog brewed an idea in his mind. "No, I don't."

When he solves one problem, two more crop up to takes its place. Is there no end in sight?

South Central Los Angeles: a residential neighborhood, known for liquor stores and gun shops on opposing corners. On all the windows, there are bars. Nights, you could drive through South Central and find things on fire and no one coming to put them out. As long as the flames don't spread past a box of streets protecting Downtown and Hollywood to the north, industrial areas to the south and east, and the Westside and Culver City to the west, those fires can burn themselves out. This box is the purview of the LAPD, and the LAPD's strategy for the area is one not of enforcement, but of containment. What happens in the hood, stays in the hood.

Over a decade ago, the city changed the name from the more infamous "South Central" to "South

Los Angeles," hoping to overwrite the stigma. Gentrification nibbles at the edges of the box, but deep in those streets the citizens are left to fend for themselves.

Something big moved through the dark and shuttered neighborhood. A cat dashed out of a side street, running for its life. There was a rumbling and a scuffling. The cat sprinted toward a tree. One second behind the cat, the big, dark shape filled the street, moving fast. It roiled like powerful muscles under taut skin. With no streetlamps, the impenetrable shape hulked with a humped back and horned head. The dark thing lunged for its prey. The cat leapt. Too late. The cat was snatched out of the air. The scuffling, amorphous shape swallowed it up as it wailed.

Lights snapped on and illuminated the scene. The massive shape in the darkness fluoresced in the glare and revealed its constituent parts. It was not a single, rumbling creature, but a mass of snarling, awful, matted, mongrel mixes of Pit Bulls, Shepherds, Rottweilers, Dobermans and dogs of every other breed. The Pack.

The Pack tore the cat to pieces. One dog looked away from the carnage, into the lights. The color of orange flame, with golden eyes, livid scars, and broken ears, it had muscled, outsized shoulders like a hyena or a cage fighter. It bared its teeth and growled. The Leader.

Alex sat in the cab of the idling truck with Yucky at his side. With wide eyes, he considered the flashing teeth and mangy haunches of the Leader, glowing like a campfire in the headlights of Alex's mumbling pickup. Though Baba had told him what to look for, Alex now knew there was something to be suspicious of in everything the old man said. Or something new to be suspicious of. It had been comforting to place his fate in the hands of Baba's guidance. But now he knew he had to be his own guide to his redemption. Baba could point him toward a task, but it was up to Alex to find a way to make that task move him forward, and not just be a sacrifice to Baba's agenda. Or Inanna's. Or whatever the hell was going on.

One thing he knew for sure, that made sense to him as a man who worked with his hands, who built and repaired things: balance matters.

Being out of balance is like a bad electrical connection. If it's not tightened right, or if the resistance is wrong, the circuit still works, and your light still goes on. But inside the walls the equilibrium is off. Every time you flip the switch, a little extra energy goes where it shouldn't. A little extra heat makes a loose connection a little looser. Still, everything works. But a looser connection causes a little more extra heat. A little more heat causes a little charring. And charring is a semiconductor, so it lets a little more energy out. The connection gets warmer and looser and carbonized and then warmer and looser still. It can take years, but someday, that bad connection becomes so hot it glows. On that day, you won't know you're out of balance, but your house will burn down.

Being out of balance was the spike in his neck. It had taken years for the spike to grow so big and sharp it pierced his nerves, spasmed his muscles, chased him from sleep, and sparked his temper. To offset that, he had to find what was out of balance and fix it. The more out of balance it was, the more fixing it would bring balance to his neck, to his temper, and to his family. Like moving weights closer and further from a fulcrum. He just had to find those weights.

He looked at Yucky. The loyal companion's hair stood on end. He looked into the dripping, feral maw of The Pack. No doubt, the weights here were out of equilibrium, and they were dragging the triptych heads of a galactic metaphor out of alignment.

"This must be the place."

Staring into the lights, the Leader barked once. The others froze and followed the gaze of their alpha. Like dissonant sirens and the wails of angry infants, a horrible chorus of barking and howls exploded from The Pack. At some invisible signal, they charged.

Alex steeled himself to take the blow. The Pack swarmed the truck. The cab rocked, buffeted by the dogs. The whole world outside was howling, barking, scraping, growling, scratching, scrabbling, snarling. In an instant, they were gone. The pickup shook on its springs in the wake of the chaos and finally settled.

Silence.

Alex held his breath, still bracing himself on the steering wheel as if for a crash. He eased his fingers open and looked in the rearview mirror. There was nothing.

"We've gotta stop that?" He turned to look at Yucky, but his dog cowered in the footwell, nearly invisible under the dashboard. The cab stank of fear.

In the light of the following day, Alex's truck waited for him in front of a rundown community center. Rundown in the sense that there always was a struggle to find the money to keep it up. The community spirit was there. For all the crime and drugs and gangs and fear that it's known for, South LA is really a neighborhood of poor and working families. Underserved by the powers that be, the people created their own support structures, loosely organized neighborhood watches, unwritten traffic rules, and safe places for kids to congregate when school was out and parents were working.

This particular center was founded in the 1970s during a surge of reclaiming Black identity, and christened after the queen the state is named for. The outside of the building was decorated with children's murals and a six-by-six hand-painted "Califia Youth

Club" sign. Kids streamed in and out of the big double doors and hung out on the steps outside.

The youths were everywhere, from five- and six-year-olds to teenagers. Inside was a confusion of pool tables, foosball games and carom boards. The level of noise was incredible, just barely drowning out the slap-bass funk the director kept playing in the background. The hub of the place was a sign-in table near the front doors. Kids signed in and out. They checked out basketballs, pool cues, and—James Stillman was particularly proud of this—computer mice. The ten computers were useless without them. An actor who'd spent his youth at this same center donated the machines only two months ago.

Stillman had been a janitor, an exterminator, and a short haul truck driver. He'd washed out at the police academy because he was colorblind. He often told that story as ironic and funny, but he never told that he was disappointed. He found a home at the community center. He was gruff and rough with the kids, and he loved them. Some of them loved him too. Only a bit older than Alex, he looked like he could have been Alex's father. He wore a childish Califia Youth Club T-shirt, but he was comfortable in it. He looked across the sign-in table at Alex— the only white man in the room—and asked, "What made you come to me?"

"I have a tradesman's wit," answered Alex.

"What?" Suspicious, Black and twenty-one, Cleo Handle didn't have time for Alex's cleverness. She was behind the table with Stillman. Like him, she was also in a Califia Youth Club shirt, but not a childish one.

"You're a community center," Alex explained. "I want to know something about the community."

That wasn't enough for Cleo. "It's on the internet."

"Cleo," Stillman admonished her. He was curious, and he recognized Alex. Not Alex specifically—but the white man who faced him was not a cop or a lawyer or a social worker or a bean counter, he was a workingman. So was Stillman.

Alex persisted, "I want to hear it from someone who cares."

Stillman explained. "We're not used to a white man coming in." It was not an apology, just a fact. And though he recognized a fellow, he was still a white fellow, and that was usually not good.

"I'm not white," Alex tried. "I'm Greek."

"Same thing," Cleo dismissed.

"Not according to my mother-in-law."

He didn't smile, but Stillman thought that was funny. "So, you want to know about The Pack?"

Alex was relieved to finally break through. "Whatever you can tell me."

"They're not dogs," explained Stillman. "Not anymore."

"They looked like Pits and Rotts to me," said Alex.

Cleo still wasn't buying. "All Black folk gots Pits and Rotts."

Stillman admonished her again. "Cleo."

"You know," Alex said, addressing her, "Cleopatra was a Greek."

Cleo knew better. "She was Black."

"Maybe," Alex shrugged. "You and me could be related."

"Cleopatra was a queen," Cleo retorted. Just the fact that there was a give and take now was progress. "You got royal blood?"

"Not likely," Alex chuckled. "When your family was ruling Egypt, mine was probably brining someone else's olives."

She'd have to think about that. "Maybe."

Alex could have turned back to Stillman now, but he didn't. He asked Cleo, "You call them 'The Pack?'"

"We call it 'The Pack,'" corrected Cleo.

"It's been around for years," Stillman added. "Growing. Getting stronger. Sometimes it goes away. But it always comes back."

Alex asked, "No one's done anything?"

"What can you do?" Stillman wanted to know. "Kill one dog, two more come up to replace it."

It sounded like nature was out of balance, and Alex almost said it out loud, but he stopped himself before he sounded too much like Baba, or a hippy.

Cleo continued the instruction. "Fighting dogs escape, puppies get thrown away. Only the most vicious ones survive."

"And breed," Stillman expanded the image.

"When it comes. It runs the night." She didn't

sound like a teacher now. It was a ghost story, a true one, told to keep children from danger.

"Gangs are bad," Stillman wrapped up.

Cleo punctuated, "The Pack is badder."

"The gangs have guns," Alex countered.

"They also have little brothers and sisters who've been mauled, killed," Stillman explained. "They feared The Pack themselves since they were babies. Sure, they'll shoot up The Pack."

"But they can't kill it." Cleo was definite. "They don't fuck with it."

"Language," Stillman reminded her, a little harshly.

Alex excused her. "I'm not offended."

"I am," Stillman concluded. And that was that.

Back in the colorful Botanica, Baba was restocking his shelves with candles and herbs. Alex followed him through the shop, seeking guidance.

"It's not what I thought it would be," he said.

Baba asked, "What did you think?"

"I thought it would be the easiest thing I've done so far."

"Why?"

"I know about dogs," Alex shrugged. "I have a dog."

"They are not dogs," Baba said mysteriously.

Alex was a little sick of that. "No shit, Yoda. What are they?"

"They are nature—"

"Out of balance," Alex interrupted. "I got that. What do I do about it?"

Baba shrugged. "I told you."

"People have tried," Alex protested. "You can't kill it."

Baba turned on him meaningfully. "I did not say 'kill' it."

Roger and his wife and kids pulled up to their house just after dark. As he lifted himself out of the car to open the gate across their driveway, he saw a white man standing in the headlights of a weathered work truck parked on the dark street. Roger rolled the gate aside and squeezed back behind the wheel. He pulled the car forward and the kids slid the gate behind him as his wife opened the trunk. Roger hefted himself up from the car. The man was still there. Pulling groceries from the trunk, Roger called to him. "Get off the street, man. The Pack is out."

"I know they are," said the white man. He brandished the object in his hands. It was a long pole with a strong, nylon net bag on one end.

There was only one thing to say to that: "Crazy." Roger shook his head and hurried his family inside. The door locked behind him.

Alex looked coldly into the darkness. Yucky wasn't with him tonight. The plan was well thought out and there was no room for cowering.

Like sowing the ground before him with dragon's teeth, Alex tossed something into the street. It skittered and clattered to a stop on the gray asphalt. An open can of dog food. He tensed and waited.

It wasn't long. The scuffling rumble of The Pack came again. It was closing in. Alex lifted the net into on-guard position.

Silently, he convinced himself. *This is a good idea.*

Now, Alex could see it, darker than the dark of the unlit street—a giant black mass, surging forward. It must have been a trick of the darkness, he told himself, plus the image implanted by the words of the priestess. For a fleeting moment, to Alex's eyes the silhouette took the humped shape of a monstrous Brahma bull. He shuddered the vision away.

The Pack knocked over garbage cans and set off car alarms as it moved. The horrible progression of sound grew louder and louder as the beast tore up the streets. The Pack moved into the lights of the truck, revealing its viscera. Some of the dogs were still in

"They are not dogs," Baba said mysteriously.

the darkness, but the Leader stood over the open can of food, ignoring it. Its eyes were fixed on Alex.

The Leader stared at the intruder, and the intruder stared back, challenging. The intruder spoke. "Here, boy."

The Leader didn't understand the words, but it felt the intruder's contempt for its power. It bared its teeth and arched its neck into attack position, displaying its strength, size, and weapons. It took a slow, menacing step toward the intruder, challenging back.

"That's right," the intruder said.

The Leader advanced, not bluffing, but expecting the intruder to back down. Behind it, The Pack devoured the food. The Leader disregarded them and focused on the intruder, who wasn't backing up.

The intruder sprang. The Leader held its ground. It was hit by something far beyond the intruder's expected reach. Suddenly, The Leader was confined. It lashed out with fury.

Alex held hard to the pole while the Leader thrashed. He pulled sharply on a cord and the net closed like a sack. The Leader gave a bloodcurdling howl. Alex shouted back, "Yeah!"

Using the front of the truck as a fulcrum, Alex levered the pole over his head. The thrashing dog lifted into the air. Alex tugged the cord and the

Leader was dumped from the bag, crashing hard into the bed of the pickup.

Alex had spent the day removing the equipment from the bed. He'd enclosed the ladder racks in nylon netting. The back of the truck was now a cage.

The Leader charged at the intruder, but it got hung up in the undulating, binding walls. Frustrated and angry, it thrashed and wailed and struggled.

Alex turned back to The Pack. "I got your boss. Now..."

Two identical Rottweiler mixes jumped into the spot vacated by the Leader. Alex jabbed one in the eye with the pole. As it recoiled, Alex snatched up the other. His back strained and he grunted as he swung the dog into the bed of the truck. Three ravenous Pit Bulls charged into the light. A second ago, Alex had been facing two dogs—now there were four.

The Rottweiler slashed at Alex with dripping teeth. Alex jumped back. The Pits rushed in. Alex snatched one in the bag and dumped it in the truck. Another sank its teeth into Alex's ankle. Sharp points closed through the padded neck of his work boot, pierced his flesh, and held on with crushing force. Alex roared with rage and pain. If he stopped to open the vice jaws, the other dogs would tear him apart in a second.

Alex stabbed the pole at the third Pit. He trapped it in the net and hurled it up into the truck. Four more dogs swarmed in. As fast as he could, Alex snatched up dogs and filled up the bed, swinging the pole like a pendulum. Now there were more dogs in the netted cage than there were on the ground.

Finally, he turned to the Pit Bull clamped to his ankle. He pounded it with the butt of the pole. He kicked it with his free foot and bashed it with his fists. The dog wouldn't budge.

Only one thing to do. Alex darted his hand down in careful jabs. Pluck by pluck, he untied his work boot. With the dog pulling in one direction, Alex tugged his leg in the other. His bloody foot slipped from the boot.

Alex grabbed the Pit in the net, the boot still in its jaws, and swung it in the cage. The other loose dogs scattered.

He jumped into his seat and started the truck. Behind him, the bed seethed with the pent-up fury of The Pack. From its magnetic holder on the dashboard, his phone chirped out the first step of the directions for a ten-block drive to the South LA animal shelter.

The Pack bashed back and forth in its cage. The truck rocked. Alex tried to ignore it as he drove with his injured foot.

With a crash, the rear window of the truck exploded. Alex ducked as flying glass filled the cab. Dogs spilled and squeezed through the broken window. The pickup swerved and spun as Alex jammed to a hard stop facing the wrong way up on the curb. The Pack barked and snarled and howled. Alex leapt out of the truck, leaving the door open, and jumped on its roof. The Pack tore through the cab like ants through a carcass. In an instant, it was gone.

Alex was alone.

"Make a U-turn," came the electronic voice of the phone. Gingerly, Alex climbed down from the roof of the pickup. His right hand curled into an unconscious claw as the spike bit at the nerve and flared exhausted muscles. He limped to the open door. There, on the driver's seat, was Alex's bloody work boot.

Chapter 8
Already wounded, the Workingman has work to do.

No kind of wound is worse than a puncture wound. Whatever stabbed you cores a funnel in your flesh and deposits dirt, bacteria, and—in the case of a fang—rotting food. Infections can set in almost instantly. A slash is bad, but cleaning it is just a matter of irrigating the channel. With a puncture, you've got to dig down deep, keep it bleeding, and fish out the invaders with the tenacity of drawing a wedding ring out of a bathroom drain. That process hurts more than the injury did in the first place.

The stainless-steel kitchen sink was scratched up, dented, and stained. It was older than either of Alex's daughters. He didn't imagine replacing it now, or think of the smooth, poured concrete countertop he'd planned in his head—a vision he was waiting until they bought a house to share with Dara. His temper pulsed like a living thing, stabbing the spike into his neck again and again.

The water ran pink over his wounded ankle. Alex winced and swore as he scrubbed with the rough side of a sponge, fresh from the cellophane. He knew he was lucky. A dog that could bite through his boot would have crippled him if the boot wasn't there. Blood ran down the drain. Alex didn't feel lucky.

Yucky stood in the kitchen watching his master, and wondering vaguely why he had one foot in the sink. Alex felt the eyes on him and looked at the dog. Yucky smiled up at him and wagged his tail. Alex's temper flared. "Go! Get the fuck out! Fuckin' dog!" Yucky sprinted away, shocked, his tail between his legs. "Why don't you do something useful?!" Alex raged. "Go clean up all the dog shit outta the bed of my truck. Useless goddamn animal!"

He batted the dish rack with the back of his hand. It flew across the room and smashed into the wall. "Fuck!" He shut off the water and stepped out of the sink. He looked in the fridge, but he was out of Dara's selected wines. Turning to a cabinet, he pulled a bottle of Agiorgitiko and pulled the cork as he limped to the living room.

There he spotted Yucky, cowering in a corner.

"Sorry, dog." He didn't say it sweetly, but Yucky pricked up his ears. Alex flopped down on the couch. He took a deep breath and held it. He was shaking.

He let the breath go, slowly. More out of obligation than anything else, he softened his voice and called his dog. "Come here, Yucky. I'm sorry."

Happily, dog ran to Alex and climbed up on the couch. Yucky's forgiveness softened Alex for real. He exhaled again, scratched an honest apology into Yucky's ears, and poured a glass of wine so red it was almost black. From his glass, he spilled a puddle onto the coffee table. "Cheers."

Yucky lapped up the offering, and Alex drew in a mouthful so rich with minerals it tasted like blood. He watched his dog. "Maybe you can help. Why would The Pack ever go away? It's got everything it wants on those streets." Yucky didn't answer, but looked with love at his human, who had only moments before exploded with rage. *You're a dog. What would make you go away?* Alex wondered.

An hour or so later, Alex sat on the floor of the living room. The space was a shop now, his tools spread around him. He worked intently on the motorized guts of a disassembled machine. The answer had come to him as he gazed into the dog's deep, brown, trusting eyes. Yucky cowered in his corner. Somewhere Chronus lifted his lion head, but only just enough to peek on the progress.

Early in the morning, the Santa Ana winds started to blow. They weren't hot at first, only dry. As the sun came up over the desert, the air heated quickly. Alex woke with energy as the light cracked into his bedroom. It wasn't the energy of the well-rested, but of the driven. Now Alex stood in the parching wind and knocked on the locked and shuttered door of Baba's shop. He saw no one else on the street.

"Baba. Open up. Baba!" There was no answer. Alex knocked louder. "Baba, goddammit!"

Baba poked his head from a window above the colorful façade of the store. "Don't you blaspheme!" Again, Alex demanded to be let in, but Baba wouldn't budge.

"You have finished with The Pack?" he asked.

"No. I'm ready, but I can't do it 'til tonight."

Baba shrugged, "Come back tomorrow," and started to close the window.

"No!" Alex demanded. "I'm running out of time. The scales are tipping, I'm gonna lose my apartment, and I'll never get my family back. Give me something to do today."

"Finish with The Pack." Baba dismissed him.

"This is a workday, Baba," Alex chided.

"So?"

"I'm a workingman."

Baba frowned, defeated. He disappeared inside the window. Alex's gaze drifted to the aged Asian woman in a window next door, who stood watching and listening. Their eyes met for a moment. She nodded terse approval.

Baba returned with a slip of paper in his hands. "This is a parishioner." He crumpled the paper into a ball and dropped it to Alex. "He has a curse on him too." As Baba closed the window to go back to sleep, he called down, "I'll tell him you're on your way."

The dirt road ran along the edge of the acreage. Hot wind coursed over rolling hills, lifting dirt from dry fields furrowed for crops in parallel lines. The farmers squinted into the wind as particles of their own land scratched at their eyes. Neither was tall, but their bodies were wide and strong from working these fields. Now that was all they had to show for their work. They looked over the wasteland, presenting it to the stranger sent by the *brujo*.

The three of them walked as the younger farmer, Kisa Romero, explained in the accent of a woman who grew up listening to Spanish but spoke English as her first language. "People pay in advance for the crops."

Kisa's father, Romeo Romero—whose own parents were self-educated poets and whose sister was named Juliet—continued in careful English. "With each harvest they get a delivery, depending on the size of the money."

Alex was following the thread. "The investment."

"*Sí.*"

Kisa was the one who knew most about the system. "It's called Community Supported Agriculture," she said.

Alex looked at the farmland. "I didn't know there was anything like this in LA."

"It's not a new idea. It started years—"

"No. Land like this. Farms."

"Farmers are everywhere." This was something Romeo knew. "We always have been."

Kisa pointed. "From the top of that hill, you can see Encino."

"I've seen it. You grow cabbage?"

"Brussels sprouts," Kisa informed.

"I can smell 'em."

Romeo continued proudly. "And tomatoes, and olives and peas and grapes. You drink wine?"

"I'm a Greek," Alex smiled. "We invented it."

Romeo's face and pride fell. "Then you will feel my curse."

Alex nodded, understanding. "I've got one of my own."

"The curse pulls up the roots of the vineyard." Romeo seethed as he spoke of it. "*Desnudarse la col.*"

This was beyond Alex's Spanish. "I don't…"

"The cabbage buds!"

"Your curse is aphids?"

"*El Chancho*," spoke Romeo, invoking the name of a demon.

"The Hog," Kisa translated.

"A pig?"

"El Chancho!"

Kisa explained, "My father's wife lives in Mexico," as if this clarified everything.

But this was more information with less sense. "Your mother?"

Romeo grew more and more agitated. "No! Kisa's mother is a beautiful woman from Guatemala. She is here. With me!"

"And you left your wife behind?" Alex was trying.

"I said I would send for her. It took me three years. I worked. Worked hard. Earned money to bring her. She did not wait."

"Your wife came herself?"

Kisa cleared it up. "She took up with another man."

Alex felt stupid, not picking up on that. He could guess the next part.

"I sent for her. She did not come. I met Adoncia."

"My mother."

"But now!" Romeo made a fist. He could not continue the story.

Alex prompted, "Now?"

"Now, the farm's successful," Kisa tried to take the story from her father, to spare him.

But Romeo jumped back in. "And her *enclenque* is not!"

"She demanded to be brought over."

"Half the farm!" Romeo raged.

"She came," said Kisa. "She brought her man with her."

Alex couldn't believe it. "She wanted you to put them both up?"

The wronged man cursed. "*Tramposa!*"

"We chased them off."

Alex was glad to hear it. Kisa continued, "They ran to Fresno, but..."

Romeo whispered, "She sent the *bruja*."

"*Bruja* is—"

Alex interrupted, "I know *bruja*. She cast a curse on you."

Romeo nodded. "She called down El Chancho."

Kisa shook her head. "I didn't believe any of this stuff before. But El Chancho destroyed our crops."

They walked to the edge of the olive grove. Knurled trees stood in neat rows disappearing over a low hill. The Santa Anas eddied through the barren branches. Romeo shivered. "Two seasons with no harvest!"

Alex was trying to understand. "This is an actual pig?"

Anger prevented Romeo from answering. "No *vino!*"

Kisa's frustration finally showed through. Something of her father flared in her. "A pig, yes. A pig that we've shot and poisoned and electrocuted!"

"Still, El Chancho comes."

"One pig?"

"Yes," answered Kisa.

"No!" Romeo raged. "No! El Chancho is not a pig. He is El Chancho! He destroys the earth. He cannot be killed."

Something moved beyond the hill at the end of the orchard. It crashed through parched undergrowth. A tree shook. Another tree was bashed aside. Quaking, thrashing branches and flying leaves marked the progress of something big and violent. Romeo announced with reverence and hate: "El Chancho."

El Chancho rooted through the dry leaves and fallen olives on the floor of the orchard. He was enormous. A horrible, lumpish mass of muscle, the gray and black boar came up past your hip and outweighed you by a hundred pounds. He could trample you, eviscerate you and consume you without a thought.

Vicious tusks protruded from his mouth. His left tusk was six inches long and wickedly sharp. But it was the other tusk that was truly awful. It curled backward in a perfidious arc and dug into the flesh under his own right eye. Blood oozed from the perpetual wound. The eye was distended and blind.

Each time El Chancho moved his jaw, the tusk stabbed him. He flinched and spun to his right to find the unseen attacker. The muscles of his right

"El Chancho," spoke Romeo, invoking the name of a demon.

haunch and left shoulder were horribly and massively overdeveloped to forever fling him at his tormentor. As he flailed and turned toward the painful assault, eternally frustrated, he bashed trees out of his way.

Over one hundred yards off, a wave of instinct buzzed through Alex. It told him, "Run away."

CHAPTER 9
Sometimes "quit" is the same as "die."

Filtered by the trees, the desert wind and morning light brushed over El Chancho's spiny hide. He moved through the orchard, rooting for food. Pain seared again into the blind side of his face. His perpetual enemy gored his ruined eye without provocation. El Chancho charged in a tight circle at his invisible nemesis. Frustrated as always, he was too slow. His tormentor was gone. But suddenly, for the first time in his life, it spoke to him.

"Hey, Chancho."

The boar froze, startled. Carefully, he turned and saw a figure standing in his path. Its hands hefted a seven-foot pruning pole with a thirteen-inch curved saw blade at the tip. El Chancho might have been amazed, or awed, shocked, or even frightened, but if you could translate the barely coherent thought of the enraged and insane wild boar, it would be: "Finally."

El Chancho snorted angrily. He charged. The figure swung its spear. It slapped the pig in the face with the blade. Saw teeth drew blood, but El Chancho ignored it and charged straight on through. The figure leapt to its left. El Chancho lost it to his blind eye and shot past.

The eternal adversary swatted the boar in the tail. El Chancho arched his back and spun, understanding the deadly game. His foe jumped out of the way, back into the blind spot. El Chancho spun again, caught up with the figure, and laid in hard. This time, his opponent wasn't fast enough.

El Chancho crashed into Alex. If Alex fell, he was a dead man. They both knew it. Alex dug the butt of the spear into the earth and caught himself. El Chancho bore down on him. Alex got one foot under him and leapt. It was an awkward, one-legged jump, but he cleared El Chancho's back, feeling the bristles through his shirt. The man rolled and stood as the beast whirled to face him.

They battled in row after row of knee-high stalks in a ruined field. Once, there were brussels sprouts here. Now, the stalks were stripped bare. Ragged leaves jutted and vibrated in the wind. Here and there was a tuft of sprouts, but no harvest to be had.

In the expanse of the fields, Alex was under the blazing, critical eye of the sun, and in its glare, he found a measure of freedom. As on the day he first met the lion—in that elemental clash—he savored the pain of his spike, leaned into his pent-up rage and blasted out the pressure like a punctured propane tank. El Chancho charged into the wash of it and sparked the blaze.

Alex crushed through the stalks, El Chancho close behind. In the open field, the searing wind and a shadeless sky assailed them. Neither cared. Both were battered and bleeding from scores of minor wounds.

Alex stayed one step ahead. He jabbed the beast on the right side with the spear and jumped to his left, back into the blind spot. El Chancho twisted and lunged. Alex stabbed the blade into El Chancho's shoulder. The teeth bit deep. The pig gave an ugly squeal. Alex charged in to follow up. El Chancho anticipated and counterattacked. He caught Alex in the leg.

Alex slammed to the ground, not feeling the pain because El Chancho was upon him. Alex held the great boar off with the butt of the spear and kicked him in the snout. El Chancho reeled back, frustrated to see Alex roll back to his feet.

On and on they fought. The sun burned higher in the sky, watching over another decimated crop. The hot wind slowed as the day lengthened, but nothing cooled the fighters in the field. Sweet peas once grew here. Now it was rooted up and worthless. Alex and El Chancho tore up what was left of the plants and cracked the thin wooden poles as they charged and spun and dove. They were covered with blood, their own and each other's.

El Chancho charged like a freight train. Alex stood his ground. He roared and jabbed his spear into the locomotive's right side, and set himself to take another charge. At the last second, he jumped aside. Again, Alex was in El Chancho's blind spot. Blood coursed from the beast's useless eye. But what Alex saw instead was Dara and the bleeding tear from the broken mirror. It fired his rage and kept him on his feet.

Over the rise from the bean field, a narrow vineyard stretched up a hillside. Alex and El Chancho struggled through vines and poles and wires. Shadows grew on the rest of the farm. Here the sun still baked, and the scalding wind grew. Man and beast were exhausted and hurting. It was morning when the fight began. Neither was ready to quit.

El Chancho charged. He was slower now. Still, Alex barely moved quick enough to evade the attack.

El Chancho chased Alex up the hill. Alex hit the ground. But El Chancho was too tired to make the kill. He slammed his big head into Alex's side and Alex lurched away. El Chancho dug his good tusk into Alex's ribs. Hours ago, the ivory blade would have slashed him open and spilled his lungs out. Now, El Chancho barely had the strength to pierce

Alex's flesh. Alex grimaced and swatted the bloody face away. He pulled himself to his feet and lurched away. El Chancho followed. They drew closer to the farmhouse.

El Chancho and Alex burst out of the vines and onto the concrete slab surrounding the farm buildings. El Chancho charged. Alex jumped to his blind side.

Father and daughter watched as the battle approached them. A woman as beautiful as she was dark stood with them. Adoncia covered her mouth to bury an exclamation of horror. She crossed herself. Romeo stood with muscles flexed and fists shaking, as if it were him in the fight. Kisa shouted a question to Alex, but Alex didn't hear it.

Without taking his eyes off El Chancho, Alex croaked, "Is it ready?"

Romeo could only whisper. "El Chancho."

Alex barked, "Romeo!"

Kisa answered, "It's ready."

"Out of the way," Alex shouted. "Go!"

Romeo and his family fled around the side of the building. Alex and El Chancho continued their deadly dance. Alex led El Chancho after the others, a trail of blood streaking behind on the slab.

Around the corner was a raised loading dock. An idling cube truck stood in the slip with its cargo doors open. Alex limped backwards onto the dock. El Chancho stalked him.

El Chancho lunged at Alex. Alex sidestepped. The wild boar drove forward. Alex juked and lurched into the back of the truck. His breath hung cloudy in refrigerated air. El Chancho attacked in desperate slow motion. Alex retreated. El Chancho was in the truck now too.

Mist rose off the two struggling bodies and churned from their noses and mouths. The inside of the truck turned murky with chilled fog. Deeper and deeper into the box they fought, El Chancho charging, Alex jumping aside.

Like a matador, Alex concealed something behind his back. Alex lowered his guard. El Chancho saw his opening, summoned all his power, and exploded at his tormentor with all his remaining strength. Alex dodged. Behind him was a plastic crate on its side. El Chancho crashed into it, his murderous momentum tipping it back. Alex leaned in and helped it fall over. The crate banged down with the open end up, El Chancho trapped inside.

Alex heaved himself to a lever. He sunk his tired weight onto it more than actively pulling it. A hopper opened. El Chancho looked up, shocked to see an avalanche. He recoiled but could not escape. With a roaring, dumping clatter, the crate brimmed over with ice, burying the boar up to his head. He struggled a bit, but his fatigue was too great. The ice sapped the last of his power.

El Chancho looked up at Alex, grunting in anger as he grew weaker and the ice ate into his blood. His hate burned so hot he thought it might melt him free. It could not. Alex reached into the crate. The beast could do nothing, not even cringe.

Alex considered his adversary. His own rage was gone, blown out by exhaustion and by victory. Almost victory. He met the eye of the beast and knew what he had to do.

With both hands, Alex gripped the curled, right tusk. As hard as he could, he pulled. His muscles strained. The head lifted an inch out of the ice. El Chancho's good eye grew wide with fear.

Alex put a boot on the boar's cheek and pulled harder. First it sounded like snapping a bamboo skewer. Then there was a sickening pop and a deep bass crack that would turn your bowels to water. The tusk tore away at its root. Blood jetted out and colored the ice. Alex stumbled backwards, hitting the sheet metal wall with a boom. The truck rocked on its springs.

For the first time he could recall, El Chancho's blind eye was free. It receded into its socket. The lid closed over it. His good eye relaxed. He blinked up at Alex, his terrible war finally over, his vicious torturer finally dead. Barely comprehending the freedom he would wake up to, El Chancho slipped into unconsciousness with the final thought: "Thank you."

Bloody and spent, Alex walked out of the mist and onto the loading dock. Romeo, Kisa and Adoncia stepped back in awe. Alex couldn't look at them. It wasn't them he'd come to help. It wasn't they who needed balance. He understood that now.

"Thaw him out and let him go."

Romeo was speechless; in fact, he could barely breathe. Kisa started to protest. The farmers wanted vengeance. They wanted blood.

Alex waved them off. He opened his arms to gesture at the ground, to the streaks and drops and spatters that marked the path of the combat. But the farmers couldn't pull their eyes from Alex's flesh. The numerous wounds and scrapes and bruises on his body were livid and terrifying.

"It wasn't your curse I broke," he said, holding up the tusk, "it was his." Alex walked away from them, facing the setting sun. It winked out a modicum of approval as it disappeared behind the hills. "Turn him loose, or I'll have to come back to set it right again."

Back in his living room/workshop, Alex sat shirtless on the floor in front of the hissing television, fresh from a bracing shower. He wielded a power drill and bored a hole into something on his coffee table. In the harsh white of the work lights, Yucky looked at him in wonder. Alex spoke to the dog without looking up. "You shoulda been there, little guy. We made a new friend today."

He drilled a second hole and grabbed a leather strip. He laced the leather through one hole and then the other. Finished, Alex lifted up his creation. El Chancho's tusk, cleaned of blood in Alex's shower, now had the strap secured in holes at the point and at the base. With a bit of private ceremony, Alex draped the adornment around his neck. The tusk hung like a broad "U" under his throat.

Rousing himself from the solemn moment, he pulled on a shirt, covering the hard-earned talisman, and looked to his dog. "Let's go to work."

He meant it. He intended and expected to rise to his feet, march out the door, and deal with The Pack on the same day he had dealt with El Chancho. He was ready. His secret weapon was assembled. Alex willed his crossed legs to extend and propel him to his feet. They didn't move. In Alex's mind, he marched out the door and Yucky ran after him.

In reality, Alex sat slumped on the floor, gazing into the electric fog on the purling screen. Yucky padded next to him and flopped down, putting his head in Alex's lap. At the touch of the dog, Alex collapsed backwards, propped by the couch, and slept.

While the Workingman drifted in dream, other orbits continued to spin.

Making no special effort to keep quiet, the broad feet of the lion stepped silently through the dry grass. Reaching into the darkness with keen eyes, she could see as well now as when the sun was out. But even if you were there in full daylight, you couldn't have distinguished the little mound from the loam that surrounded it.

Asleep in its nest in the turf, the rabbit woke up an instant before she killed it. This was easy prey, but small. In another time and place, she would have brought down a deer and feasted for a week. In these hemmed-in, low mountains, bigger game was hard to come by; she was compelled to hunt every night. Still, it was easier now. There were enough rabbits and rats to sustain two adult big cats, but only just. Hunger, injury, illness, and poison had driven her mate to madness, but she didn't know that. She had seen him only twice since he became trapped on her side of the freeway. Once they fought, once they mated, and now he was gone. Now there were enough rabbits and rats and coyote and quail for her and the brood she carried inside her.

Alex ticked in his sleep. His right arm jerked straight at the elbow and his wrist flicked. Sleeping sitting up, the weight of his head and neck bore into the spike, jamming it deeper into his nerve. He didn't wake, but he lolled to his left with his face screwed into a grimace. Jaw clamped, his head came to rest on the floor. His left arm curled underneath him like a child and his right arm stretched straight past his hip, as if pulled down by a great dumbbell. In this new pose, his face went slack and his breathing eased. Alex tumbled back into the deep rest his body and mind could not resist.

At the same moment Alex's cheek met the carpet, a lilac-crowned parrot shot from its globular nest. Its almost identical mate sat on their single egg clutch, and that damned raven was back.

The black bird swooped into parrot territory, testing the borders. At every dawn, the incursion came. The barely glowing east illuminated the green plumage just enough to distinguish the parrot from its foe. The parrot shot into the raven's shadow with a furious trill. The raven dug one wing into the fluid air to pivot and back away from its adversary, slipping just out of reach and answering with a heady crow of its own.

The violent dance of threat and show continued, waking the neighbors, until the rim of the sun breached the horizon—cueing both birds to swoop in opposite directions, toward other tasks.

There was no sleeping in for Cleo. She was already up and drinking a glass of water spiked with apple cider vinegar. From memory, she flowed through the poses of the Surya Namaskar, no longer needing to reference the guide for the sequence. Letting her muscles warm and her joints pop, she breathed into the start of her day.

She drank another glass of water and turned over one card from her deck of affirmations. "Today I clearly see the beauty in a flower and my whole world changes." She spoke the words out loud and then contemplated them as she showered.

She pulled on a purple polo shirt with the logo of a house cleaning app on the breast, already looking forward to taking it off to trade it for the Califia Youth Club tee. Mindfully, she advised herself to take her moments as they come. She left her apartment, thinking of the easel she hadn't had time to touch in two weeks.

El Chancho braced his hindquarters into the earth and stretched his cloven forehooves far out in front of him. He rocked back and flexed his entire, lumpish body, razorback flaring. Dozens of minor wounds stung, tingled, and pricked at him. Muscles raw from yesterday's violent encounter complained mightily against the strain. He bore down into the stretch, almost holding his breath, making a keening sound as high and loud as a V8 with a faulty starter.

He straightened up and shook his massive head and hump, producing a cloud of dust that sparkled in the rays of the sun. The most tremendous ache was in his mouth, but even that was glorious. He ground his heavy jaw, producing a spring of blood.

As he contemplatively licked his lips, he smelled it.

Without checking for an attack from his blind right side, he turned to the left to follow the scent. One tusk hooked under the fallen tree and he cored it open with a flick of his great neck. The tree split with a hollow, guttural crack, exposing the colony. In no time at all, El Chancho consumed an entire generation of translucent termite eggs and pupa.

Baba knew what time it was because the bell over the door rang and Mrs. Smith tread into the Botanica on unsure hips and knees. She had a covered Pyrex dish in both hands, and the cane she refused to actually use swung from the crook of one elbow. Today's lunch was a stirring of seasoned ground beef, potatoes, raisins, olives, and tomatoes—a simple dish that, as ever, smelled amazing.

He admonished her for not using the cane and thanked her for the food. She waved off both sentiments, but she accepted the parcel containing the poultice of paraffin oil and herbs. She was to wrap the concoction around her joints with brown paper and sit motionless for an hour a day until the parcel was empty. She could listen to her weird fiction podcasts. But that was a long time to be idle, and grandchildren, great grandchildren, nieces, and nephews all needed tending, one way or another.

She left, satisfied. Baba savored the food, standing at his counter, knowing his prescription would barely be followed. But Mrs. Smith would be back next week, and he could admonish her again, which was part of what she came for.

Lunch complete, Baba packed up the dish, flipped the sign on the door to "CERRADA," and set the lock. He disappeared into his back room and gazed at his altar table. The golden girdle seemed to glow at him from among the figurines and icons. Reverently, he lifted it from its place and undid the catch.

Baba slipped the Belt of Power around his waist and breathed into its tightness. He poured a glass of mezcal, lit a cigar, and let the smoke spiral, expand, and speak to him. But it wasn't Chronus he consulted.

The afternoon sun crept a ragged square of light across the brown carpet, turning it golden in its path. The halo dazzled across Alex's face, threatening to pull him from his slumber before he was ready. But Yucky intercepted the beam, casting a cool shadow on the face of the man. The dog soaked the sunlight into his black and white coat, letting it blanket him in its warmth and lull him into a trance.

Luna pushed herself away from her desk and stood. She peered down at her monitor. She always proofed her writing from afar, staring down her nose as if she were sneering at it.

Now that she was retired, her weekly arts and society paper, *The Valley's Edge*—where she'd once supported a roster of stringers, interviewed Alice Bag, and covered Screamin' Jay Hawkins playing the Palomino—had evolved into an email newsletter aimed at her readership of likeminded women of a certain age. Typically, she still published on Thursdays so they could read it before the weekend, but she was a day late this time because she'd scrapped her original editorial, inspired to compose something new.

One thing she hadn't done in a long time was write about her son. Compelled by an encounter she could not put out of her mind, she focused this week's column on the shock she felt when he came home with his first tattoo.

Of course, there was a girl. She lived in Stonehurst, deep in the East Valley, where charros still trick out their horses, saddles, and outfits with the same care and pride as the lowriders over the hill in East LA. The girl's brother did not like Luna's son, but the girl was determined to prove her *wedo* boyfriend was worthy.

The *escaramuza* girl gave Luna's son a three-minute lesson and a horse, and though he was not skilled, he had great balance and no fear. Impressed by his success, the girl and then her brother paired him up with a less docile animal, and then another.

They promptly overmatched him and got his nose broken, his chin split and his head cracked.

To celebrate and commemorate the three wounds, the brother's best friend pulled his tattoo machine out of the barn and freehanded a sugar skull with a fantastic mustache on Luna's son's forearm. With relentless banging from a bootleg cassette and his bell still ringing, Luna's son egged them on, until one skull became three and they grew a rattlesnake's tail that wrapped down to his wrist.

Luna couldn't actually remember how or when her son broke up with that girl, but when he came home with his face bashed in, it was his swollen, bloody arm that had truly set her back on her heels. No one gets a first tattoo that big and in such an obvious spot. They hadn't even shaved his arm and hair caked into the seeping ink and plasma. At least the work was done with an actual machine, even if it was in a corral, so the ink was deep and the lines were not too scratchy.

Luna cleaned the area with extra virgin olive oil and roundly admonished her boy. But when he shook his principal's hand with his right and accepted his rolled-up diploma with his left—the skulls grinning and the snake rattling out from under the flowing black sleeve of the gown—Luna smiled with pride and self-satisfaction at the barely-muffled whispers of the mothers who had never raised a boy alone. In her mind, he had achieved his rite of passage many years earlier, but on that day the world knew her son was a man to be contended with.

Luna looked down at her column with a sort of nod, frown, and tiny shrug Alex would have recognized as approval. She knew it conveyed the tone and iconoclastic parable her ladies would love. And though he had many other tattoos, she couldn't stop thinking of that three-headed serpent, swinging as her son made his way.

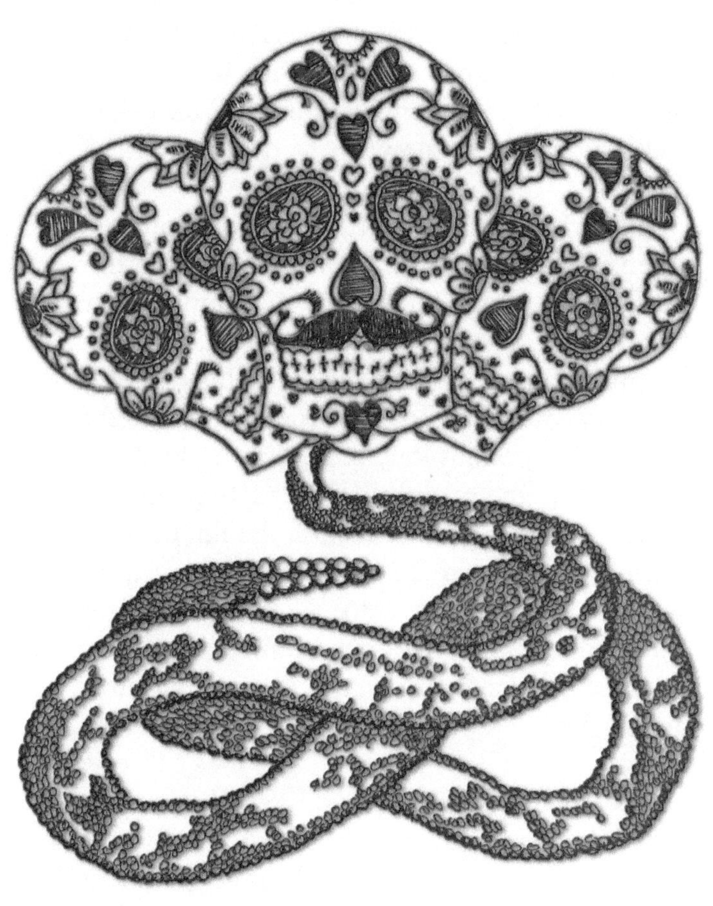

*One skull became three and they grew a rattlesnake's
tail that wrapped down to his wrist.*

As Luna hit "send," Inanna opened one heavily-lidded eye and then the other. Carefully, she lifted her head, last night's rites replaying in random order. She relished the remembered images, flavors, smells, and sensations, but now it was time to begin a new day.

The priestess sidled without rolling. Someone had fallen asleep cradling her round bottom, and the limp hand clung to one buttock as she slipped away. The fingers dragged against her movement, slid down her hip and dropped into the sheets. Inching through the tangle of covers and acolytes, Inanna navigated to the edge of the specially-ordered emperor-sized bed. She executed a single pushup, racked back into child's pose, and finally put her feet on the floor.

Shaking out her hair and invigorating her scalp, she shrugged into but didn't tie her pearlescent robe, and padded into the bathroom. There, she peed, splashed her face with water, and rubbed down her breasts, belly, and between her legs with a warm, wet towel.

The robe flowing behind her, Inanna moved to her kitchen and gathered her materials. By eye, she measured sugar and water and coffee ground as fine as flour into a copper *briki*. She turned on the stove and set the vessel over the flame.

The little pot came to a boil and Innana rested it on the counter to cool. After a moment, she returned the *briki* to the burner, but didn't set it down. Holding it by the long handle, she danced it gently over the heat, coaxing it slowly back to life. The coffee boiled and the priestess raised it high in the air to settle down.

Inanna eased the *briki* back to the heat a third time. The coffee crested to the lip of the pot with a hiss. Before the foam could subside, she poured the liquid—as brown as a horse's eye—into a thick, tiny cup with no handle.

It was too hot, but the demitasse felt good in her hand. When it had cooled enough to hold comfortably, she agitated it gently without breaking the foam, and let the aroma fill her sinuses. She put her lips to the rim and sucked in air and foam and coffee. Satisfied, she drank down the cup in a slow, deliberate draft. The viscous, velvet liquid flowed around her tongue, spiking her senses with rich flavors, sweet and bitter.

The cup drained, she tipped it to one side, careful not to let the thick residue of grounds spill out. Three times the priestess rotated the cup, coating the whole inner surface. She placed the little saucer upside down over the cup, then inverted them both and set them down, letting the saucer fill and the grounds set.

Inanna waited patiently, opening her mind, and finally turned the cup over. The dark patterns arced and divided and curled like filigree against the white enamel. Each separate course told a different, branching story. Inanna followed the plotlines. "Twin towers," she heard herself say out loud. The deeper into the cup, the more uncertain the future—but the towers extended from the rim to the bottom. One thing was clear: the towers were not exact twins. They were slightly out of balance, and at the top of one was a fulcrum.

Thoughtfully, she dragged a finger through the grounds. She could erase the stories, but not what was coming. "Shit."

The bologna and cheese sandwich tasted exactly like her childhood. Dara used her tongue to coax the white bread and mayo from behind her front teeth. Her laptop sat open in front of her, but Aunt Alice peered over the top from across the table.

"Thanks for the sandwich," Dara offered.

"I noticed you didn't break for lunch."

"I guess when I'm working from home, I forget." Dara realized what she just said. "I mean, working from…remotely."

"I know." She scrutinized her niece with eyes so dark they were almost as black as her hair. "You want some juice?"

Although she loved the woman, Dara knew the beverage her aunt offered would be unnaturally iridescent and definitely not juice. "No, thank you."

"I do," Thea spoke up from the couch in the next room.

"Who broke your legs?" Alice asked.

With performative huffing, Thea lifted herself from the couch and lurched into the kitchen. A moment later she collapsed into a chair across from her mother and aunt. As if it weighed forty pounds, she delivered the plastic bottle of orange liquid to the table and announced, "I am so bored."

"You know the difference between bored and boring?" Alice chided.

"Nothing." Dara and Thea answered together, both too familiar with Aunt Alice's old saw.

"What about your reading list?" Dara asked. But Thea had spent her morning reading.

"Well, don't bother your mother about it. She's got waste management to do."

"Is that what you think I do?" asked Dara.

"Don't you?"

"Recycling. For a winery."

"Fancy," Alice said.

"Besides, I wasn't working. I was studying for my certificate."

"You're going to school on purpose?" Thea crinkled her face.

Dara looked from her work module to her aunt and daughter, then to that bottle of juice. Decisively, she closed her laptop.

"Thea, get that box that was delivered."

After an eye roll, Thea did as she was asked. With a struggle, she shuffled into the dining room gripping the black cardboard box. She tried to heft it onto the table but couldn't quite clear the lip, so she set it on the floor next to her mother with a thump.

Dara held out a hand to Alice, who understood the unspoken request and handed her a knife from a place setting. "I get one of these a few times a year so I can know what I'm talking about." As Dara slit the clear packing tape from the flaps of the case, she questioned her daughter. "How old are you?"

"Seriously, you don't know?"

"I have a lot to keep track of."

"Thirteen," she answered, obviously.

Dara asked. "Where's your sister?"

"With Uncle Scotty. With the horses."

"Okay. She doesn't need to know about this."

Finally, Thea was interested. "About what?"

Dara sorted through the open box and drew out the bottle she was looking for. "Okay," she quizzed. "What are we eating?"

"Bologna and cheese," Thea answered first.

"So, the meat is salty, fatty, a little smoke, a little paprika."

"The cheese is yellow-tasting," analyzed Thea.

"Right. Really, really smooth-tasting. Almost like butter, but a little tangy."

"Don't forget the mayo," reminded Alice.

"Also a little tangy and fatty." Dara paused, checking to see that the curiosity of the table was sufficiently piqued. "When you take a bite, you can feel all those fats and flavors sticking to the inside of your mouth, right?" Her students nodded. "Now, Alice, that 'juice' is very sweet, and also sort of thick."

"Yellow-tasting," Thea repeated.

"Good. So, it's not going to contrast enough with the sandwich. It's not going to help you wash it down, or to taste it better." She started to open the selected bottle. "If there was mustard, or maybe potato chips on it, I might go for a dry, cold Riesling."

"But we don't have chips," led Thea.

"No. Now you might think I'd go for a Viognier or even a Sauv Blanc. But I'm opening a Grenache." As she spoke, she poured a sample into three empty juice glasses. "It has low tannin for a red, and just a bit of sweetness, but it has a really light body and the right acidity to cut through the fatty feel of the food." She tore the corners off a slice of sandwich and offered them to the class. "Eat that," and then after a moment, "now sip this."

Suddenly, Thea was worried and unsure. "Mom?"

Alice intervened. "You're a teenager now. Better here with us than behind the Mi-T-Mart."

"Well, that was pretty specific, but yes," smiled Dara. Cautiously, Thea put the glass to her lips and let the wine slip into her mouth. "Let it fill your mouth and literally clean your palate."

"Pepper!" announced Alice with surprise.

Thea held the liquid motionless in her mouth, frozen and unsure what to do. "It's okay," her mother reassured her. "You can spit it out if you want to." Slowly, Thea shook her head. The wine swirled a bit and she tried to talk.

"It's…" a drop escaped and dribbled down her chin. Her hand jumped up and reflexively, she swallowed the rest. "It's like ketchup."

Dara was intrigued. "Really?"

"How is it like ketchup?" Alice prompted.

Thea searched carefully. "You know…you know how you put ketchup on something to make it taste better? And, it was sweet, a little, and spicy, a little. And like…" she waved her hands like her father did when he was searching for a word. "Like Nerds," she concluded thoughtfully.

"Sour?" her mother offered.

Thea waggled her head in an exaggerated figure-eight that indicated "sort of."

"Tangy?" asked Alice.

The waggle continued.

"Vinegar? Like salt and vinegar chips?" tried Dara.

"I hate those!" Thea announced emphatically. "Like those, but in a good way. Like ketchup."

Dara's face blossomed into a great smile. "That was perfect, Thea."

Thea smiled proudly back. Then the worry crept back in. "Am I going to be drunk now?"

"Not really. Not from a few sips," Dara reassured her.

"But don't go driving anywhere," warned Alice.

Thea rolled her eyes, but without malice. Dara took in her growing daughter, and a warmth spread through her like the wine hitting her system. She knew she was staring, and that Thea would call her on it in a second. She forced herself to break the cord and reached into the case for a different bottle.

"What do we think would go with ranch dressing?"

Thea sprang from the table to retrieve the condiment from the kitchen.

"I didn't think I liked wine," Alice commented. Dara shrugged, happily.

Alice said "So that's what you do."

As the day came to an end, the ripples eddied and stacked up in a tide that gathered and weighed on the coils of the serpent. Incrementally, the lion lifted, and the bull waned.

The sun went down, and Alex opened his eyes. Carefully, he eased his weight off the floor and tested his shoulders. He felt the painful creaking and grinding, but nothing more than he could take.

Yucky stretched, yawned, and looked to Alex quizzically. Alex scritched his ears and started to get up. "Whoa, I think I fell asleep for a minute." He shook his head and gathered his wits. "Let's go to work."

Chapter 10
The Workingman's been here before and failed. Now he's back for more.

Roger couldn't believe what he was seeing. The same white man with the same tired, black truck was parked in front of his house again. This time, he wasn't even armed with the ridiculous net. Roger shook his head and called out from his porch. "You didn't get enough the other night?"

"I didn't do enough," the man corrected him.

The Pack was coming. Roger stopped wondering about the man. If you asked him, he'd say he'd heard The Pack, but he hadn't. For now, The Pack was silent.

Roger was a civilized, urban man and possessed no skills as an outdoorsman. He didn't even like Griffith Park. Like most city men and many country men, he held no cultural memory of the stalking, hiding, foraging, fleeing survivor his brain and body were built to be. There are even avid hunters who insert themselves into the wild places that dismiss—or fail to notice at all—the tingles and twitches and inklings and hairs standing on end that communicate unseen dangers around them.

He couldn't hear The Pack, but Roger had lived here all his life. Though he couldn't hunt or trap or fish or climb or run, he could sense The Pack as the Ashanti ancestors he knew nothing about had sensed the lion. His family possessed a worthy protector. He closed and locked his door behind him.

Alex looked up at the quarter moon, winking like a pearl button on a hastily done-up shirt. Alex was in a hurry himself, and the moon reminded him why he was participating in this insanity. That moon was shining over Dara.

Seventy miles away, at the far edge of the county, Dara stepped out on the ranch house porch with the glass of warm milk and honey Aunt Alice had mixed up for her. She looked up at the sliver of moon and thought of Alex, with his shirt badly buttoned. It made her smile.

In the cab of Alex's truck, Yucky barked wildly. Alex knew what that meant. He peered into the darkness and whistled.

The seething mass of The Pack stood out against the night. It swung its huge and horned head around to meet the call. Its massive body roiling, hooves churning the pavement, it charged.

Alex stood his ground. The Pack closed in. The air vibrated with its growling. Its taurine form loomed at the edge of the light from Alex's headlights. Yucky froze, still and noiseless.

The Leader detached from the shadow body and stepped into the light. It looked at Alex with a challenge in its yellow eyes.

"Look at you," Alex scoffed. "Leader of The Pack."

The Leader growled and bared its teeth.

"I know your secret."

"I know your secret."

Shoulders flaring, The Leader stepped closer. Saliva dripped from its jaws.

"You're just a dog."

Alex reached behind him and flipped a new switch on the hood of his truck. With a terrible wail, an electric motor whined on. The Leader froze. The Pack fell silent. Alex dashed to the driver's door and jumped into the truck. He fired up the engine, but the electric howl was even louder. Another new switch. New lights came on, bathing the street in light. The entire Pack was illuminated, disappearing the bovine shadow and exposing the dogs.

In the shine of the lights, the whining machine on the hood of the truck shimmered: a vacuum cleaner. Souped-up and enlarged and fixed to the grill and bumper like the cattle catcher on a locomotive, the horrible contraption thrummed and wailed and growled. Wide-eyed, and ears pinned, the dogs were paralyzed in the light. Alex revved the engine. The Leader's tail sank between its legs.

The truck lurched forward. The Leader barked—this time in fear. Alex eased on the gas. The pickup crept up to the Leader. The Leader bolted. It charged straight back through the mass of The Pack, splitting them apart. The Pack disintegrated.

With the terrible vacuum screaming between the headlights, Alex pursued the dogs through the streets. He homed in on the Leader. The Leader juked to the left. Tires chirping, Alex followed. As the Leader sprinted away, it pushed the other dogs of The Pack ahead of it. Dogs leapt fences and squirmed under parked cars. They shoved themselves into storm drains, hid in trashcans. Two even climbed trees. Anything to escape. One by one, they disappeared, and were not replaced. The Leader sprinted down the street faster and harder than it ever had in its life. The truck shrieked after it.

The Leader zipped around a corner. There were only a handful of dogs with it now. The vacuum chased them down an alley. A dead end.

Just like that, The Pack was gone. Now it was only a group of terrified dogs fleeing in all directions. At the end of the alley, only the Leader remained. Pinned against the wall, it stared at the awful machine. Alex stopped the truck. Yucky barked and barked. The Leader cowered.

Alex stepped down from the truck with a length of rope in his hands. He shut off the vacuum. The sudden quiet held only the barking of the one dog and the whimper of the other. Alex walked slowly toward the petrified animal. "Easy, pup. No more Pack. You're the leader of nothing." In submissive stillness, the dog let the rope loop around its neck.

The man led the shrinking dog back to the truck. "Jump up. Up, up, up!" The dog jumped into the bed it had fought to escape only two nights before. The man put out a strong hand, palm forward, in a universal gesture the dog could not help but comprehend. The word burned into association with the hand. "Stay."

Yucky stood on the seat and looked out the broken back window. He lorded over the frightened dog in the bed. The dog cowered.

In the circle of light from a pitted outdoor sconce, a man stood in front of Baba's Botanica and waited. He did not pace or shift his weight. His left hand held both a bottle and a lit cigar. He almost always kept his right hand free. Strong and tall and muscular and at ease, he wore the kind of pencil mustache of twin checkmarks that takes fastidious attention to maintain, and the slightest smile. Chango was his name, and he blew smoke into the mouth of the bottle of golden rum. He spiced the rum himself with cinnamon and cloves and allspice and peppercorns.

Chango sipped from the bottle and watched Baba with eyes that appeared much older than the rest of him. Baba slid the security gate closed across the front of his shop. He turned to Chango, ready to say, "Let's go," but then stopped. Someone was coming.

Chango watched a man approach. He too was muscular and strong, which are not always the same thing. His hair was dark and clipped short for ease. His beard was trimmed, but not fussed over. His sleeves were rolled up, his slacks were triple-stitched,

*He spiced the rum himself with cinnamon
and cloves and allspice and peppercorns.*

and his boots were practical. One of them seemed to be repaired with duct tape. Wounds and cuts and bruises—the most lurid a set of three parallel slashes, sutured shut from his ear to his cheek—marred every inch of exposed flesh. No, they didn't mar it, they marked it. In fact, they appeared as much a part of him as the tattoos on his arm and hands. He walked with ease and purpose, and a slight limp. Two dogs ambled with him on leashes. One white and black, the other amber. Chango liked the man immediately.

The man walked to Baba with the dogs. "Baba, I brought you a puppy."

Baba jumped back, afraid. "From The Pack?!"

Chango laughed, and the man gave the perfect answer: "There is no Pack."

Baba began to protest, but the man interrupted him. Challenged him. "You didn't think I could do it."

Chango couldn't help pitching in. "Of course he didn't," he said. He offered the man his right hand. "I am Chango." The man took his hand but did not squeeze it. He held it for a one-pump shake, a comfortable display of nothing to prove. Chango was pleased.

"I'm Alex," said the man.

"I thought you were," answered Chango.

Fixated on the dogs, Baba missed the entire exchange. The mustache twitched and curled. Sensing his fear, the dogs stared at him. "How?" he whined. "Cut off its head, two more replace it."

"I didn't cut off its head," Alex explained. "I cut off its body. Now it's just a bunch of dogs." Chango clearly loved that, and Alex turned to him. "You work for Baba?"

"Sometimes. Sometimes he works for me."

Baba was still focused on the dogs. "This is its head?!"

"It was. I call him Phobos." He offered the leash to Baba. "It means 'fear.'" Baba shrank back. "What's the matter?" Alex tortured him a bit. "Don't like dogs?"

"He can't believe it," Chango explained.

"You don't want him?"

"No!" Baba insisted. He gathered himself and said more reasonably, "No."

Chango laughed again. "Dogs don't like him."

Alex smiled back and said innocently, "I can't see why not." Chango offered his bottle to Alex, who courteously refused.

Alex looked back to Baba. "You got anything for me?"

"For tonight?"

"No. Not for tonight. I already did this tonight."

Again, Alex offered Phobos' leash to Baba. Again, Baba retreated from it.

"For tomorrow," said Alex.

"No! I haven't seen it yet."

"Really? Even with the Golden Girdle?" Alex looked to Chango. Chango shrugged, and turned to Baba for the answer.

"It isn't instant. I—" Like a man trying not to gaze at a woman's breasts, Baba flicked his eyes unconsciously to Chango and instantly, forcibly, flicked them away. "I'm working on something."

"Are you?" asked Chango with a hint of mockery.

Baba ignored that and continued with his didactic tone to Alex. "It isn't like turning on your TV and getting an instant picture."

"I don't have a picture on my TV," countered Alex. "I have the shockwaves of the universe."

"Ha!" Chango let the explosive laugh escape. "Looks like you have Saturday off, Workingman."

"Tomorrow's Friday," Alex corrected him.

Chango smiled at that. "See? This is what happens. The universe doesn't care about days of the week, and that's who you've been working for. But here in the world, its Friday night, and it looks like you lost a day somewhere."

Surprised, Alex considered that. "Saturday?" He smiled, a little plan forming. "I guess I'll go enjoy my weekend."

"Good," Baba perked up. "Go do that. Take the head with you."

"Phobos," Chango reminded him cheerily.

"Good to meet you, Chango," said Alex, as he headed off with the dogs.

Chango toasted him with the smoky bottle and called after the man. "Sleep with ease. You earned it, Alex."

Not much later that night, Alex removed every stitch of clothing and let the cool air play against and around his flesh. Goosebumps stretched every wound and abrasion. It all felt good, dancing on the edge of pain. Chango's parting words drifted through Alex's head. Unlike the night and entire day before, he did sleep with ease. Lying atop the covers, he drifted motionlessly away into unrestless slumber. At the foot of the bed, Yucky and Phobos curled up in a pile of blankets. All three snored quietly.

Chapter 11
When it feels like everything's all right, it's time for the Workingman to look over his shoulder.

The next morning, showered and shaved, Alex stood at his broken mirror. He shifted his position to best catch his reflection in the shards. His claw marks were healing into a livid tightness around the stitches. His lips were chapped and split, and the freshness of his grooming highlighted the bruising on his jaw, cheek, and eye. But he wasn't badly swollen, and Dara's haircut had grown out only as far as a trim neatness. His dozens of reflections looked him over with mild approval.

A sort of rested, ready energy filled his lungs and energized his blood. He counted in his head. The lion. The eggs. The girdle. El Chancho. The Pack. Five. Baba told him he had ten tasks ahead of him. Alex was halfway through. In as much time as he'd already spent so far, maybe less, he'd be done with this insanity and have his life back. When he repaired the mirror, he would install hinged wings, so Dara could see her profile.

As tight as he could cinch it, Baba wore the zoster and breathed shallow breaths. The brazier burned with barley and laurel, carving the little back room into horizontal strata of haze. Baba read through the layers of smoke like pages, finding a story—but not the plot. Finally, he saw the reverse cascade rise and delaminate the blue-gray sheets with twin columns of smoke that towered up to the ceiling. Now he knew what had to happen. But "How?"

Spend some time looking at signage around the United States, and you'll see a trend: "In business since..." "Established in..." 1946, 1948, 1953, even 1957 or 61. These places all came to be in the wake of the War. Not every business was established by a man who slogged through four years of combat to return home and realize the American dream. They weren't even all veterans. But the surplus of money, and opportunity, and more than anything, vigor—purchased by the Depression, the deprivation, the deaths and finally the sweeping victory—pushed the country into booms in every facet of its life.

Ray Balentine was not in the infantry. He'd been a seventeen-year-old cook. But there was no rear area at Anzio. He'd lost two fingers to enemy action, and not on the same day. No one knew this, not even Ray, but one of them ended up in the soup.

When he finally came home, he took out a loan and rented a storefront. With pots and pans from the Army Navy store, and a flat top grill made from the engine cover of an M10 tank destroyer, he opened the doors at "Ray's." That was in 1948, and two mornings a week he still gets in front of that flat top now.

This place was mostly a long counter, with a few tables lining the walls. Nothing had changed much since opening day, including the staff. A little bell rang as Alex walked inside. He looked good, all cleaned up. The scratches and bruises were showing, and the stitches on the side of his face, but he was rested and out of his work clothes. You don't dress up to go to Ray's, but Alex put on a fresh Veruca Salt t-shirt because he had Dara on his mind, and they were her current favorite band.

Alex watched Ray, hardly noticing the missing middle and pinky fingers on the old cook's left hand, as he twirled a spatula and flipped a pat of hash browns the size of a pizza. The old man looked up from his hot work and noticed Alex. He fixed the younger man with confused and judgmental eyes.

"Alex? Good morning." It was almost a leading question.

Alex was in too good a mood to notice. "Morning, Ray. My table open?"

Ray mused, "I guess. I don't know."

"Okay?" Now, Alex noticed Ray was still staring at him. Alex wasn't sure what was up, and he wasn't sure he wanted to know, so he sat at the counter and ordered. "I'll have the "Two, two, two and two—"

"With the eggs scrambled," Ray interrupted. He turned his back and set about preparing the food.

Keely White was seventy-two. She claimed to hate Ray, and she'd worked for him since 1964. When she saw Alex, she stopped in her tracks. "Alex?" She said it as if she were testing him.

Alex smiled at her. With him seated at the counter, they were at about eye level with each other. "Morning, Keely. Coffee?"

Was she sneering at him? Alex wondered.

"On your table." She marched away.

No point in fighting with such an opponent. Alex got up from the counter and walked around a little corner to his regular table for two by the window. Now he stopped in his tracks. Dara was there. She sat at the table looking up at Alex, her finished breakfast plate in front of her.

Keely put down an empty coffee cup across the table from Dara and filled it. "Alex, sit," said Dara.

Without taking his eyes off her, Alex sat. Her eyes were locked on him too.

Alex was brimming. His heart pounded as if he'd never before asked her out but was about to. "I'm trying not to giggle. I'm so happy to see you."

Dara seemed immune. "I just came for biscuits and gravy."

"Kind of a long drive." Alex was grinning.

"Your face looks better."

"How are the girls?"

"Fine," she said. "Thea was sick."

A little bit of concern crept into him, but not much. If anything was really wrong, this wasn't how she'd tell him. "With what?"

"Nothing serious. Niki never got it, but she pretended she did." Normally, she would smile at that, but she forced herself not to. Still, she said it.

"They're okay now?" He knew.

"Yes."

"Good." He couldn't stop his grin or even dim it. Actually, he didn't even think of trying. "You look good. I miss you."

"You're not exactly playing it cool, Alex." She admired his choice of T-shirt, but she didn't show it.

"I don't have to. That's how cool I am."

She would have laughed at that too, but she brought herself back by asking, "You seen any more of that woman who doesn't remind you of me?"

Alex batted that woman away with a gesture. "I forgot about her. Since then, I've had two more big jobs."

Not impressed. "Make any money?"

"That makes five. I'm halfway through." He admitted, "No money."

"When you do these five more jobs"—she really wanted to understand—"then you get the money?"

"I don't know." And still he smiled as he said it.

"And this gets me back?"

Alex didn't have an answer. Keely came with Alex's breakfast and shoved it in front of him. Two pancakes, two slices of bacon, two links of sausage, and two eggs, scrambled. Dara pushed her chair back, took out some money and showed it to Keely. "I'll get this. He doesn't have any money." She put her cash on the table and stood up.

Keely looked harshly at Alex. He ignored her. Dara started to walk out. There was no smile on his face now. He was serious. Alex announced, "I'll get you back, Dara."

Dara stopped and turned back to her husband. "What makes you think so?"

Alex rose and walked close enough to touch her, but he didn't. "Your Aunt Alice makes the best biscuits and gravy in the state."

Dara looked Alex in the eye. That deep connection, that pull—it was undeniable. She didn't deny it, but she said, "Maybe. But I won't let you kiss me."

He smiled again at his wife. "Not today."

He impressed her by not trying. They broke away from each other as if from a passionate embrace. Dara turned and left the diner. Alex headed back to his table.

Keeley was definitely sneering at him now. "What are you smiling about?" she asked.

She couldn't get him down. "It's all coming together," he let her know. He stepped past her, sat at his table, and started his breakfast.

Later, Alex's truck pulled into the carport at his apartment building. Over the years, he'd done his best to secure all his tools and equipment, but a carport is not a garage. The space was crowded with locked gang boxes and projects nearing completion. Dara always had to park on the street.

As Alex stepped off the running board, a brown Mercury Mystique with a bad muffler and a rattle like a bike with a baseball card in the spokes squealed to a stop with urgency. Baba leaned from behind the steering wheel to shove open his passenger door and shout at Alex. "Get in!"

Baba explained as he pushed the car hard, racing through the pass on the busy freeway. "You know what is a 'changeling?'"

"A baby stolen by fairies?"

"The changeling is the baby left in the abducted child's place," Baba clarified.

"So, what happens to the baby?"
In answer, Baba drove to Century City.

Century City makes a good attempt at being a second downtown. The land was sold off by 20th Century Fox when it became too expensive to keep a massive back lot. The sets had been torn down, and the law offices moved in. Hundreds of them. About a hundred acres of land, almost all of it built up—and almost every building filled with lawyers, or the facilities to support, feed and entertain them.

At the center of it all, two identical prisms loom into the sky. Forty-four stories tall, the twin towers lord over the Westside. Black glass, three-sided skyscrapers, featureless and imposing, they rise from a concrete plaza as blank as their façade, giving no clue as to their contents.

Alex and Baba stood at the base of the buildings. Alex looked up and concluded, "I don't get it."

Baba answered as if it were obvious. "You need to rescue her."

The skinny Latino with long arms and fingers, in a billowing, black guayabera shirt and cargo shorts, knees almost white with calluses, and the muscular, scarred and battered Greek in Carhartt pants and a concert shirt, could hardly have looked more out of place as they rode up this mahogany and mirrored elevator that moved so smoothly it felt like it was standing still.

Alex was still trying to get a handle on the situation. "So, someone in this luxury office tower is practicing black magic and kidnapped a baby."

Baba was relieved. "Exactly!"

"And," Alex continued, "they left another baby in her place, so her parents don't even know she's gone."

"They didn't know," Baba corrected. "Then they came to me. And the Golden Girdle helped me see the towers in the smoke."

"And I have to get her back."

"That's it," answered Baba, proud of the man.

The doors opened silently. Alex and Baba stepped out into the lobby. All brass and tanned leather, this room projected the power of the men who worked here to all who entered.

Alex whispered, "Where do you keep a baby in this place?"

CHAPTER 12

The gentle touch of a soft hand pulls the Workingman from his work.

Neville and Stephen, both young and fit and perfectly dressed, sat behind the curved blond-wood reception desk, artfully lit from below. The desk was on a slightly raised platform, giving the visitor the impression of looking up to high and powerful gatekeepers. The one long, leather-paneled wall facing the elevators countered the curve of the desk, making the room into the shape of an eye. There were no visible doors leading out of the eye. The two men in its pupil traded off answering silently ringing phones.

"Niemand, Amoodo and Blank... hold please."
"Niemand, Amoodo and Blank... hold please."
"Niemand, Amoodo and Blank... hold please."

Baba hung back by the bank of elevators. The mustache wavered. Alex approached the desk, unsure of how to start. He tried, "I'm here about the baby."

Neville didn't miss a beat. "And what is your name?"

"Alex Cides."

"Stephen," Neville turned to his colleague, "Mr. Cides is here about a baby."

Stephen looked up from the phones and blurted, "My God, Neville, look at him." He smiled at Alex and asked, "Where do you work out?"

"Stephen," Neville prompted, "the baby."

Alex returned the smile. "I don't work out, Stephen, I just work." Maybe even more impressed by the repartee than the physique, Stephen flared his eyes as Alex turned to the other man. "What about the baby, Neville?"

"Well, for that," Stephen said with authority, "you need Mr. Blank. You have an appointment?"

"He should know I'm coming."

Stephen produced a raised finger to request a moment and spoke into his headset. "Leilata, there's a Mr. Cides here for Mr. Blank."

"Leilata?" Alex asked.

"Leilata's Mr. Blank's assistant," Neville let him know.

Stephen was off the line. He sized Alex up. "You'll like her."

"Do you want a water?" Neville offered.

"Or a soda, or anything else?" Stephen suggested.

"What I could really use right now is a beer," Alex commented.

Neville jumped in. "Stephen's not single, you know."

Alex nodded, "Neither am I."

Neville settled the matter. "Then, water for you both."

A hidden door opened in the leather paneling… and in walked Leilata. She was twenty-three, and long ago she had learned to control the boyish bounce in her step. She moved with a lithe stride and a roll in her hips that never once made a man think of his mother. Her hair was the color of sun-bleached wheat, and you just knew it would flow like silk if you unclasped it from the jade clip confining it in a knot on the back of her head. Her eyes perfectly matched the clip, and her skin would be so smooth to touch. She wore a professional suit that was not cut especially low to reveal her supple cleavage or slit especially high to show off her long and strong legs.

The magnetic effect pulled Alex's eyes to her. Stephen chimed in, "See?"

Alex nodded. "I'll take that water."

Leilata was efficient and professional. "Did you get Mr. Cides something to drink?"

Suddenly, Baba spoke urgently from the back of the room. "That's her!"

Alex asked, "What?"

"That's her!" Baba insisted.

Alex was confused. "The baby?"

Leilata didn't like being called that. "Baby?"

Baba continued, almost frantic. "She was a baby. Twenty-three years ago."

"What's this about?" Leilata asked.

Alex and Baba went on, as if they were alone. "Twenty-three years? You said this just happened."

"I said her parents just came to me." Baba urged, "Well?"

"Well, what?" Alex asked him, irritated.

"Yeah," Leilata added. "Well, what?"

Baba ordered. "Grab her!"

Leilata didn't hesitate. "Stephen! Neville!"

Neither did the receptionists. They leapt over the desk. Now Alex could see they were strong and tall. They flanked him in ready positions that were not yet on guard but could be in a split second.

Baba furiously pushed the elevator button, shrieking, "Get her! Get her!"

Alex squared off with Stephen and Neville. "Don't do anything stupid," Stephen warned Alex.

But Alex ignored the others. Without turning to Baba, he chided him angrily. "This was it? Just 'Get her?'"

Baba insisted, "Rescue her!"

That gave Leilata pause. "Rescue?"

Neville waited for her direction. "Leilata?"

She decided. "Get him."

Stephen and Neville charged. They were fast. Alex ducked and weaved.

"Don't let them take you!" Baba directed uselessly.

The mustache shrank in fear, showing teeth. The elevator opened. "Alex, quickly! Bring her!"

"Just a second," he answered. The receptionists were on him. In self-defense, Alex threw the first fist and caught Stephen in the eye. Stephen rocked back, but Neville was right there.

Neville planted a knee in Alex's gut. Alex doubled over and saw his next target right in front of him. The tan, duct taped and blood-stained boot bit down hard on a blue, wrinkled calfskin, Ferragamo loafer. Neville hopped back. Stephen checked Alex into the wall. Neville recovered and slammed his shoulder into Alex's side.

Baba stepped onto the elevator and called out something like, "Don't let them take you!" But Alex was too busy to pay attention. Baba held the "Open Door" button down, as if pressing it harder could help Alex move faster.

The weight of the two men pinned Alex to the wall. He gathered himself and strained against them. With all his strength, he dragged the two men toward the elevator. His shirt didn't tear, but the collar stretched with a little pop, and El Chancho's tusk sprang free.

Leilata called to her gatekeepers. "Get him too." She pointed at Baba.

Stephen struggled just to answer. "We can't get them both." Alex pulled the men closer to the elevator. Baba didn't exactly cower, but he did step back from the elevator panel overly quickly. He let the doors go.

Alex roared, "Baba!"

"I'm sorry."

"You son of a bitch!"

Baba threw up his hands. "I'm so—" The doors closed and cut him off.

With a furious surge, Alex broke free. He spun and drove a knee into Stephen's liver. A vicious right to the jaw laid Neville flat.

Alex turned on Leilata. "What the hell?!" he demanded.

"Who are you?!" she wanted to know.

A violent crash hit Alex hard from behind. A swarm of uniformed security guards enveloped Alex and dragged him through the hidden door as his head swam into darkness.

Alex slipped unsteadily toward consciousness. He tried to think, to lift his head. A tightness in his face told him there were new bruises. A buzzing backbeat at a nauseating off tempo prevented his vision from clearing.

He flinched a little. Something had touched his mouth. Lips. Lips on his lips. He took in the kiss and returned it. The warmth, the electricity of it softened the rhythm in his head as the blood ran to other parts of his body.

A cool hand eased under his shirt and ran up his bruised back. It felt so good to be touched. His own rough palm cupped smooth flesh. A soft moan whispered in his ear like a perfect breeze on a hot afternoon. A sweep of wavy, golden hair drew across his eyes like a curtain, and Alex became aware of a lush room, warmly lit and dim.

Eyes of rich malachite gazed into his through the bleary haze of unconsciousness. Alex knew those eyes, or he though he did. Told himself he did. The comfort there was such dreamy relief.

White teeth flashed like pearls against ruby lips as the delicious mouth mirrored Alex's growing, drunken smile. Those lips spurred his longing and made him forget any fear or any purpose—though he still remembered that he shouldn't forget. Struggling to recall, Alex tumbled back into those lips and a burning desire that they would kiss him again.

The red lips parted in a silvery, musical laugh with a treble that made you lean into the joy of it, and a bass that pulled you down into passion. Alex tried to rise to capture the sound with his own lips, but the crimson smile teased away from him, drawing him deeper.

His head was still swimming. Alex lay back and exhaled slowly, trying to still the room without breaking the spell. He looked out from under

A soft moan whispered in his ear like a
perfect breeze on a hot afternoon.

his eyelashes in a delectable agony of enchanting anticipation. He could feel the movement of her breath on his cheek. Honey-sweet, it sent a tingling through his nerves that eddied around the spike.

Alex couldn't tell if he was afraid or simply unable to open his eyes completely. He sensed as much as saw the woman bending above him as she went to her knees, lips and eyes gloating with deliberate voluptuousness. The thrill of it battled the memory of his mission. She arched her supple neck and licked her lips, moisture shining on the scarlet pout and the pink tongue, and Alex forgot again.

Lower and lower went her head, delivering tiny kisses, trailing cool spots on the hot flesh from Alex's mouth to his chin to his throat. She paused, and Alex reveled in the breath on his neck. His skin tingled as nerve endings reached for the expected sensation, each hoping to be the next target of the probing mouth.

Alex's fingers tunneled through silky masses of lustrous hair. They found her ear and ran around the rim, gently traversing the helix to stimulate the nub at the opening of the canal. Alex could feel the sparks he set off in her flesh.

The soft, shivering touch of the lips parted from the sensitive skin of Alex's throat. He closed his eyes in languorous ecstasy, easing a hand under the hem of a satin shirt. Caressing up from belly to ribs, he found her breasts. She flexed her shoulders to help him spill them over the tops of the low, lacy cups.

Gently, he pinched a nipple between his middle and index fingers. The closed mouthed hum of a moan vibrated from her lips.

Alex slid his other hand along an easy thigh and pushed a skirt up to the point of a hip. He inhaled deeply. That honey-sweet smell of her flooded him again. It was glorious, but it was wrong. It buzzed at him. The ringing in his ears returned, along with the pain in his shoulder. The spike twitched. That honey smell worked at his struggling brain. Her kisses continued, but the fragrance was all wrong. Not bad—just wrong. Reluctantly, he formed a question and forced himself to speak. "Dara?"

Like a key opening a padlock and dropping a chain to the floor, the name broke the spell. Alex's head cleared and his eyes popped open. "Dara?!" It couldn't possibly be. Alex struggled to his feet. "What are you doing?"

Leilata looked up at him from the leather couch. "You came here for me. Don't you want me?" Her jacket was off. Her blouse was undone to her navel. Her breasts rose free of the delicate balconette. Her skirt bunched perfectly in her lap to cast a mysterious shadow in the cleft between her legs.

Alex fought the syncopation between his head and his loins. "Want you for what? This is what you do here?"

"I work for Mr. Blank." She did not cover herself. "I do what he tells me."

"He told you to do this?"

She said, "Yes," as she undid the last button of her blouse.

"Why?"

"I didn't ask." She took hold of the clasp between her breasts. "Why do you ask?"

"Stop it."

"You don't mean that." The clasp popped and Leilata rolled her shoulders, easing herself free. She stood and reached out. Tenderly, she followed the line of stitches on his neck with a fingertip. "Your scars itch. Let me scratch them."

Alex stepped back. "You asked me who I am."

"So?" She continued to caress Alex's face and neck, and found the leather strap.

"It doesn't matter. I'm here because of who you are."

"You are interested in me," she purred. She slipped her fingers around the tusk and traced its curve.

"You were kidnapped."

"No, I wasn't," she fought on.

"You wouldn't remember. Your parents sent me."

"My parents are dead."

Twenty-three years ago, not many people lived in Century City. There are more now, but even with the new condos, there are almost no children. Leilata had grown up in a corporate world of adults and privilege and tutors. She was guided and trained. She could jump a horse, select the finest wine, or discuss important art as easily and as well as she could use her body to perform whatever task was at hand. All these things she had been taught well, but never warmly. Secretly, she wondered at the intimacy shared by people who get to go home from work.

Still, she said it proudly when she let Alex know, "Mr. Blank raised me."

"He named you, too?" She was maybe starting to listen, and Alex thought he had stumbled on a way in.

"It's a Greek name," she mused.

"I know."

"It means, 'Treasure.'" She stepped back a bit, so he could see all of her.

"No. It doesn't."

No one had ever resisted her like this. Alex's words disturbed her. Leilata was finally paused, but she insisted. "Yes, it does."

"He's your father, and he ordered you to have sex with me?"

"He doesn't order," she defended.

"Still," Alex pointed out, "your top is undone." Suddenly shy, Leilata started doing up buttons. "I have to get you out of here."

She was confused and she didn't like it. "But—" Alex interrupted. "*Thisavros* is treasure."

A wave of juvenile fear almost prevented her asking, "What's *Leilata*?"

"Loot."

That hit her hard. Years of tiny, ignored questions flooded back to her.

"You know my mother?"

"No."

"My father?"

"No."

"But you know who they are?"

"No."

Alex didn't hide or apologize for his answers. His stark honesty shook Leilata.

"Where are they?"

"I don't know."

"But they're looking for me?"

"Yes."

"And they sent you?"

"The man you saw me with sent me."

"They went to him for help?"

"Yes."

"To rescue me?"

"Yes."

"And you trust him?"

"No."

Leilata was silent, a tumbling of new and old questions crowding her mind. For the moment she pushed them aside.

"But I can trust you." It wasn't a question.

"Yes."

She made her decision. In as little time as it takes to straighten your clothes, Alex and Leilata rushed into a long, lush and secret hallway with just one door at the far end. As she led them toward escape, Alex asked her, "Are there cameras?"

Leilata looked worried. "Everywhere."

Chapter 13

When the Workingman thinks he understands the job at hand, it all goes to hell.

Arrow-straight, the corridor shot through the hidden backways of the tower. Here, all was carpeted richly in gold, with matching, felted wallpaper. Footfalls were silent, and voices sounded like they came from inside your head. Alex and Leilata sprinted toward escape.

The far door banged open. The pair skidded to a halt as Neville and Stephen shouldered through and blocked the hall. Alex sized them up and stepped in front of Leilata. He'd almost beaten them once before. He balled his hands into fists. Neville and Stephen moved in. Alex set himself.

"Wait," said Leilata. She pressed a panel on the wall. It swung open. A door. She pulled Alex through.

A startled accountant jumped up from behind his

desk as Alex and Leilata burst through a door in his office he had no idea existed. They ignored him and rushed across the room to the now-unhidden entrance. As they disappeared, the stunned accountant began to sink back into his chair, mouth hanging open. Before he had time to wonder, Neville and Stephen crashed in. The accountant dove under his desk as Neville and Stephen knocked over furniture racing through the room.

The gatekeepers exploded out into the next hallway. This one wasn't secret. People leaned out of sepia-toned, translucent-walled offices to see what was going on. Neville and Stephen clattered down the black marble floor, following the sounds of Alex and Leilata's flight. They rounded a corner and the hall widened into a space of bubinga café tables and bentwood chairs, discrete refrigerators, a soda fountain, espresso machines, and a corkboard covered with messages and fliers.

Lawyers and paralegals scattered as Stephen flew first into the break room. Before he could take more than a step, Alex buried a hard fist in his ribs. Stephen doubled over as the force fired off deep nerves and froze his diaphragm in place. Neville crashed into Stephen. The tangle of bodies swept over Alex, and the three men toppled to the floor.

They sprawled through the room. Alex scrambled across the marble, making eye contact with his dark reflection. It gazed back, looking disappointed in him. Neville pounced on his legs. Alex jerked and kicked to free himself. Keening out of rhythm, Stephen sucked air, trying to get his wind back.

Leilata didn't know what to do, so she watched. Alex fired off an unaimed foot and good luck landed it in Neville's face. Neville rolled up like a rubber band snapping back. Alex jumped to his feet.

Recovering as one, Neville and Stephen started to get up from the floor. Alex knew he had only a second. He spotted the biggest thing in the room, the soda fountain on the counter. With all his might, Alex wrapped his arms around it. Straining against brass fittings and plastic pipe, he tore it free. The base splintered away from the counter. Jets of varicolored soda rainbowed through the air. The soda fountain crashed onto Neville and Stephen.

Alex grabbed Leilata by the wrist and they ran out of the room. Neville and Stephen struggled out from under the decapitated machine on the now-slippery floor.

Associates, assistants, and clerks popped their heads above their low walls in this vast bullpen of cubicles. Alex and Leilata dashed through the big room, filtered sunlight glowing golden off the maze of partitions. From the far corners of the labyrinth, hidden doors swung open. Black uniformed security guards thundered in. Leilata guided Alex through the twists and turns. The phalanx of guards converged on Alex and Leilata, carving the room into giant wedges.

Soaked and stained, Neville and Stephen appeared back at the entrance. They sprinted into the office staff. Leilata turned Alex toward a broad set of stairs. Only three steps up, they covered one whole wall and led to a set of heavy double doors that dominated the room. The guards were almost on them. Neville and Stephen began barking orders. Alex shouldered the doors open.

They spilled into a room that was surprisingly small compared to the grand entrance. Alex slammed the massive doors behind them. Leilata ran behind a mirrored desk lit by a sphere of light that appeared to float equidistant between the floor and the high ceiling. Alex started to drag a heavy leather chair to block the doors. Leilata pushed a button on the desk. The doors locked with a chunky click.

Alex looked at her, questioning. "This is my office," she explained. From the outside, the doors shook, and the gatekeepers shouted.

"They really don't want to let you go," noted Alex.

"Another reason to believe you," she agreed.

There was almost nothing in Leilata's office but the expensive and uncomfortable guest chairs and her desk, which reflected you back at yourself while you sat and waited for her attention. The only other feature was the subtly vorticose moldings that pulled your eye irresistibly to the uncomfortably off-center double doors standing behind the desk. Alex's feet were planted, but the play of the room tugged him by the gut toward the doors as if he were falling.

This time it was Leilata who forced them open. "Mr. Blank!" she demanded.

The room was vast and dark and red. Polarized windows subdued the sunlight to rosy dimness and turned the glass to lucent mirrors. Shifting light and shadow undulated on the walls where barely discernable images of massive bulls rolled in expressionistic bas-relief. Leilata stood her ground in a spot of glowing light that illuminated any entrant into the room. She confronted a portly, balding, corporate man in his fifties who sat another three steps up behind an oversized desk. Calmly, he addressed his assistant. "Leilata, I hear you're leaving us."

"Don't call me that." The desk on its raised platform forced her to look up at him, but she was unintimidated.

Mr. Blank scolded himself, mildly. "We taught you so many languages over the years, but never Greek."

"It's true?" she demanded. "Loot?"

By way of an answer, Mr. Blank raised his focus to meet the sweating, angry man hanging back in the open doorway. "Mr. Cides." He gestured as if to a subordinate he was sure would follow his direction. Alex did follow, reluctantly stepping into the light with Leilata. The doors closed behind them. "I guess we didn't count on you," said Mr. Blank.

Alex was no stranger to a stinging retort, and the one he was about to deliver would help him recover his footing in the weird room of half-light and no answers. But before Alex could speak, Mr. Blank stood up behind his desk and into shadows.

The man completed the move, but his silhouette continued to rise. Alex froze. A trick of the light? The shadow form of the man appeared slimmer, fitter, taller. The red tip of a cigar that hadn't been there before glowed as he drew in the smoke.

Alex almost sat on the floor. His feet ached, rooting him to the spot. Something snapped in his head, the tendon that keeps your brain from floating from the sane to the insane. It was not Mr. Blank facing down Alex from the shadows behind his desk. The man in the shadows was Chango.

Chango continued his rumination. "I should have guessed, though. You were inevitable. Why else would we have given her a Greek name?"

Alex tried to force some sense into his head. "Chango?"

"Such a cliché, *el momento de la verdad*, especially in English. But do you know where it comes from?" Alex didn't know, and even if he had, he couldn't have answered. He was locked in confusion and disbelief.

"Bullfighting," Chango answered himself. "It's the moment where the matador must stand in the face of the charge and allow the hot bulk of the bull to come as close as it will ever come. This is the moment that tells whether he has it in him to plant his feet and guide his sword with elegant precision, over the head, between the horns, to dive the blade between the neck and shoulders, and pierce the heart to deliver instant death. Or it tells that he does not." Chango sized up the man standing before him. "You're in the middle right now. In the middle, but still not in balance. Tell me I'm right."

So much had been said to Alex about balance, about tasks, about forces and powers beyond understanding. Cosmic pulses rang in his brain like the throbbing of the impinged nerve that never left his body without pain. Chango was right. If that was Chango. Could it be Chango?

"It seems," Chango continued when he got no answer, "you have already been pierced between the neck and shoulder."

That broke Alex from his existential fog. His pain. That was real. He focused on it. It rooted him back to the world and out of the aether. He relished his pain, gritted his teeth, and made eye contact with Chango.

Chango knew exactly what Alex was doing. In answer, Chango held his fist high in the air. Alex froze. He didn't know what was about to happen.

Leilata knew. "No!"

Chango brought his fist down and slammed it hard on the desk. With the mighty boom, the spike in Alex's neck became visible. Alex didn't have time to wonder at its appearance. An unseen force drove the spike deep into Alex's flesh.

Alex roared out in pain. His knees turned to water, and he collapsed. His hands groped at his neck. His fingers closed on nothing.

Chango hammered the desk again. Boom! The spike shot deeper. Alex crumbled. Chango raised his fist a third time. Alex knew what was coming. He cried out, but not for mercy.

"Chango!" Alex challenged. "You forgot one thing." Chango hesitated. "I'm not the bull." With all his strength, Alex charged.

He roared with rage and fury. In the wicked light of the room, Alex's shadows on the floor and his reflections on the windows were suddenly those of a lion. The lion tore across the writhing bulls etched in the walls. Chango froze for an instant, surprised. It was exactly enough time.

Alex cannoned his shoulder into the desk. The impact jarred him to the heels. The spike stabbed deeper, and excruciating numbness shot through to his fingers. The desk flipped over with a crash, blasting Chango back into the wall.

Alex lurched to his feet and called to Leilata, "Door!"

Leilata ran to a wall and opened a hidden panel. The shadow lion rushed out of the room with them and was gone.

No artful, moody lighting or leather panels decorated the steel stairwell. Harsh shadows slashed through the long, long, narrow flights. As fast as they could, Alex and Leilata sprinted down and down and down. Alex's useless arm flapped against the handrails, each downward step a drumbeat of neuropathic pain.

Chango froze for an instant, surprised.

Leilata focused on not breaking an ankle, taking two stairs at a time to escape the tower.

On the flat plane of the concrete plaza a nondescript door banged open. Alex and Leilata burst out into white bright sunlight. They were alone. Stunned, Alex looked around.

"Baba!" There was no answer. "Baba! You bastard!"

Leilata squinted into the emptiness, knowing their pursuers could not be far behind. "Where's your car?"

Half an hour later, Alex and the girl sat on a crowded bus moving slowly across town. Alex was seething. She was lost.

Alex could move his arm now but doing so burned, like sweat hitting the million tiny wounds inflicted by fiberglass insulation.

The girl had escaped, but every lurch of the bus took her farther away from the only home she'd ever known. She turned to Alex and gasped, "There's blood on your neck." Alex put his hand to the sore spot and his fingers came back red.

"The spike..."

Alex raged, "There's no damn spike! It's from hitting the desk."

"But I saw..."

"Saw what?!" Right then, only anger kept Alex from falling apart. "You don't know what you saw."

"Mr. Blank..."

"There's no fucking Mr. Blank!" Alex's temper refluxed like vomit. His elbow lashed out in the confined space. The bus window splintered in a frozen sunburst with the impact. The blow boomed through the seats, and the shocked silence of the passengers was like a scream.

The bus jerked to a halt. The furious driver marched down the aisle with a six-inch billy club, illegal in the state of California. Alex threw himself out the back doors.

Knowing no one else in the world now, the girl followed him.

John and Jacqueline stood in the sun outside Baba's shop, because it just smelled too funny in there. Still, they hadn't been too disdainful to seek and accept his help. For years they'd struggled. Desperation had broken down a wall of prejudice, and they were relieved to finally hear Baba's answer. It wasn't their fault.

Their advisor looked up the block and pointed. They followed his long finger and saw two people walking wearily down the sidewalk.

Alex stopped on the pavement and put out a hand to the girl who was no longer called Leilata. She took it. Neither had said a word since the bus. Hesitant and afraid for the first time in years, she looked down the block. She saw a colorful little storefront with a painted sign and a window full of fantastic wares. Standing in front of the shop was the dark Latin man who had come to the office with Alex, and a couple in their forties who were not colorful at all. Not colorful, but excited.

Jacqueline rushed to her with arms extended. "Baby. You're beautiful." She started to cry.

The girl looked on them, unsure. She did not accept the embrace. "What's my name?"

John answered proudly. "Candy."

She didn't like that at all. "Are you serious?"

"Oh, Candy!" Jacqueline couldn't wait any longer. She threw her arms around the girl.

The girl froze. "Is it short for something?"

John almost jumped up and down as his wife crushed the girl in her arms. "We knew it. We knew it. You had to be out there. When Candy, the other Candy, kept running away, she just wasn't right. She couldn't be ours."

The girl stepped back from her mother's arms and asked, "Why'd she run away?"

Jacqueline threw up those arms in a dramatic gesture. "Who knows?"

"Candy," John explained, "the other Candy, is in jail now."

"Oh."

"Meli," Alex stepped in. He literally stepped in too, separating the parents and the girl.

"What?" John took in the beat-up-looking man for the first time. The man did not wither under his gaze.

"I call her Meli," Alex informed them with authority.

"It's Greek," the girl expanded. She looked a secret *thank you* to Alex.

Jacqueline tested the name. "Meli?"

John tested the ethnicity. "Greek?"

Baba weighed in with a smile and a pat on both their backs. "Well, all is set right now."

And that was enough for John and Jacqueline. "Thank you, Mr. Baba. Thank you."

Alex and Meli looked at Baba, unsure. But the parents swept up their daughter and the little family headed off down the street. Meli glanced back at Alex, unhappily. In a moment, they were out of sight.

Alex turned angrily on the priest. "What the hell was that, Baba?!"

Baba put his hands up as if bats dove at his head. "I know! I know. I couldn't let them capture us both."

But Alex swatted that aside. "Not that! Your friend. Chango."

"Chango?" Sometimes Baba pretended not to understand in order to appear more mysterious, but not this time.

"He kidnapped her! He tried to kill me!"

Baba was a little shaken. "Chango was there? Actually there?" The implications seemed to mean something. "I see."

"You see? 'Cause I don't. He's Mr. Blank? Or not. Or what?"

"There is so much," Baba began to dismiss, panic, backpedal and explain at the same time. "In due course, the universal resonances will make clear..."

Alex had no patience for Baba's elliptical wizard-speak. "He drove the spike into my neck, Baba."

Baba's eyes flared and the mustache bristled with electricity. "Did he?"

"Meli even saw it. Saw it, Baba!" Alex tried to gather himself. "Did he put this curse on me?"

"No."

That didn't help at all. "What the hell?" Alex finally realized, and it hit him harder than Gate had, harder than Neville and Stephen. He reeled as his arm seized up. "There really is a curse."

"Of course."

Punch-drunk, Alex leaned on a mental turnbuckle, trying to get his bearings. "I knew there was something wrong. Out of balance, whatever. That makes sense."

"It is all the sense there is," Baba interjected.

Alex rolled on as if the old man hadn't spoken. "But a curse?! Black magic?! This shit is for real?!"

"I thought you knew."

"It's a goddamn metaphor!" Alex raged.

"No," Baba countered simply, "it isn't."

"I know! It's a fucking spike in my neck. I saw it!"

"That's good," said Baba hungrily.

"That's good?!"

"Yes! It's coming closer to the surface, like a splinter. You're becoming the man you're needed to be."

"Needed? By who?!"

"Haven't you been listening? Do you think if any other man walked into my shop that day he'd be where you are now? You think you're the first? Look at Heracles. Look at Arthur. Look at Hunahpu and—"

But Alex rejected that litany of heroes. "Bullshit, Baba! Magic, science, crystal therapy on a cosmic fucking scale, I don't care. That lion was out of balance. So was the giant pig. The parrots don't belong here, so I guess that makes sense, maybe. But the girdle? And that girl? She has nothing now."

"She has a family," Baba protested.

"Nothing, Baba! What did I balance? How did I help her?"

"She didn't belong—"

"Or, what did I hurt? Was that the point? Because I don't feel the scales tipping in my favor over this, even if I did see a splinter coming out."

"The mysteries—"

"The mystery is why I trusted you."

"Trusted me?"

Alex pared back to the core of the question. "Why. Was. Chango. There?"

"Chango takes on personas…"

But Alex was beyond that. "Not how. I get it. The magic is real, and Chango was magically there. Why was he magically there?"

Baba blurted, "I saw the towers. Then her parents came. I didn't know he would be there!" All truths, and Alex could hear the earnest plea in each sentence. He could also hear there was more he would never be told.

Instead of forcing another round of non-answers, Alex marched toward Baba's rattletrap. "Take me the hell home."

So, Alex sat steaming in the passenger seat of the buzzing car with his arms folded across his chest. He let himself be mesmerized by the meandering passage of the lines and cracks in the road so he needn't think of anything at all. The undulations brought to mind the writhing of a snake.

On some cosmic plane, the great metaphor tipped its three heads on its serpent body. And though the chosen hero of this age had completed his task exactly as told, the heads did not tip in his favor.

Baba started to open his mouth, but not enough to part his lips. He did this several times. There was so much he wanted to tell Alex. More than that, he wanted to ask him questions. Baba drove on in silence with the distinct impression that if he spoke, Alex would kill him.

Baba's car churned into the parking lot at Alex's building and stopped. Unsteadily, Alex climbed out of the car. Before he could close the door, the muscles in his arm locked up again. His whole body jerked so hard it was like he didn't move at all.

Alex's eyes were fixed on the parking spot in his carport. He adjusted his vision again and again to try to see that he was wrong, as if deciphering an important message obscured by inexact handwriting. All the pieces of information were before him, but what they added up to was impossible. His truck was gone.

He looked hard at the spot where it should be, as if he was somehow just not noticing it. But in the truck's place, the ladders and tools and equipment he kept in the back had all been lined up neatly in his parking spot by the repo men. The "Electric Man" sign from the door sat at the end, like the dot on an exclamation point.

CHAPTER 14

If the Workingman's fate is in the hands of others, who pulls the strings?

Baba paced in the aisles of his shop. Things were getting out of hand. Barely halfway through his tasks, he was now assaulted on three fronts. Alex was ready to kill him, someone was coming, and the jangling jangling of his landline palpitated from behind the counter.

In a sort of dissonant rhyme with the telephone, the sudden clang of the bell above the entrance announced not only that someone had arrived, but how hard he had opened the door.

Chango bit the cigar between his lips and demanded from the doorway. "Where's my rum?"

Baba had more important things to think about. "I knew you were coming."

But Chango sniffed like a chef testing a steaming pot and declared, "I doubt that." Then he reminded Baba about the rum.

"On the altar." Chango headed into the back room.

Baba continued to pace. As the turbulence of the doorbell ebbed, the phone continued its discordant chiming and Chango's voice barked from the other room, "Answer that!" He returned with an unlabeled bottle of clear booze and he ordered, "*Tilo!*"

Distracted by self-doubt, Baba picked a green sphere from a shallow bowl on a shelf and tossed it to Chango. He caught it in his fist and snapped open a switchblade, then sat back on a stool and placed his feet on the counter. Was Chango's casualness a mask?

The piercing peal of the phone rang on. With emphasis, Chango set the phone on the counter but didn't answer it.

Baba picked up the receiver. "Botanica D'Baba." The interrupted bell sustained in the air as Baba grew icy at the voice on the other end. The mustache sneered, but out loud Baba attempted an unconcerned, "Oh. Hello, Inanna."

Chango quietly commented. "I'm not here."

On the far side of the city, Inanna sat on her throne with her phone set to speaker so she could clench and unclench her fists. In the strangely bare room, she was dressed in her priestly robes, but of course, no zoster. With no acolytes and no camera there to see her, she did not pose just so in her practiced performance of anger, designed to be both seductive and irate. Instead, she seethed deeply and truly. Baba's innocent greeting pushed her further. "You can take your 'oh, hello,' and go to hell."

Not taking his eyes off Baba, Chango sliced open the *tilo* with his knife. Captivated by the dripping blade, Baba almost missed his chance for a comeback, so he gave his next words extra weight for a harder blow. "I've been there."

But Inanna knew he was covering. "This isn't a joke, little man."

Chango produced a tempered glass beaker, poured a measure of rum, and listened to Baba's side of the exchange.

Baba hissed into the phone. "What do you want?"

The priestess answered, "Just keep pretending you don't know. First, you sent the Workingman to steal my Belt of Power."

Chango slid open a refrigerated display case, noting the priest's dismissive defiance as Baba challenged, "So?"

"So," Inanna countered, "I gave it to him."

"Gave it to him?" scoffed Baba. "He beat you and your guards—"

"Is that what he told you?" she scoffed right back. "Losing your grip on him, little man?"

"No! I—"

"I could see the path you put him on. We needed him on that path. The balance was tipping, and it was time for the lion. The zoster is just a symbol, but if you really needed a placebo that badly..." She let the anger ease from her voice and hit him coldly with, "But you got selfish. Didn't you, little man?"

Chango dropped a handful of ice into the beaker, making Baba jump at the crystalline clatter. Baba tried to maintain his bravado. "You didn't call me that when we were together."

Inanna was growing tired of the gaming. "How dare you use the Workingman for your own ends?! You used my zoster to find a hidden hoard?"

"Hidden hoard," mocked Baba. "This isn't The Hobbit."

"Interesting," observed the priestess. "Because what was important about that hoard wasn't the treasure, it was the chink in the armor. Is that what you sent him there to find?"

Baba tried to retreat to the dismissal, "You don't know what you're…"

But Inanna rose to her feet with anger, ending the banter. "He thinks he's fighting for his own balance? He thinks he's working for you?!"

POP! Chango opened a bottle of effervescent, amber liquid. It crackled as he poured it over the rum. Again, Baba flinched with distraction under Chango's gaze and the judgmental clatter of his concoction. "He is working for me," Baba both insisted and stammered. "You didn't even have the power to—"

"I have the power to send an envoy to collect my zoster and reset the scales. The Workingman has upset the balance too far the other way."

"He didn't upset—"

Inanna rose to her feet with anger, ending the banter.

"No, Baba. You're right. He didn't upset anything. You did. You made him your tool, and you sent him to the towers to take something that wasn't yours, just like the first hero raiding the cedar forest—not to right the scales, but only to make a name for himself and to loot lumber. But you haven't got the gonads to go up there yourself, so you sent him instead."

"I did go up the tower myself!" Three-quarters of the way through his boast, Baba realized what he was saying and who could hear him.

Chango clacked the beaker down onto the glass countertop, clinking ice like an exclamation point. Baba dared not look at him.

"Did you now?" trilled Inanna. "Then there's no way you didn't know. It wasn't balance you were trying for. It was power."

"You don't know…"

"Hubris, little man. Finally making your move for the seat at the top. You're just lucky Chango hasn't found out." Baba couldn't stop his eyes from flicking to Chango, who was focused on preparing his potion. He was drawn back to the phone as Inanna dropped her voice and delivered the threat with extra venom, "Since you can't set it right, I will."

Baba hung up on her, hard. It was an old phone, and he hoped she could hear the bell ring with the force of the slam.

Chango asked him mildly, "So, what did she want?"

"You know," covered Baba. "Always bitching about ancient history."

"Right," agreed Chango ominously. He slid the beaker down the counter to Baba and stood from his stool. "Something's coming," he pronounced.

Baba looked into the hissing glass, worried now, as Chango headed back to the door. The bell rang and Baba barely heard Chango's parting toast: "Cuba libre."

When that something came, Alex got the call. With nowhere to go and no way to get there, he sat on the green, manicured grass of a neighborhood park, watching Yucky and Phobos snarl, bite, grapple, and wrestle. It was a perfect, blue-sky day, with only a hint of dark clouds on a far horizon. He tried to take in some of their joy, but there was no hope of that. He was not startled or even very moved when his phone rang. A resigned thought like now what? washed over him. The screen on the phone told him, "BABA CALLING."

He answered the call, anger rising like heartburn. "This better be a solution." Suddenly, he sat up. "What?!" The dogs stopped their game and stared at him.

In still one more corner of the county, another phone rang. It was cold in the desert. Black clouds rimmed the sky, though it was blue overhead. In the old house where Dara was staying with her aunt and uncle, Thea picked up the ancient handset and recognized the voice of her father before he'd hardly spoken a word. "Dad!"

She dropped her adolescent guard long enough to exult in the bubbling exchange.

"Hiya, Thea," Alex grinned into the phone.

Niki was just behind her sister. The eight-year-old danced and jumped to get on the line. "Here! Here!"

"I can talk to you both for a minute." In his mind, Alex wrapped his arms around both girls. Their feet dangled off the ground. Niki laughed. Thea groaned as if being crushed.

Dara's voice appeared in the background. "Is that your dad? Please give me the phone."

Alex caught a thrill as she took the phone, even though he knew what was coming.

"Alex, we didn't even eat breakfast together," she chastised. "Why are you calling me?"

But Alex was ready for her admonishments. "No offence, Dara, but I wasn't calling to talk to you."

An hour or so later, Scotty Anderson sat in the cab of his very old, very well-maintained, heavy-duty pickup. In seventy years he'd never been east of Omaha. He'd traveled west to Japan, Vietnam, and the P.I., and he'd cowboyed from Arizona to Montana, Idaho, Washington, and down to California. In all that time, he had never worked on his own spread. Finally, he called in all his markers and bought a place. He raised alfalfa and broke wild mustangs rescued from the open range. He sold the horses at Southern California prices after feeding them on his own hay for a year and had just about broke even.

He'd met Dara's aunt Alice at a craft fair, where he demonstrated saddle making and she sold her beadwork. That was the day he'd started planning his horse ranch/alfalfa farm.

Scotty chain-smoked as he drove. Alex was silent in the seat beside him. Neither man had spoken for twenty minutes or more. Through the windows, they watched the sky, darkening with threatening clouds. Alex had expected the old cowboy to play outlaw country, but Scotty surprised him with 1980s dance-pop, tuned so low it barely competed with the wind. In the narrow rumble seat of the extended cab, Yucky and Phobos held their heads out opposite windows like sentries on a parapet.

Scotty was never good at broaching a conversation; he knew people found him too abrupt. So he said, "That's a good-looking dog you picked up."

"I thought you'd like him. He needs a new home."

Scotty nodded, completing the deal to take Phobos back to the ranch and satisfying the opening requirements of the talk. He continued, "So, there's a woman?"

Alex didn't like the road this was going down. He answered, "In a way."

Scotty made an unappeased "Hmm" sound.

"I've never cheated on Dara," Alex jumped in quick. "Not even a little."

"That's good," Scotty declared, and then fell silent again.

Scotty left a thread for Alex to pick up, so finally Alex asked, "You ever fool around on Alice?"

"You know,"—Scotty didn't take his eyes from the road, and he didn't raise his voice, but he enunciated clearly, so as not to be misunderstood—"'fool around' makes it sound so harmless. And, if I ever did, her uncle would kill me."

"I see."

Scotty started again. "So, there's a woman."

Alex had to agree with that. "There is a woman."

"And she wanted you."

"At first, she did. But that's just her way, I guess."

"You put her off." Not a question, more like a demand.

"I actually broke in to steal her girdle."

Scotty nodded. "Course you did."

"I guess she's pretty mad about it."

"She take your truck?"

"No. That was repoed."

"Been there." This didn't all exactly make sense to Scotty, but he knew when a man was lying, and Alex wasn't. The details were unimportant. "So, she wants to get even."

"Yeah."

"She's got a hell of a way about her."

"That's why I called you."

Unlike the rest of sprawling Los Angeles, downtown is dense with office towers, street traffic and pedestrians. The tallest skyscrapers in the state cluster together with City Hall, and with bridges and tunnels and brick buildings that are actually old. For a few blocks in any direction, you might turn a corner and think you were in Chicago.

The sky was dark with the approaching storm. Amidst the big city noise and clutter, something felt different. Car tires screeched. Someone screamed. People scattered. Traffic halted.

Something big and black charged between the cars. Cloven hooves thundered on the pavement. Rock-hard horns swung into a car window. Glass burst in a shower. And then, a second bull careened around a corner.

This was no apparition, like the shadow of The Pack taking form in darkness. Two identical black bulls tore through the streets. Massive shoulders topped with powerful humps of muscle carved through frozen traffic like the dorsal fins of orcas. Wicked horns crowned their heavy heads.

Chapter 15
Usually "the horns of a dilemma" is a metaphor; for the Workingman, it isn't.

Cars jockeyed to back up and clear out of the suddenly violent streets. Only one vehicle drove toward the bulls: Scotty's truck. No point in looking for a place to park. Scotty jumped the curb and stopped on the sidewalk. The two men stepped down from the cab. Yucky and Phobos spilled out and ran expectantly back past the tailgate.

The old truck was towing a trailer. A horse trailer. Scotty nodded toward the bulls. "She doesn't kid around, does she?"

Alex shrugged, "Neither do I," and pulled the back of the trailer open.

A minute later, Alex was swinging up into the saddle of a strong cow horse named Sabbath. He was born in the wilds of Idaho and taken late off the range. By the time he was poached from the hills, he'd started his harem and sired a foal. Somebody beat him up bad, and when Scotty got him, he was a wreck. Scotty named him Sabbath because putting a horse like that under saddle was a sin. But it was a sin that saved Sabbath's life. He was trained up right, and he knew cows.

Yucky and Phobos barked up at Alex, begging for direction. Alex looked questioningly over to Scotty, already mounted on a rangy paint. Scotty caught the look but didn't take his eyes off the bulls. "You remember everything I taught you about riding a horse?"

"Yeah."

"Well, forget it. You got bigger things to think about." And they spurred their mounts toward the beasts.

The twin monsters charged up on a sidewalk. People scattered and hid. Just like that, the streets became deserted. The bulls had no targets. Their unleashable violence needed fodder. Compelled to exercise their raw power, the brothers turned on each other. With a crack like a rifle shot, the bulls locked horns. Straining for leverage and dominance, they shoved back and forth. Cars crushed and juddered aside. Storefronts bashed and shattered like mesquite trees.

Alex and Scotty looked on. Alex was transfixed. Scotty sized up the situation and nodded. "You take the small one." He moved in on the bulls. Alex looked closer at the awful twins, trying to tell them apart.

The bulls spun each other into a mailbox, ripping the blue steel out of the ground like a rotten tooth. Alex and Scotty approached at the walk.

"Talk to them," Scotty counseled. "Be polite." He demonstrated, "Howdy, bull."

"Hey, bull," Alex greeted. The bulls stopped, startled. They turned to the men on horseback. "Now what?"

"Just tell 'em what we're here for."

In a calm tone, Alex addressed the respiring combatants. "Okay, bulls, we're gonna head you over to that truck and put you in the trailer." The bulls watched him and seemed to be listening. Alex was encouraged. "It's only about a block." The twins looked at each other, considering. "Okay?" The bulls turned back to Alex. One of them snorted.

Quietly, Scotty said, "Oh, shit," and the bulls lowered their heads and exploded at Alex.

Scotty ordered, "Get behind 'em!"

Alex kicked his horse, but Sabbath already knew what to do. He wheeled to one side. The bulls shot past. Alex and Scotty got in behind the bulls.

Alex turned to his coach. "Now what?!"

The older man shrugged and said rationally, "Well, we tried polite." He slapped his coiled lasso against

One of them snorted. Quietly, Scotty said, "Oh, shit."

his leg, making it pop. "Hey, bull! Get up!" He spurred his horse and charged after the bulls.

Alex followed with a war cry of his own. They chased the bulls off the sidewalk and into the street.

Yucky was not trained for this. He wasn't trained for anything more than being a good dog. But he was half border collie, maybe more, and herding was something he thought he understood. Phobos wasn't even a good dog, but he knew what it meant to intimidate, to corral, to push. The dogs darted between the legs of the bulls, snapping at hocks and tails.

"Block 'em there." Scotty pointed. Alex and Sabbath raced ahead and got between the bulls and a side street. The bulls veered away from the now-blocked outlet. They crashed through cars as Scotty closed in. Toward the truck and trailer, they forced the bulls up the block.

Alex cut off the path behind the bulls, moving up the street like a closing gate. It was working. He couldn't restrain himself. "That's right! Head for that trailer!" he crowed. One bull cocked his head toward Alex.

Scotty saw it and warned, "He didn't like that." The bull pivoted and turned on Alex. "Here he comes."

Lowering his head like the ramming prow on an ancient bireme, the bull charged. Sabbath rolled back on his haunches and spun at the last second. The brute smashed past him and into a car with full force, taking the blow between the eyes. He was not stunned. The second bull followed his twin and rumbled toward Alex.

"They're hungry for you, Alex."

"I see that, Scotty!"

"Okay," Scotty decided, "if we can't push 'em, we lead 'em."

With the new strategy, Sabbath leapt ahead of the attacking bull. Alex lurched and held on as he shouted his question. "Around the block and back to the trailer?"

"Right," Scotty answered. And he added, "Just don't let 'em get you."

Alex nodded at the obvious directive. He and Sabbath loped ahead again. The brothers were close behind. Scotty filled in after them. Yucky and Phobos continued their dance in and out of the hooves. They were totally ineffective in guiding the bulls, but drew off ounces of their fury as the monsters spun and twisted and tried to ward off the persistent pests. Most importantly, they managed not to get killed.

Each time Alex avoided a charge, the bulls clawed just a little bit closer. They destroyed a bus stop and scattered trash cans in the effort to reach their target. Each charge edged them closer to the goal of the trailer.

Sabbath cantered and skidded around a corner, fighting to keep his feet under him and the rider on his back. Alex righted himself in his seat and looked up. The bulls hadn't torn up this street yet. Cars and pedestrians went about their business, hoping to get indoors before the rains came. For a split second, Alex reflected on how all that was about to change.

The bulls hit the corner and slipped on the same slick patch that almost brought Sabbath down. But they outweighed the horse by a thousand pounds each and they hit the ground hard. At full tilt, the pair slid into a bus and rocked it on its axles. A flinch radiated in all directions from the impact. Drivers jumped in their seats and slammed on their breaks. Pedestrians gasped and then froze. For a moment, this street was as motionless and quiet as the deserted one around the corner.

Everyone started screaming. The bulls untangled themselves and lurched to their feet. People on foot scattered in all directions. A messenger on a motorcycle rode his bike up an outdoor escalator. Half a dozen cars shot away. Others were hemmed in and trapped. The bus driver uselessly slammed his doors shut.

With a shriek of sirens, the police finally arrived. They popped open doors and drew 9-millimeters, a shotgun, and an AR-15, but there were too many people in the way to open fire. Besides, it looked like there were actual cowboys taking the lead.

The twin brutes scanned the scene and came to the same conclusion as the cops. They homed in on Alex. His horse saw them coming. Sabbath and Alex surged out of the way. The bulls wheeled and charged again. Alex turned the horse to get away. They almost made it.

The recurved horns missed, but the muscular black shoulder slammed Sabbath against a car. Alex was pinned. Sabbath barked out a quick, high keen like a cornet. The second bull arrowed in for the killing blow.

The bull lunged. Alex braced himself. Sabbath shrunk away as far as he could. At the last second, the bull thrashed and spun away, a lasso wrapped and jerked tight around his horns. Scotty dallied up the other end of the rope on the horn of his saddle.

Sabbath pitched free of the other bull. Both bulls charged at Scotty. Scotty unwrapped the lasso from his saddle and tossed the loose end to Alex. Alex grabbed the rope and held on hard.

The bull hit the end of the rope. It slowed, but the lasso dragged through Alex's hands. The four-strand nylon coil burned his flesh like a torch. Alex's fingers sprung open. The bull slammed into Scotty's paint.

The horse reeled back and Scotty crashed from the saddle. Alex urged in Sabbath and charged between Scotty and the bull. Scotty staggered half to his feet. Flailing legs, reins, stirrups, and tail, the paint scrambled and righted itself.

Alex was out of cowboy knowhow. He did the only thing he could think of. He kicked the bull as hard as he could in the eye. The bull veered to one side.

Scotty had just enough time to mount his horse and spin out of the way as the second bull charged in. He didn't break from the fight to chastise Alex.

"Goddammit! You can't hold onto a bull like that! Dally that lasso around the horn!"

"I'll remember that next time I'm herding two giant bulls!"

Alex and Scotty swung their horses in a wide arc through the street. The bulls pursued. They turned another corner into a new neighborhood. Behind them, the LAPD scrambled back into their cars.

Halfway down the block, the bulls caught up to the riders. Yucky and Phobos barked uselessly and nipped muscled hocks, but the bulls charged in. Alex and Scotty started to counter. They were too late. An angry voice boomed through the street. "STOP!"

The men, the horses the dogs and the bulls all stopped. All eight of them looked to the source of the voice. A skinny, irate Mexican stood on the sidewalk, waving knobby fists in the air. Baba. The downtown, financial district had given way to the barrio. Baba stood in front of his shop. "What the hell are you doing?!" he shrieked.

"What does it look like?" Alex wanted to know. "You told me to get the bulls off the street."

"You!" Baba emphasized. "I told you to take care of the bulls."

Scotty interjected, "Who's your friend, Alex?"

"And here I am," Alex insisted.

"Not by yourself, you're not."

Alex picked up Scotty's question. "Scotty, this is, Baba. I work for him." And he turned to his boss to ask, "So?"

"So," Baba chided, "it is you out of balance. Not the cowboy."

Scotty bristled. "I don't like the way he says 'cowboy.'"

Baba concluded, "This task cannot count."

Alex was floored. Scotty was curious. "Count for what?"

Baba made shooing motions. "Get these bulls your priestess sent off my street."

"My priestess?" Alex was livid. "You sent me there!"

"You're the one that made her *hambriento*." Scotty laughed at that, but Baba continued, "Get rid of your bulls."

Alex didn't have to think about it for a second. "You think I'm too stupid to know what *hambriento* means, and too stupid to know that's not why she sent those bulls." He gestured to Scotty. "I don't work for nothing." Scotty knew exactly what he meant.

Scotty turned his horse and rode around behind the confused and waiting bulls. Alex gave Baba a hard look. He and Sabbath turned away and headed for the abated brothers.

Baba praised the dutiful decision of his man. "That's right."

Alex spoke not to Baba, but to the bulls. "Get up!"

Alex and Scotty rushed in on the animals. The bulls tried to evade. Scotty, Alex, Yucky and Phobos closed in on the back and sides. They found all paths blocked but one. The bulls pushed up onto the sidewalk.

Baba shouted, "Hey!" and dove out of the way. The bulls rushed past him. Alex and Scotty crowded the pair. There was only one way for the bulls to go. They saw the opening, and they took it.

A deliberate gap opened between Alex and Scotty. The bulls rushed through and saw a storefront with an open door. They charged into Baba's shop.

Shelves and merchandise exploded through the little space. The bulls crushed their way through the wares. Votive candles burst like fireworks and a confetti snow of greeting cards filled the air. The figure of beheaded Saint Denis, patron against frenzy, made a taunting target. It burst aside with the hook of a horn. The severed head cannonballed through a glass case. Chest-high shelves bashed like dominoes, ejecting herbs and rosaries, ceremonial cups, and figurines into a confusion of carcasses strewn across a battlefield.

Outside, Baba was still half-curled into a ball after his dive. Alex looked down on him from Sabbath's back. "Call me when you've got a job that pays."

As the bulls tore the hell out of Baba's shop, Alex rode away. Scotty, Yucky and Phobos followed.

Baba turned back to the Botanica, rose up to his full height and entered without fear. Skirting the thrashing animals, he moved behind his counter and grabbed a large glass jar full of red powder. The bulls charged him. Baba threw the jar. It burst in an

"*Call me when you've got a job that pays.*"

explosion of red dust that was mostly asafetida, for exorcism, chili pepper, for hex breaking, and—believe it or not—sesame, for controlling lust.

The dust settled. The bulls reappeared. Motionless, they sat on their haunches staring blankly. They were made of stone.

These were the twin statues that had flanked the throne of Inanna, Priestess to the Goddess most High. Baba looked at the carved images, now back in their proper state, one with a lasso still looped snuggly around its horns. Baba frowned. "Hubris my ass, *Puta!*"

CHAPTER 16

When it rains it pours. The universe is getting literal with the Workingman.

There's no rain like desert rain. When the storm finally comes to the parched land, it's that much stronger for the waiting. Los Angeles is a desert. For the better part of one hundred years, it's hung on at the edge of drought. But there's a reason we call it the LA Basin. It fills up. Floods scour the canyons, mudslides bury houses, and every year somebody drowns in the Los Angeles River.

Rain pelted down outside a dim and quiet pub. Beer mugs with faces on them lined the shelves. Union Jacks and football pennants hung from oak rafters. But this wasn't England, and the weather kept even committed drinkers at home. With the place all to themselves, Alex and Scotty sat at the bar, each nursing a beer and weathering the ballad the bartender played, designed to lift no one's spirit.

Alex absently fingered the seared strip of his palm where the rope burn turned his flesh to leather. He counted out his labors. "The lion, the birds, the girdle…"

"That came back at you."

"The pig, the dogs and the girl."

Scotty piqued, "Another girl?"

"I don't want to talk about that."

Scotty accepted that and reminded Alex, "And the bulls."

"No," said Alex, angry and frustrated. "The bulls don't count. I'm still at six. I gotta go all the way to ten."

"Four more."

"If they count." Alex drew off his beer, disgusted with himself. "I can't believe I bought into all this magic crap."

Scotty looked at the man, watching for the truth. "Did you?"

But Alex was on his own track. "I'm quitting Baba and getting a real job." Alex swiveled around in his stool so he could look out into the rain. He'd mentally performed the roll call of his tasks so many times it was like a song stuck in his head.

The lion, the birds, the girdle, the pig, the dogs and the girl. The rhythm of the recitation beat in time with the throb of the invisible spike digging at his neck and shoulder. But was it invisible? Not to say that chronic pain doesn't hurt, but it was such a constant—so simply part of his existence—that on most days, if you asked Alex if he was hurting, he'd say "No."

The lion, the birds, the girdle, the pig, the dogs and the girl. He wasn't ignoring the pain, or fighting through it, or blocking it out. Working around the debility it brought on became as routine as washing your hair in the shower. Sometimes you stand there and can't remember if you've washed it yet or not. It was only with the flare-ups that his pain was front of mind.

The lion, the birds, the girdle, the pig, the dogs, and the girl. Of course, that had all changed. He had seen it. He saw the invisible spike and so had Meli and so had Blank or Chango or whoever the fuck that was. Since that moment, there was no routine, no compartmentalization, nothing that could make him forget.

The lion, the birds, the girdle, the pig, the dogs, and the girl. The white noise of rain flooded Alex's brain. He tried to wrap his senses around the wash of sound and draw it into himself, to drown his thoughts and overtop the beat of pain. Instead, the throb imposed itself on the chaos of the rain, and the splash of each drop became a voice in the chorus of his pain.

The lion, the birds, the girdle, the pig, the dogs, and the girl. Each one was supposed to take him closer to the end. Closer to his victory. Closer to ending the curse. Closer to balance. But nothing was better. The pain was still here. Dara and Thea and Niki were still gone. He was losing, he was hurting, and he was wrong.

The lion, the birds, the girdle, the pig, the dogs, and the girl. Just like the voices formed from the churning of the storm on the pavement, the spike was a hallucination. It had to be. Desperation and pain had finally broken him, and he'd latched onto the words of some crazy old man, his mind manifesting the spike like a piton to grab hold of.

The lion, the birds, the girdle, the pig, the dogs, and the girl. Maybe he'd swivel back to the bar, climb into that beer, and stay there.

The cowboy wetted his lips from his mug and looked into the mirror behind the back bar. "Remember I told you Alice's uncle would beat hell outta me?"

Weary, Alex answered automatically. "I didn't touch the girl."

"Forget that." The force of the words jerked Alex out of his reverie. In the window's reflection, he could see Scotty gazing into the mirror behind the bar. The older man continued without turning, knowing he had Alex's attention though they sat back to back. "Alice's half a Piute. Her uncle's full-blooded and serious about it. When I asked Alice to marry me, she introduced me to him."

"He like you?"

"Not a bit." Scotty paused—even Alice didn't know this. "He took me out to Death Valley. Stuck me in a *wickiup* and started a fire."

"Sweat lodge."

"You bet. I thought he was going to grill me about my intentions, but he didn't say a word. He just watched me 'til I passed out. When I woke up," Scotty's reflection looked Alex's reflection in the eye. His voice sank as if in church, "we were in Shin-au-av."

"Shin-au-av?"

"Secret, ancient Piute city. I saw things there I can never tell you about. Coyotes that'll talk your head off." Memories and images buzzed through and shook him like a sneeze that wouldn't come. "I'll never cross Alice or her family, that's for sure."

Alex started to interject. To make some kind of light comment like how he wouldn't even argue with Alice after that, but Scotty waved him off.

"That's not my point, Alex. My point is, all this magic you're talking about doesn't surprise me. This world we live in only makes some kind of sense if you know that."

Another man who had seen such things. And not just any man, but a resolute, no bullshit cowboy who wouldn't even go to the movies because they were too unreal. Maybe Alex wasn't insane. *The lion, the birds, the girdle, the pig, the dogs, and the girl.* Though the spike stabbed at him, he almost laughed aloud with relief.

Scotty continued, killing the laugh. "Whatever quest you're on. Whatever tasks you gotta do to make things plumb and square, you go do it."

Memories and images buzzed through and shook him like a sneeze that wouldn't come.

The magic may be real, but it didn't change the realities of a workingman. "And get cheated outta the credit, like today?"

Scotty dismissed that as a useless gripe. "You may hate that skinny *curandero*, but remember—" Scotty didn't talk about these things. He wasn't going to say any of this again. Scotty's eyes lanced into the mirror. In the window, the rain seemed to swirl around the cowboy's face, fixing Alex's eyes to the center of the vortex. Scotty made sure he had Alex's attention before he continued.

He had it. "It's not really him you're working for."

So, an hour later, Alex sat in Scotty's truck, parked at a curb with gushing gutters. On the way to drop him back at home, Alex had told Scotty the story he hadn't wanted to tell. The tale of Leilata weighed more heavily on him than being cheated out of credit for the bulls. He didn't share the image of the three-headed serpent, but he could feel Chronus tipping out of his favor. As he re-watched in his mind the young woman who was no longer Leilata sadly disappearing with the family she didn't deserve, he felt his quest for redemption slipping away. The betrayal of the bulls cemented his loss.

Scotty interrupted. "Two things," said the cowboy. "You used that word 'redemption' in a manner that sounds like going back to a way things were." Alex expected him to elaborate, but Scotty concluded, "That's one." Scotty let that hang for four beats of the windshield wipers. "Your magic Mexican isn't just changing the rules of the game, he's not letting you know what game you're playing. That's two."

"Stop playing the game?"

"Nope. Find the real rules."

There was not actually a crack of lightning and peal of thunder at that, but Alex's phone did ring. With a morose chuckle, Alex accepted the emergency call from Baba. Scotty offered to help, of course, but the rules were Alex had to do it alone. They diverted from the path to Alex's place and parked on this street Alex had known his whole life. He thanked Scotty and gave Phobos a final scratch on the head.

Alex jumped from the truck and ran through the rain with Yucky on a leash. They dashed up to the porch of a house with perfectly maintained wiring and plumbing, a clean, sky-blue and white paint job, and a lawn made of rough, green, volcanic pebbles because Luna just couldn't be bothered with plants. Besides, there was a park down the street where the city mowed the grass, and if the child Alex had wanted to play, he could play there.

Alex knocked on the door. After she examined him through the peephole, as he knew she would, Alex's mother opened up.

"Look at you, Alexander. You're soaking wet."

"It's raining, Mom. You said I could borrow the car."

She seemed to be reconsidering. "You get a job?"

"That's where I'm going."

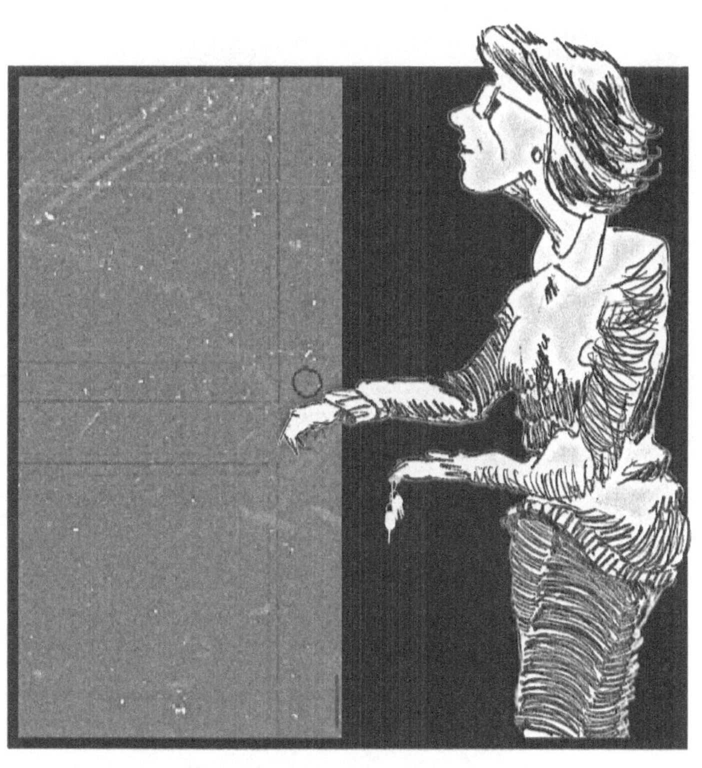

"Look at you, Alexander. You're soaking wet."

Luna nodded, but not in an entirely positive way. "With your dog?"

"Yes," Alex concluded.

"Dara's cowboy can't take you?"

"No," he answered simply. "Can I have the car?" He threw it out there like a challenge.

Saying yes would be too much like giving in, so she said, "Put a towel over the seats."

A spine of hills cuts the city in two. Up until the middle of the last century, the gullies and canyons were home only to exclusive estates, an art deco observatory, and cattle. The expansion of the 1950s saw the estates parceled up, the cattle kicked out, and homes crushed in, from the ocean to Elysian Park. No matter how steep the hillside or narrow the canyon, there are houses.

The Santa Monica Mountains were pushed up through the Earth by the great seismic forces that famously threaten to drop the city into the sea. But the canyons were formed by the rain.

Rain beat down hard enough to batter the hat off your head. It slashed at the Greco-Roman-scripted sign—perched atop twin columns of marbled tile—

that either welcomed you to or warded you off from this semi-gated community of neo-classical midcentury exceptionalism entitled "Mt. Olympus." Lording high above the Sunset Strip, the homes built into the steep hillside of the wooded canyon now stood on the banks of a growing river.

The entire length of the street had been scoured of garbage cans. They swirled in the eddies as they were sucked down toward the boulevards at the base of the hill. Compact cars parked at the steep curbs strained against emergency brakes and shuddered slowly downhill.

At one house in the path of the flood, Myron and Rivi stood on the porch, still dry for now. For thirty years they lived in this house, and never had the water been so bad. Once, they'd lost the porch, and twice all the landscaping in the back yard, but today they feared for their home itself. So they called Baba, and Baba sent the workingman.

He was soaked to the skin and working hard, stacking sandbags to hold the flowing water back. He had driven up to the house in his borrowed car and seen what needed to be done. There was an introduction, and he handed them his dog on a leash. Then he got to work. The only other thing he said was not to help him.

The man dropped a sandbag into the foam and rushed to the porch to grab a new one from a stack. Myron was seventy-eight years old, and he hadn't had a physical job since his teens. He was not as strong as he once was, but he was not weak. He was also not a man to stand back in a moment of crisis. He started to pull a fresh sandbag from the stack.

The man barked at him, "Don't. Don't you help me, Myron."

"Sorry," Myron snatched his hand back. "Sorry."

The yoke of muscles in his back stood out through his soaked shirt as the man pulled the wet, heavy sandbag to his shoulder. It slapped like a dead body. The ghosts of tattoos seemed to move like cartoons under the wet fabric as the man's muscles tensed and flexed. Myron comforted himself a bit by thinking that he really wouldn't have known what to do, and he'd have killed himself lifting those bags. Rivi put a hand on his shoulder that said the same thing.

They watched the man slog through shin-deep water to the edge of the yard where the river raged down the street and eddied up the property. The man added the sandbag to the wall he was building. As he worked, he talked to them, to make up for snapping at Myron.

"How do you know Baba?"

Rivi didn't answer the question. Instead, she prodded her husband and the man at the same time. "He won't believe you."

"I'd believe almost anything." The man smiled as he grabbed another sandbag.

So Myron told him. "Our rabbi introduced us."

"Sure," the man accepted, without stopping his task.

"At an interfaith conference," Rivi reminded her husband.

"In Las Vegas," Myron said it as if it were a punchline.

The scarred and bearded workingman was unphased. "That's what I thought." He dropped a final sandbag like an exclamation point. The wall of sandbags complete. The man stood back and looked at it. The river of the street continued to foam and rise, but the sandbags formed a levee. Water raged and licked at the levee, but it couldn't encroach on the yard.

The man took a satisfied breath and turned to his dog. "What do you think, Yucky?"

Yucky was just happy to be addressed. He smiled and barked and sort of skipped in place. Myron was charmed by the man and his dog, but his wife nudged him. "The side yard."

Myron protested, "The man's soaked to the bone."

"Baba sent him," Rivi argued.

Hot from work and chilled by the water, the man stood steaming in the calming pond of the yard. Through teeth starting to chatter, he jumped in on their debate. "Rivi, what do you want him to tell me?"

Myron answered for his wife. "Sometimes it floods in the side yard."

The man stepped to the edge of the property and looked down the side of the house. As he did, Myron and Rivi heard a roar like a fire hose filling up a five-gallon bucket. Water cascaded down the hillside and funneled into the narrow space between the side of the house and the steep slope that led to the neighboring house above it. It gushed through and attacked the sandbag wall from the rear. The man had built the levee strong and tight, and now it held the water in.

The yard filled up like a pool in front of the house. He tried to run up the side yard, but the current between the hillside and the wall was too strong. His eyes darted through the torrent, assessing this new set of challenges. Quickly, he turned to Myron. "Axe?" he asked.

Rivi urged her husband, "He wants an axe!"

"I have an axe," he told her. "It's in the tool shed."

Rivi addressed the man directly for the first time. "That's in back."

Without hesitation, the man ran full tilt onto the porch and through the front door. The couple parted to let him pass. The dog strained at his leash to follow him. Through her open door, Rivi watched the man leave a path of mud and water on her floors as he sprinted through the house. She didn't mind a bit, and the thought made her smile.

The water out in the back yard was waist-deep and ice cold. The man sucked air through his teeth and jerked rigid for an instant as the torrent lapped above his groin. Fighting it, he slogged his way to a brown plastic tool shed and pulled the green door. The whole shed surged toward him. It was floating.

He braced his foot on the rocking wall and tugged the door again. The door popped open and the shed spun in the current. With no intention of boarding the doomed craft, he tipped the structure toward him to reach the tools hanging on the back wall. Straining as far as he could, he grabbed an old axe with a rusted head. He released the shed and it rolled back like the head of a mother bird, vomiting him out to feed her young. He dashed back into the flood to see if he'd be devoured.

Water gushed down the side yard, covering the stairs that led to the kitchen door and shooting toward the front of the house. Now, the front yard was deep and growing deeper with brown, swirling water encroaching on the porch. Yucky whined and skittered his paws away from the ugly surf. Myron and Rivi strained at the side rail to see Baba's man.

There he was, on the hill above the house. In the driving rain, he swung the axe. He chopped into a great cypress that clung to the hillside. He grunted and strained, moving fast to complete this desperate gambit before the water rose too high and the cold sapped his muscles of their strength.

With a boom audible above the storm, something big hit the water. The tree. The trunk crashed across the flood funneling into the side yard. Water groped up the scaly, green-black thicket of tight branches, but couldn't climb over. The angry tide spun off into the back yard. The tool shed whisked away in the deluge, but the surge was turned away from the house.

Held back by the dam, the gouts of water from the side yard died, but still the rain slashed down. Muddy water rose up to spread onto the porch. Myron and Rivi stepped back. Yucky cringed. The rapids surged above the doorsill.

The man dashed back into the front yard. He sloshed waist deep across to his sandbag wall. The level of water on this side of the levee was now higher than the surface of the river in the street. At the corner of the wall furthest downstream, he furiously tore away sandbags. The wall breached. The pooling water in the yard was sucked into the raging river.

The sudden current gripped on to boots and pants and pulled like it was trying to undress him. The man was jerked off his feet. The force of the water twisted a fist into his shirt and tugged him down. He splashed hard and went under.

Yucky saw his master's distress. Myron held hard to his leash, but the dog yanked forward and tore the strap from his hand. He dove into the water and arrowed toward his man.

Yucky surfaced with the man's shirt in his teeth. Swimming like a live anchor, the dog held him back from the violent drag of the river. In the middle of the tug o'war, the man towed up to the surface. He gasped for air. Yucky gave a mighty wrench, and the man got to his feet.

Yucky surfaced with the man's shirt in his teeth.

The choppy pool of the yard drained into the river. The water level fell rapidly to the man's knees. Myron and Rivi could hardly believe it. Their house was saved.

The man turned with a smile, but not for them. "Good dog," he said. But his dog wasn't there. "Yucky?" The dog was gone.

The man splashed through the murky water and called the dog again. A chill more gripping than the rain held Myron and Rivi. The man saw something and dashed out into the current. He could barely stand, but his voice raged over the torrent. "YUCKY!"

The couple followed the look of the man. And there, across the raging rapids in the street, caught in the branches of a fallen tree, they saw it. The limp body of the dog, soaked, battered, lifeless. Yucky was dead.

Through all the things he'd seen and done, the forces he'd tackled and defeated, it had taken this sixty-pound dog to save Alex's life. Now all his strength was useless. He could not even force his way across the foaming rapids to retrieve the ruined body. Wind trembled the black ears and the rushing water swung the white tail in mockery of the innocent life sacrificed to Alex's curse. He could do nothing.

The white noise closed in around him. His lips tingled. His knees gave out. Alex collapsed and sat where he landed, waist-deep in water, staring at the nothing that seconds ago had been his loyal and constant shadow.

On walks, Yucky would glance over his shoulder every ten or twelve paces to make eye contact with Alex, checking to make sure all was well. On off-leash excursions to wide-open spaces, Yucky would roam and explore with delight, but always found a hillock or stump or other higher vantage or would leap above the spraying tops of tall grass to catch sight of Alex and get his bearings on the man who was the center of his world. He loved and would play with the girls, would cuddle with and obey Dara. But Yucky had been a joyful, loyal little soul because he knew that Alex would always be there to protect and care for him.

Every moment those deep, brown eyes had reached out to him pierced into Alex now. Every time Yucky had looked to him and found reassurance cored into his chest. The cumulative trust of each of those moments of connection amounted to a thing that was very like religious faith. And Alex had betrayed him.

A hot, stinging wave rolled up through Alex, and he thought he might vomit. But the wave reached his face and crashed there. Alex wept. As unrestrained as a child, he sobbed three massive sobs and fell silent. He did not suppress further tears; he was spent.

"I...I..." A voice stammered beside Alex. Myron stood in the water at his side. He hadn't heard the old man's approach and was still hardly aware of his presence. "You saved our house."

There was a wad of dirty wet leaves forming in the dog's open mouth. Yucky would hate that. He would hack and shake his head, and Alex would laugh.

"Look, Mr. Cides...Baba let it slip about your truck. I want you to take this." Myron held out a roll of folded bills.

An eddy of wind and rain cleared the debris from the dog's lifeless mouth. Alex was glad.

"I was going to give it to you anyway. It's not for—" Myron started to gesture toward the soaking carcass but stopped himself. "Get your truck back."

Without changing his gaze, the Workingman took the money.

CHAPTER 17
When the Workingman goes for broke, he goes broke.

Without any joy or even relief, Alex retrieved his truck from the repo men. There were no recriminations at the auto yard. Alex was not a social climber with a Ducati he couldn't afford. He was a workingman, and so were they, which is why his tools were so delicately dealt with when the vehicle was taken in the first place. The fact that Alex was there with his mother shamed the repo men, and there was no small talk of any kind.

Having said that, he was not getting the silent treatment from Luna. Yesterday's rain was now a slow, heavy mist that clung to them as they walked through the lot to her car and his waiting truck. "You know, I've always been supportive, no matter what you decided to do with your life."

Alex's shoulders hunched up against the cold drizzle and the lecture he knew was on its way.

"I knew from the time you were a boy. Special. Remember that day at the park?"

Alex did not remember, but he'd heard the story so many times it was as if he did.

"You were just this little guy, with your head in the clouds. But then that homeless man approached me. All of a sudden, you stopped your fantasies because you could see he was dangerous." Luna smiled to herself at the memory. "You walked your little self between him and me and stood up as tall as you could. You stared him down and he backed away because he knew you were serious." She nodded, agreeing with her own story. "He knew you were special. And I knew it. You were special."

The story always made him uncomfortable. It was a lot to live up to. Alex had peaked before he was four years old.

"It wasn't easy, raising you without a father. You weren't easy. But I knew you were special. You'd be special."

Here it came.

"And you decided to be a handyman."

Alex was an electrician and Luna knew it.

"And that's just fine." She paused exactly long enough to clarify that it was not fine. "If you're not making enough to make your car payments. Well, that's not how I wanted to spend my money, but I was happy to help you."

Luna had not spent any of her money today. But something had been killed inside of Alex. There would be no sparring now. His hand was already on the door of his truck. He angled his body as if to turn and face her, but it was just a token gesture, and their eyes did not meet.

"Thanks for the ride," he said. He climbed into the cab and left her in the mist, disappointed again.

His truck hissing over the wet pavement, Alex pulled up to his building, not happy to be home. Since the death of Yucky, the only thing he'd been glad of was to part company with Luna. The pickup sighed to a stop in front of its spot. Alex stepped down from the driver's seat and reloaded his tools and ladders because if he didn't do it now, he'd have to do it later, and he wouldn't want to do it later.

Alex trudged up to his front door and turned the key in the lock. The door didn't open. Alex shoved. Nothing. He stepped back and focused his eyes for the first time since he looked away from the lifeless little body.

A bright new hasp and padlock secured the door. There was a note too. Alex didn't read it. The content was obvious. Evicted.

By the time Alex charged across town to Baba's shop, the sun was going down and the mist was clearing. Venus shined in the east, heralding the passing of the storm. Alex didn't see the evening star, only that the security bars were shut, and a sign announced "CERRADA" in the window. Dim lights from a few displays shown through the glass, but the inside was still a wreck since Inanna's beasts tore through it like a bull in a botanica. Alex cared nothing about that. He shook the bars, more for the clash of metal on metal than in hope of opening them. "Baba! Baba, you son of a bitch! Baba!"

Before Alex could tear the cage from the wall, a woman stepped out of the storefront next door. She was the same Korean woman who had spied on them from the window when Alex received his El Chancho assignment. To get Alex's attention, she clapped once. He spun toward the sound and recognized her. In lightly-accented English, she looked up at him and announced, "He's at Chango's place."

"Chango's?"

She pointed up the street. "Gas station. By the bridge thing." Alex looked at her, unsure. She eased his mind. "You're not the only one who doesn't love Baba."

Alex nodded and jumped back in his truck.

It was not a bridge, but a vast culvert of the Los Angeles River. The building at the center of the service station seemed hardly bigger than a changing room, but there was somehow space for shelves of snacks and gum and candy and air freshener and for some reason, aphrodisiacs—all in aggressive circus colors. There was a cardboard standee of a curvaceous swimsuit model, selling either beer or motor oil. Though the evening was growing, it wasn't dark yet, and the clerk hadn't closed the Lexan shield across the counter.

Five years ago, he came from Turkey. He was Armenian and barely five foot one. Someday he'd own this gas station and tiny market, but for now he worked for Chango. Surely, his name was not Kevin, but that's what it said on his shirt.

Kevin jumped. A furious and muscular man slammed through the glass doors. Poised to slap the bulletproof glass into place, Kevin held still—thieves were not usually angry. The intruder barked at him. "Baba!" Relieved, the cashier pointed to a door at the back, past the restrooms. The madman muscled his way through the colorful racks.

There was an office in the back. The room was hardly large enough for a desk and file cabinet, and how the furniture had gotten through the narrow hallway and door was a mystery. The white walls were entirely unadorned but for an oversized clock constantly set ten minutes fast and a much-written-on calendar. Though the room was spare, and though even the calendar was a free one, you wouldn't get the impression that business here was poor. There were stacks of cash on the desk and on the top of the file cabinet. Neatly organized on the floor, more bundled money filled the corners of the room.

Baba had just picked up his takeout when he was called to Chango's office. He stood in front of the desk with the bag held in both hands, as if to protect his genitals. Chango rocked to his feet from a desk chair that was the most expensive thing on the property and dug silently into Baba's bag. He barely unwrapped the Quarter Pounder with no cheese and no pickles before he bit it in half.

The moment Chango threw the other half of Baba's burger in the trash, the door of the little office burst open. Alex stood framed by the open doorway. Chango didn't flinch. Baba jumped behind the desk. Sincerely, Chango greeted Alex "I'm sorry about your dog," spilling a bit of dry beef and ketchup from his mouth.

Alex advanced on Baba. The mustache spread in a mollifying smile. Baba rationalized, "At least you got another one," but for some reason, that made Alex even angrier. "What?!"

"The head," Baba tried to clarify.

Chango changed the subject, impressed. "You turned back the flood."

Veins under Alex's flesh pulsed visibly. "I lost my home."

Reluctantly, Baba had to inform him, "The flood. It doesn't count."

That bounced off Alex like a spent bullet, but it made Chango's eyebrows jump.

"Nothing has gotten better. You haven't helped me."

"I'm sorry." Baba knew the man must be made to

understand. "You accepted payment for it. You did it for the money. Not the balance."

"Balance?! My dog is gone. My home is gone. My family is gone."

"I don't make the rules," Baba shrugged hopelessly.

Chango nodded. "He doesn't." He looked to Baba, as if to check on him. "In fact, I called him here to remind him of that."

Alex nodded too. It was so simple, he wondered why he hadn't done it before. "I'm going to balance up with you." He lunged across the desk. The fist marked "T-H-I-S" balled in Baba's shirt and dragged him across to the other side.

Baba wailed, "Chango!"

For an immeasurable instant Chango considered leaving Baba to his fate. He flicked a finger across his upper lip, correcting the already perfect checkmarks of his mustache. But he didn't want Alex to take a man's life, and Alex was in a killing place. Chango jetted to his feet and jerked Baba out of Alex's grip. Baba collapsed in a corner.

Alex didn't care who he killed today. "Fine!" He cocked back his arm and fired his powerful fist into Chango's jaw. Chango reeled back. Alex charged in. Chango struck forward and head-butted Alex hard.

Alex shivered with the blow and sparks flew in his vision. He crashed into a wall. Chango buried a knee in his gut. Alex doubled over. Chango wound up for a final blow. "Alex, it's too soon for this. I don't want to end you."

Alex looked up from the spasm in his gut and through the swimming points in his eyes to the fist cocked back like an arrow in a bow. Fuck you, Chango, was what he said in his mind, but the sound he made was more of an animal roar.

Alex started to straighten. Chango was disappointed. "Maybe you're not the fulcrum after all," he said. He released the held back blow.

But Alex didn't actually rise up. Instead, he stayed under the punch and kicked hard into Chango's shin, raking lug soles down the bone. Chango hopped back, bloodied. Alex shoved him and Chango toppled behind the desk.

Alex straightened up and took a deep breath. Chango struggled to his feet. Alex set himself, ready. Something hit Alex hard from behind. Baba.

Baba tackled the Workingman, but the confined office left no room to fall. They smashed a dent in the drywall. Alex shrugged off the wiry priest. Baba hit the desk. He came up, swinging furiously with a letter opener from the scattered desk set. He charged like a lancer, blade outstretched. Alex crouched and drilled his shoulder into Baba's chest. The witch doctor folded. Alex stood and flipped Baba over his back. Baba hit the wall and fell in a heap.

Back on his feet, Chango crouched into a fighting stance. Alex faced him and raised his fists. The Workingman was taking this so seriously it made Chango laugh, and his laugh plucked at Alex's taut temper. He did not see red or shout or rage. He hated. Hate drove the spike deeper into his flesh. White-hot venom filled his blood. He charged like a wounded lion. No defense. Only attack. Powerful blows he never felt fell on his face, his ribs, his ear and his belly. Like a B-17 ignoring the flack, Alex powered through. With fists and elbows and knees and every other natural weapon he had, Alex drove Chango back.

The back door of the gas station burst open. Chango retreated into the grimy strip of land between the station and the barrier along the bank of the LA River. Alex charged after his prey. He slammed a fist into Chango's face. Chango stumbled and fell. He hit the greasy asphalt hard, but he laughed.

Alex raged, "Son of a bitch!"

Chango got to his feet and chided, "I wouldn't talk about my mother, if I were you." Again, he laughed. Watching the fury of the Workingman, Chango anticipated Alex's charge. He spun aside and knocked Alex in the back of the head. He watched Alex's anger rise.

Alex closed. Chango anticipated again but was surprised by Alex's speed. And Alex wasn't throwing a punch. He grabbed Chango by the head like a bulldogger. Alex flexed his powerful arms and Chango felt rock-hard muscles compress his skull. The world blurred. His hearing focused to a single whine. Suddenly, the ground leapt at him, and he hit it hard. His head free of the vice, he felt the cool wind on his face, and he laughed again.

That should have ended it. Alex was shocked when Chango jumped back to his feet, ready. Recovering in an instant, Alex was on him. Blow after blow, the two powerful men tore into each other. For a fourth time, Chango hit the slick ground. Still, he laughed at Alex. "You keep knocking me down." He climbed to his feet. "But I won't stay down." The laughter boiled at Alex. Chango called him out. "Come on, worker bee."

Alex's anger flashed over. He charged in. Chango was knocked back, but still he chided, "Stupid." He fended off Alex's blows, laughing all the time. "Just a dumb hammer." Alex drove in with punch after punch. "Whose hammer are you? Beating me at whose bidding?" His every blow blocked, Alex was getting nowhere. "Where's your balance now, ballpeen? Nothing but a tool."

Suddenly, Alex stopped. He fixed Chango with his angry eyes. "You know what, Chango? I don't think I will knock you down again."

Chango smiled at that. "I don't think so either."

Alex charged in again. Chango put up his guard. Alex didn't throw a punch. The only headway he'd made was with the headlock. Alex was in a rage, but he could still engage his most potent power. Find his enemy's weakness and, like Scotty said, change the rules. He slammed into Chango and wrapped his arms around his body. Chango's laugh cut short.

Alex's arms bulged and strained as he squeezed Chango as hard as he could. Chango struggled, but his arms were pinned to his sides. His chest compressed.

Inside his ribcage, his lungs could not expand. They pressed on his heart. Chango's veins swelled. A wash of purple filled his face. Blood couldn't drain from his head. Alex growled as he squeezed harder and lifted Chango off his feet.

Alex backed up to the rail at the river's edge. The rain was gone, but distended and green from the storm, the water raged against its confinement in its concrete channel. Chango saw what was coming. He thrashed as hard as he was able. Blood could barely deliver oxygen to his muscles or wash away the lactic acid burning fatigue into his limbs. His hands tingled and he couldn't feel his feet. Alex's closing grip was inescapable.

Alex leaned back. Chango's struggling form rose up. Braced on the railing, Alex tipped Chango still higher. Through almost sightless eyes, Chango looked over Alex's head to the foaming water. Alex let go.

Gravity grabbed Chango, flipped him over Alex's head and tugged him toward the center of the Earth. Alex spun to watch. Unmoving, Chango simply hit the water and disappeared.

Exhausted, Alex sunk to the base of the low wall. He inhaled but couldn't fill his lungs. Pain stabbed at him as he raggedly drew uneven breaths. Every blow and cut and bruise were catching up with him. Breathing shallow, he stumbled to his feet and guided himself around to the front of the station. *Had he just killed a man?* He had to get away.

Alex's anger flashed over.

As if to compensate for the violent storm, the sky in the west was neon blue with clouds of fire pink and magnificent orange. The glowing clouds wrapped the city in tones of amber and gold. The majesty was so spectacular that the colors spread all the way to the opposite horizon.

Alex drove his truck, squinting into the sunset. On any other evening, he'd have called Dara to tell her to check out the sky. She'd step outside with the phone, and they'd watch the display together. Now he could not call her, and he did not see the beauty. He thought about air. His breathing was labored and strained.

He tried to sit back in his seat. Pain shot through him and made the entire truck lurch. Leaning forward, he tried to reach back to his right shoulder blade. He couldn't quite reach, but something was there. The spike? He could feel it. Almost grab it. If he could speak, he would say, "Fucking curse," but he couldn't speak.

No. It wasn't the spike. It was something cold. It vibrated when he breathed. He reached again and brushed it with a fingertip. Baba's letter opener. The blade was buried deep in Alex's back. The handle brushed against the seat as he drove.

Alex's exasperated sigh sounded like the word, "Dammit." He drove painfully on.

Hawwa Abdurauf had already been in her chair behind the counter for eight and a half hours. Normally she didn't work the desk, preferring to actually care for patients rather than sort them. The emergency room had quieted down after the car accidents of rush hour, but she'd still be here for the dinnertime burns and knife wounds and drunk drivers. Staff cuts and a shortage of nurses had her pulling a double. Still seated, she shifted and set her weight on her feet. It was time for her break, but before she rose more than a millimeter from her chair, a man came and stood at the reception desk. He looked like he'd spent an hour or so in a tumble dryer. His eyes were dark and deep, and he looked into hers with energy that barbed her like a harpoon.

"What is your emergency?" she asked. He didn't answer. Hawwa started to grow impatient. But her name meant "Eve, servant of the Compassionate One," the eighty-third name of God. She reminded herself of that and asked the man a second time.

He seemed to be mustering his strength. His mouth opened and his breath rasped, but he gave up as if not knowing how to explain. Hawwa waited. Finally, the man turned his bloody back and pointed with a tattooed finger.

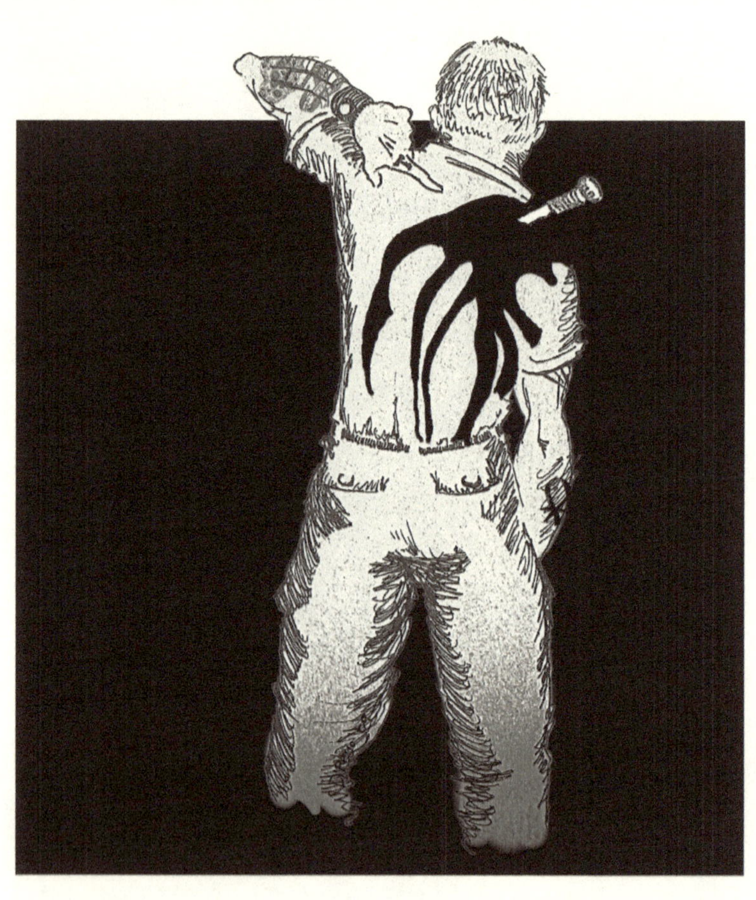

"What is your emergency?" she asked. He didn't answer.

Face down on a gurney, Alex's shirt was gone, and blood flowed across his back. He noticed that although it was a cool night outside, the air conditioning seemed to be running on high. It vibrated and whined, and he shivered. He was so cold, but he had no opinion about it.

Clad in green and pink and white and blue, doctors and nurses milled around him. His vision was not dull, but he couldn't move his head, so only their waists were accessible to him. Their voices came with the muted distance and hyper-clarity of the first risers at a quiet, early morning campsite. They were calm and professional, nothing frantic or frenzied, and there was something soothing in that. They've done this a thousand times. The gurney moved through corridors.

"Let's go. Scissors. Jones. Okay, somebody get his BP."

"Oxygen."

"Can I have an ABD pad?"

"Can you move your hand?" Alex realized that was to him, and he was trying to reach his wound. He let his hand drop.

"Punctured lung?"

"Somebody get X-ray."

Alex wasn't on the gurney anymore. He was on a bed or a table. And he wasn't in the hall either. He didn't remember shifting from the one surface to the other, and he guessed that meant it hadn't hurt. He tried to look up at the doctors and nurses surrounding him, to be a partner in their activity. He couldn't tell who was saying what. Which were the doctors and which the nurses? He felt left out and useless.

"Suture. Ligature."

"Here you go."

"What is it?"

"Three-O."

"What's his BP now?"

"Scissors."

He wanted to follow what was happening. They were so calm. Nothing like on TV. There were hands reaching inside his body.

"Down to 90 over 70. We started the blood."

"Sponge. Suture. Kelly. Scissors. Help me tie this."

Impassively, Alex shifted his gaze. At his bedside, someone leaned down to look him in the face. Baba. A surge of fear gripped him. He was helpless. Alex struggled to get up.

"Metzenbaum, please."

"I thought he was unconscious."

"Hold his arms."

Alex squirmed. His eyes went wide and he tried to cry out, to alert the doctors and nurses. "Boofff!" was all he said.

Baba opened his hand. In the palm were two small, hard-boiled eggs, slimy and slightly green. Pickled parrot eggs. Eggs of the dragon bird.

Alex had to get away. He pictured it. *Put your hands flat under your shoulders. Push up. Rise to your knees and slap the eggs away.* He didn't move. Baba reached for Alex's face and pinched his jaw. Alex panicked and wondered...*why aren't they stopping him?*

Baba forced the little eggs into Alex's mouth. Choke or swallow. Alex didn't get to choose. Instinct that didn't even reach his brain made him swallow the slippery things whole.

"Now he's dropping."

"Pick up."

"Pulse is also going up now."

"What was it pre-op?"

"BP pre-op was 140 over 90."

"How much blood do we have here?"

"Retractor."

Alex noted a new intensity in the medical team. They were not panicking, just upping their game. No one shouted or even raised their voice. Alex was impressed. *They're losing you,* he thought.

"We have four here. We've ordered four more."

"Mayo, please. This is the subclavian."

"Here's your wipe."

"Thank you, Beth."

"I can't get a BP?"

"Go."

They were working fast now, but still with practiced ease. Alex looked over at Baba. Baba smiled at him. He waved and walked out of the room. The finality of it was terrifying.

"Do you want to defibrillate again, Dr. Barber?"

"Not now. Not with that complex."

"Somebody in—"

An irritating BEEEEEEEEP filled the room. Alex winced as if at an alarm clock.

"How much bicarb?"

"Yeah, fifteen..."

"Go ahead, push it in."

He was fascinated by the professionalism and the deft precision of their work. He wished he knew better what they were talking about.

"You want some more after this?"

He thought he'd look up medical terminology when he got the chance.

"Draw some up."

"Any pupillary reaction?"

"No. Dilated and fixed."

But then he thought, *never mind.*

"Get some calcium up too?"

"Twelve units."

"What's that now? What's he got?"

"No activity."

"More epinephrine?"

"Half a milligram. Push."

Chapter 17

But that didn't help. Someone, probably the doctor in charge, shut off the flatline alarm. The room went silent. Alex was so glad.

"What time is it?"

Everything washed out white.

Chapter 18

An easy job for the Workingman. All he has to do is die.

It is a silent, early morning. Iron clouds stretch across the sky and filter the light. There are no shadows. Alex stands in the dirt yard in front of the high desert ranch house where Dara and his daughters shelter from him. It appears to be deserted. It is eerily quiet. Alex's boots crunch on the ground and he notices there is no wind.

He's confused. He takes a deep breath. His chest expands and his lungs fill. There is no pain.

Alex starts to walk to the house. Something darts at him from around the corner. He freezes as the black and white, mostly white, streak charges toward him. It's Yucky. The dog rushes to Alex and crashes into him with glee. Alex rubs Yucky's ears. "Hey, Yucky. How you doing, dog? I thought you were..." Alex stops himself. Here is his dog and here he is.

The weight of it sinks down on his shoulders. "Oh, shit."

Alex looks around, trying to get his bearings. He sees no one but Yucky. He walks around behind the house.

Here too, the light is dull and the air is still. Alex finds himself in a wide, open field. He's on horseback. Yucky darts in and out of the tall grass as Alex rambles without purpose on Sabbath's back. Someone rides up beside him. A beautiful woman on a beautiful paint. It's Dara. She guides her horse next to Alex's. They ride knee to knee.

Dara looks him over and says, "You look pretty bad, Alex."

Alex smiles at her. "You look outstanding, but..."

She shrugs and interrupts. "It's good to see you anyway." She laughs a happy laugh.

Her joy radiates through him like the spreading warmth of a sip of wine. "I love you." Alex drinks in her words and the massive relief they bring. But Dara's laugh trails off. She stops her horse and turns seriously to Alex. "I'm going to miss you so much." Alex stops a few yards ahead of her. Her eyes are fixed on his and the earnest gravity of her look turns that flowing warmth to ice, even before she speaks. And then she speaks and makes it even colder. "The whole world is against you, Alexander."

"The whole world is against you, Alexander."

The words hit him like a frying pan. Alex is stunned, head ringing from the blow. Dara's horse starts to back up, nervously. "Dara?"

"I can't," she explains. "I'm not dead. I'm only dreaming."

Alex doesn't know what she means. He looks down and realizes his horse is hoof deep in flowing water. Dara's horse shies away from the edge of this wide river.

A tug like the current of the flood pulls at him and Alex is compelled to ride deeper into the flow. With one final look to Dara, he spurs his horse. Sabbath thunders across the shallow river.

Just like that, it is night. Scrubby trees and close chaparral throw a cage across the sky and make a jagged maze of the woodland. Alex's horse is gone. He stumbles through the undergrowth. The chugging throb of pain strokes through his shoulder and neck. His back spasms. Alex reaches up and pulls his shirt off.

The spike stands out, real and solid and visible. At the point where his neck meets his right shoulder, the spike stabs through the muscle, drawing flesh into the wound. It glows with a strange, white light, encompassing every color in the universe. As he crashes through lacerating branches, Alex reaches for the spike, but can't get a grasp.

Something moves on Alex's back. The dark form stalks and spreads and reaches and makes him quiver.

In the scattered moonlight, the lion tattoo lunges across Alex's back. With determined fury, it paws at the spike. It tears at Alex's flesh. The spike doesn't budge. Claws dig at the wound, trying to extract the curse.

Alex thrashes in pain as the great, inked beast rakes and tears through muscle and bone. He can't escape the curse or the lion. He loses his footing and falls.

Alex tumbles through empty darkness. With a rending crash, he bursts through a ceiling and thuds to the floor. Shaking, he pushes up on his hands and finds himself in his own apartment. Furious and frustrated, the animated lion stalks around the immovable, glowing spike. It bites and tears a frayed and bloody channel around the terrible barb but cannot find the root. Alex struggles to his feet and looks around. He's home, but still alone. He staggers into the bathroom.

In the broken mirror, the spike is reflected a hundred times in crazy angles. He tries to turn and see the raging battle on his back. Only the edges of the action are visible to him. Frustrated, Alex reaches out and leans on the shattered mirror, seeking a better angle. The glass moves. Alex peels the jagged shards aside like a curtain. Behind it is a dark void. Compelled, Alex hoists himself onto the counter and climbs through.

At the far end of a long dark hall, Alex spies a lighted doorway. He forces himself into a ragged jog and almost reaches the door. Something blocks his path. Dripping wet with muddy filth, a snarling, vicious dog guards the door. It's Yucky.

The dead dog's eyes shine with blind aggression. He growls and bares vengeful teeth. Alex must get through that door. He reaches out for the knob. Yucky lunges. Alex snatches the dog by the scruff and flings the raging beast down the hall behind him. The dog springs to its feet and charges, but Alex ignores him and marches through the door.

The sun shines warmly through the trees. A stream flows over a waterfall. The door leads not to a room, but to a lush and rocky grotto. Atop the waterfall, sitting on the rocks like a throne, is Chango. Hunched and bristling, Yucky crouches at Chango's knee, glaring at Alex. The lion settles angrily on Alex's back, glaring ragefully at the spike. Here in the sun-dappled grotto, the spike juts from Alex's shoulder in the back, and its sharp point protrudes from under his collarbone in the front. Alex strains against it.

He looks up at the man and points at the snarling Yucky. "That's my dog."

"Not anymore," answers the throned man. "Now you're both dead."

"I killed you?"

Chango indulges Alex with a smile. "No. I was here already. But you did beat me. I didn't think you could do it, but I should have known. That's your seventh task done. Two more to go, according to Baba."

Alex looks up at the man and asks, "Who are you?"

"Ask your mother." Instead of explaining that, Chango adds, "Your next task is to rescue him."

"Him?"

"Baba."

"From what?"

Chango answers as if it's obvious. "From me."

"You?"

"The imbalance is bigger than you are, Alexander," instructs Chango. "It's taking in the people around you."

"You are my curse?"

"No." Chango bobbles his hands, trying to come up with an explanation. "The curse put a mark on you. Brought you to the attention of the universe. Pinned you to its fabric." Alex puts his hand to the glowing spike, speared through his shoulder. "Exactly," confirms Chango, pleased that Alex is getting it. "Literally."

"I'm not out of balance?"

"Oh, you're out of balance. The whole universe is, and the curse pithed you to the weight on the metronome." Chango looks down on Alex with affection. "I do root for you. But I can't help you. I'll even stop you if I can."

"Why?"

"Balance doesn't come without pushback."

"I thought you wanted balance."

"Not what I want. I'm just the arbiter, the adjudicator of the needs of the powers that be."

"I don't know what that means."

"The priestess was right. So was the cowboy. It wasn't really Baba you were working for. Baba forgot that. He's been trying to take advantage of the imbalance to seesaw himself above me. And he thought I wouldn't know. But I'm not the boss either," Chango explains, "and sometimes the boss requires the worst of me. I'm just an agent. My client is the universe."

"The worst of you?"

Chango gestures to the waterfall. "The universe is like water. It always takes the easiest path to its end. Baba got caught up in the current." Chango leans in, to be sure Alex gets this. "Equilibrium comes whether you win or lose. The universe doesn't care. But if you lose, you lose everything. The whole world does."

"The lion or the bull. Whoever comes out on top, the universe keeps on ticking."

"You got it. And the easiest path is if the lion just gets swept away. It'll even take Dara and the girls if that's easier."

A charge jolts through Alex. "What?!"

"The universe has you backed into a corner."

"Yeah?" Alex stands his ground. "Well, it's my corner."

"Then, you're going to have to force the universe into balance."

"Fine." He's heard enough. Alex is ready to take on all comers.

Chango tests to see if Alex is ready for one more push. "Your mother was right. She's not a grandmother. Ask her about the spike."

Alex doesn't rise to the bait. Chango is secretly pleased. He orders with deep authority, "Go!"

Alex bristles. "You're wrong, Chango."

"Oh?"

"If beating you was my seventh task, I have three more to go."

"What do you think this was?" Chango laughs. "Besides," he shrugs, "I'm afraid Baba's numbers were arbitrary. How many times to you have to adjust a gate post to set it straight and level?"

Alex scoffs at the notion. "You don't. You set a gate post one tick out of plumb, so the gate swings shut by itself."

"Interesting."

Alex acknowledges this by marching toward the door. He steadies the spike with one hand like a terrible swagger stick. "If the whole world is against me, then everybody'd better get the fuck out of my way. Come on, Yucky." The dog's ears perk.

Chango rules, "He's not going with you."

"The hell he's not." Alex pats his thigh with a pop and looks at neither Chango nor Yucky as he disappears down the dark hall. Chango's authority overridden, Yucky springs into the darkness.

Alex woke with a start, swaddled in bandages and lying in a hospital bed. The room was beige, the curtain surrounding the bed was rigid and blue, and the air hung with nauseating cleanliness. A woman sat at his bedside, watching him. Luna. She saw him stir.

"Alexander?"

"Mom?" His voice scraped and burned with terrible fry. It hadn't sounded like that when he was with Chango. When was that? He was parched. He wondered how long it had been since he'd spoken. And then he wondered… "Are you dead?"

"No, Metaki." Her son was wrong, but unlike every sparring session they'd ever had, Luna didn't jab him for it. "You were. For thirteen minutes."

His muscles felt like he'd spent three days over-lifting at a gym. His arms strained and his back ached, but he sat up. "Where's Dara?"

"We think she's on the road. Your cell phones were suspended."

Resigned. Alex shook his head, "Ananke."

"What?"

Alex looked at his mother. She was about to go on, but his seriousness captivated her, and she fell silent.

"You really aren't a grandmother."

That visibly struck her. With a tremble, she started in with, "That's just—" But she wasn't sparring, she was evading.

"Who is Chango?" Alex interrupted.

If she hadn't already been in a chair, Luna would have had to find one. Her son's question hit her like a physical thing. "How do you know that name?"

"You tell me." Alex didn't relent, but he was almost moved by his mother's lack of fight.

"Alexander Papachangos," she said.

"Alexander?"

Luna explained, "You were named after him."

That didn't make sense. "He's not old..."

"He's your father."

"What?!" Alex sat up further and it didn't hurt a bit.

Luna shrank. "I think."

"You don't know?" Alex demanded. "There were other men—"

"No!" she said with sudden passion. "There was Papachango! He loved me. I loved him. He...he brought me a baby."

"Don't be coy."

"He brought you," she insisted. "He said you were his. Then, you were mine. You were called Alexander after him, and Cides after my father."

"You're not my mother?" Alex was lost.

"Of course I am!" she snapped back at him. "I'm just not really..." she trailed off but then found her strength. "You are my son."

Her son's question hit her like a physical thing.
"How do you know that name?"

"He left me with you." Alex started to pick up the threads. "He come back?"

"No."

He wove the fibers of the story into a picture that started to make sense. "And you raised me for him."

"I loved him then." She said it with a pain that confirmed his picture.

"But he left you." His mother nodded, ashamed. Alex tied up the last of the threads. "And that's when you put this spike in my neck."

Luna's eyes filled, horrified at her own weakness. "No."

"You hated him, and you cursed me for it."

"No! Not a curse. I needed help. I was alone. I went to my Yiayia Magissa, but she wouldn't do it. I found a man. He said I needed something of his— of Papachango's—that I valued more highly than anything. That was you!"

"So, your Greek witch wouldn't do it. Let me guess, you found a Mexican one."

Luna was shocked he could have guessed that. She tried to explain. "Yes. I love you. I'm sorry. He put a mark on you. That's all. So he could spot you. Like a standard, he said. A flagpole."

"More like a pike."

"I thought he'd come back for you. Back to me. Follow the signal. Maybe a guide to make him come back."

"Oh, he came back."

"I was so young."

Alex didn't have time for any more of this. "I have to find Dara."

A thrill ran through Luna. She could help. "Her uncle said she and the girls were on their way home."

But her boy was not pleased by her news. "Your curse didn't hurt Chango a bit, Mom. Now it's gonna get my family." Alex threw the covers off the bed. He had work to do. "Where the fuck are my pants?"

Luna shrank back from him, suddenly afraid of her son. "They burned them. The blood…" she held out all she had, as an appeasement, an offering. "All that's left is these."

Alex swiped the keys from her palm and tugged the tubes and wires from his body.

"What are you going to do?"

Alex cinched his gown shut with the sensor wires and leaking IV tube. "I'm gonna beat the universe into balance." He marched out of the room.

Luna put her face in her hands and cried for the first time in forty years.

Chapter 19
The Workingman meets his match.

Days of violent weather purged the city and the sky above it. Every scrap of mist or cloud or smog was gone. Stars shined down with telescopic clarity through air cold enough to make you clench your teeth. Alex sped through the crisp night, racing to get home.

It's only pain, thought Alex. The churning in his shoulder was worse than ever. The muscles visibly twitched and cramped. As he closed in on the apartment, he reached back to massage the spot. The actual wound there stopped him. He gripped the wheel, gritted his teeth, and rocked in time with the throbbing, as if that would ease the pain and urge the truck home faster.

Toward the same point, from another direction, Dara drove on the edge of hurry. She'd had a strange and somehow terrible dream. Mounted on a pale horse, she had told Alex she'd never see him again.

The dream hung on her with the terrible clarity of a too-high-definition image. The resigned finality of it shook her like no dream ever had. She had to talk to him.

Their cell phones being suspended, she loaded the girls into the car and told them they were going to see their father. Niki sensed the tension or fear in her mother, but Dara was so outwardly calm the girl wasn't sure how to process it. Thea was glad to be going back to the city, but she saw the anxiety in her mother and confusion in her little sister, and she took it upon herself to do something about it.

Thea sat in the passenger seat, lit by the glow of her tablet. She was too old for the game, but she knew it was what they needed. "A noun," she prompted.

Niki piped up from the back seat. "Poop."

Without a smile, Thea entered the word and continued, "Adjective."

"Poopy!" Niki sang.

Thea was trying to be an adult, but she couldn't stop herself from being thirteen. She was exasperated by her little sister. "Niki!"

Dara stepped in. "It's my turn, Niki."

Appeased, Thea repeated, "Adjective."

Dara answered, "Poopy."

Niki laughed. Thea rolled her eyes.

Dara protected her daughters.

Headlights illuminated the empty parking spot at their building. Alex wasn't here. Dara pulled in, knowing that meant something was wrong.

The hall outside the apartment was dark, the dead lightbulbs unchanged. Cautiously, Dara approached their home, holding Thea's hand in a protective chain with Niki holding onto Thea's other hand. With the caution of someone in a Halloween fright house knowing there was a scare in store, she inserted her key in the lock and turned the knob of the front door. It didn't open, and the scare didn't come. She sighed, releasing some tension. "He's not here."

Suddenly, a new figure appeared out of the darkness.

Dara jumped back from the door, startled. "Who are you?"

"You have not heard of Baba? Alex has kept you all to himself."

Chilled by the implications of being shared, Dara asked, "Alex works for you?"

"That's right." Baba leered and though it was dark, Dara knew it. "I can open that door for you."

With a crash, the front door shook on its hinges. Dara and the girls flinched away from Baba. He kicked the door again. Without the deadbolt set, the padlock ripped out of the hastily installed screws, and the door banged open. Baba reached out and grabbed the first wrist he could get a hand on. Thea. He dragged her into the apartment and threw her to the floor.

Dara advanced on Baba with fury. Niki ran in behind her mother.

Baba stood over the fallen girl. "Your man won't stay dead. I'll settle the balance with you instead."

"I don't think so." Dara backhanded Baba across the face. The reedy man spun and stumbled away. Dara pulled Thea to her feet. "Are you okay?" Wide-eyed, Thea could only nod. "Take your sister. Run!"

Thea turned to Niki, but Baba was faster. He ran to the door and slammed it, throwing the deadbolt. "Now we're cozy."

Dara wrapped an arm around his waist and flung him away from the door. She twisted the lock open. Baba rushed back in on her. Her backhand split his eyebrow and stumbled him away from her girls. She threw open the door.

Baba caught his balance. "You can beat me up," he announced, "but you can't beat me." He dashed to the kitchen and cranked up a dial on the stove. The sparker tick, tick, ticked. A blue flame jumped up on the burner. The glow slashed coldly through the priest's eyes. Baba lifted a towel with a snap. He cast it into the flame. Fire grabbed the fabric, curled it, lifted it.

"Son of a bitch!" Dara ran to the kitchen. The flames grew, jumping from the towel to a potholder to an empty cardboard wine bottle six-pack Alex had left on the countertop. Focused on the growing fire, Dara didn't see Baba dart in at her.

His hands closed around her hips. He spun her like a psychotic dancer. She lifted off the ground and crashed into the smoke. The particleboard counter rushed at her. She could do nothing but turn her head. The impact turned her off like a window slamming shut.

United, the sisters shouted for their mother. Baba ran out of the burning kitchen to the front door. He wasn't trying to escape. He slammed the door again.

Instantly, BOOM! The door blasted off its hinges. Alex was there. Baba reeled back. Thea and Niki watched their father stride into the smoky apartment in his cinched-up blue hospital gown. They knew he would make this right. "Mom's in the kitchen!" Thea let him know.

"Tell her I'm coming." Alex grabbed Baba by the throat and pinned him to a wall. The fire burned hot and fast. It climbed the kitchen shelves, consuming food and paper. The heat and light danced crazily on Alex's bare arms and legs. He ignored it.

Baba barely struggled. With unveiled smugness, he crowed, "You can't beat me. I'm the agent of—"

"Of this?" Alex reached up to his own neck. Baba's eyes went wide when he saw it. Glowing with hot, white light, Alex grabbed the cursed spike.

Thea and Niki saw his strong fingers close on the spike. They saw it. Light spilling from his clenched fist as he drew it out like pulling a blade from a sheath. It glowed like burning frost in his hand. The sharp and awful weapon dripped with their father's blood.

Baba thrashed to break free, but Alex held him firm. He raised the spike, illuminating livid lion claw lash-marks and furious eyes. He slammed the supranatural knife into Baba's chest. The point popped through his skin and wedged the ribs apart. Baba screamed so hard his jaw dislocated. His body shuddered and his punctured heart deflated.

Now a bubble welled up in the fabric of the universe. The irresistible pressure built and burst. The great force exploded from the head of the spike. Alex was blasted back off his feet. Thea and Niki tumbled to the carpet as the wave crashed over them. Baba crumpled to the ground.

There was no wound. The spike was gone. No, that's not true. Instead of the spike, a powerful, dark figure now loomed against the wall where Baba had stood.

In the swirling smoke and fire, its form jumped and flickered, part of this world and part of another. Muscled and horrible, with thorny claws and knotty flesh, its body was a grotesquery in the form of a man. Its ridged and bony head was long and blunt, and topped with heavy, sharp and curved prongs. They glowed white against the red blaze of the fire. Alex gazed at the creature and recognized it. The terrible implement that had pierced his flesh and tortured him for so long was never a spike at all. It was a horn.

Alex gazed at the creature and recognized it.

Thea climbed up to one knee, shaking her head clear. But then she looked into the flames. She saw the Minotaur, and screamed.

Alex snapped back to life, lunging to his feet. The creature spread its arms and flexed peaked shoulders in a threat display, making a wall between Alex and his daughters. Alex roared at Thea. "Go! Get out! Take Niki!"

Thea protested, "Mom!"

Alex assured her, "I'll get her."

"But…" Thea hardly knew where to begin. "What is…everything?"

That was exactly the right question, but Alex had no time to answer it. "Go, Thea!"

Thea grabbed her crying sister and rushed to the door. The Minotaur pivoted on broad, cloven hooves, gouging the floor and blocking the girls. Alex propelled himself into his nemesis. As their father crashed into the beast and slammed it to the wall, a safe passage opened up. The girls ran for the door.

The spiny hair of the fiend bristled against Alex's face. They grappled for dominance, one pushing toward the door, the other deeper into the apartment. Reflected in the monster's eye, Alex saw Thea leading Niki. He watched them disappear through the door. Frustrated, the Minotaur gave up on the girls and pivoted again. Alex overbalanced and tumbled past his foe, deeper into the fire.

Alex roared. Light from the flames and glowing horns cast sick and dancing shadows. Unlimbered by the removal of the spike, the shadow of the lion exploded across the walls and tackled the silhouette bull. In furious battle, the cosmic manifestations tore through the burning apartment, splaying the terrible shadow play across every surface. Horns and teeth and claws and hooves tore into shade forms, scattering tufts of shadowy pelt and spatters of dry blood.

Back and forth they raged. The lion sank dagger fangs into the bull's muscled hump. The bull bucked and twisted, catapulting the lion. The bull reared and angled its head down at its sprawled enemy. Curved horns gored through the lion, pinning it through the shoulder.

Alex was already wounded before the fight even began. He was losing. The Minotaur beat him back, deeper into the fire, preventing him from reaching Dara. It spun him around and clamped a bark-hard arm around his neck. As the creature squeezed, Alex ebbed.

Through the smoke, Alex saw Dara's unconscious body on the floor. A gush of fury rose and charged his arms and legs. Alex reached up and found the gnarled hand of his living curse. He peeled a finger from his throat and forced it backwards. The bone torqued and buckled. Tendons snapped. The creature didn't flinch, but its grip weakened. Alex broke the monster's hold.

With that split second of freedom, Alex ran for Dara. In the burning kitchen, Alex felt his skin singe with instant sunburn. It didn't slow him. He heard the terrible crack. Compromised by fire, the ceiling caved in. A heavy beam tore from a burning bracket. Dara lay in its path, waiting to be crushed. In an instant and without hesitation, Alex dove under the beam.

The beam hammered him down, carving its weight into his shoulder. Blood sprang from the reopened wound. Alex crashed to one knee but held the killing blow away from Dara. With all his strength, he rose up like a pillar. The Minotaur rushed in on him.

Alex called out, "Wait!"

The Minotaur stopped.

The weight of the beam was crushing him. He could barely speak. "Let me save her."

The Minotaur moved in.

Alex stopped it with a question. "You promised Baba the world of the bull, didn't you?" The Minotaur hesitated in confirmation. "Baba above Chango. You, free in the physical world." Another silent confirmation. "But do you want that body?" Alex looked to Baba. The Minotaur followed his look to the crumpled, skinny, aging man. "Or this one?" The Workingman's muscles bulged and strained. Ripped away by the combat, his hospital gown hung in tatters like an ancient exomis, one shoulder bare, torn fabric stretching across his hips and legs. Tattoos and battle scars shone in the firelight. Sweat and blood dripped from flesh made strong by years of toil.

His massive strength at its ultimate end, holding back the crushing weight of the beam, Alex stood tall. "Let me save her, and I won't fight you."

The Minotaur cocked its head, considering.

"I can't reach her." Alex was slipping. "You want me, right? I won't fight you. Easy balance for the universe. Just let me save her."

Balance. No fight or struggle. Easy as water. The Minotaur didn't actually nod, but it moved in. It put a hand on the beam. It took on the strain, and Alex ducked out from under the pulverizing force. The beam rested across the Minotaur's shoulders.

Alex rushed to Dara and dragged her free of the flaming kitchen. In the relative safety of the living room, he put his face to hers. Her skin was hot to the touch, but she was breathing. Alex could have wept with relief, but instead he looked back to the Minotaur, straining under the weight of the beam. The Minotaur put out its broken hand and made that languageless gesture that means "Come."

Before Alex could accept or the Minotaur could demand, something exploded from the shadows. Like a fiend from hell, the fearsome creature sprang to the Minotaur's chest and tore at its throat. The Minotaur staggered back, swatting at its new attacker with one hand. It was Yucky. Yucky.

Yucky rent flesh with fangs and claws. Amazed, Alex gazed wide-eyed at his returned companion. The shade bore into the neck and shoulder of the horned beast. The Minotaur tried to dislodge the dog but lost its hold on the weight above it. Yucky vanished. The beam collapsed, driving the creature into the floor.

Pinned under the great weight in the burning room, the Minotaur felt the pendulum swing toward the lion. It knew. Just like water, fire always takes the easiest path. It struggled, trying to make the universe work harder for equilibrium.

Alex looked into its desperate eyes. "I said I wouldn't fight you, you son of a bitch!" The Minotaur bellowed in rage and pain, consumed by flames.

Alex lifted Dara and carried her out of their burning home. They disappeared through the broken door. Approaching sirens wailed in the distance. After a moment of hesitation, Alex reappeared. He peered through the mounting smoke and spotted what he came back for. He grabbed Baba's depleted form and dragged him outside.

From outside and in, firefighters attacked the burning building. Fire trucks and ambulances lit the night. Flashing lights strobed and sparked red and white in the artificial rain, kicking off from hoses and backwashing out the windows of the apartment. Dissonant flashes of blue added an out-of-sync undercurrent to the lights.

Sitting close to her sister in the open passenger door of a black and white cruiser, Niki repeated over and over that there was a monster upstairs, and Thea explained that she had no idea why their father's boss had tried to kill them. The officers didn't ask her about the monster at all, and she knew they wouldn't.

A wheeled stretcher rolled smoothly toward an ambulance, attended by two paramedics and a cop. Someone lay perfectly still on the thin mattress, one wrist cuffed to a chromed rail. Baba. He was shrunken, crinkled and gray, like sodden paper, but he was alive. Inside his chest, his heart pumped and blood flowed, prevented from bursting out by a tiny plug of keratin. The cracked-off little wedge filled the hole in the essential organ, burrowing like a seed with every throb.

Already in the back of another ambulance, Dara sprang up in a cold panic with an oxygen mask on her face. She reached out for her children as if they were all still upstairs in the fire. Her own team of medics hovered close and calmed her, assuring her that everyone was safe. Soot streamed from her nose and eyes as she wept in rage and fear and relief.

Watching all this unfold with exhausted hyper-clarity, Alex sat on the wet asphalt, wrapped in a silver blanket like the cloak of some science fiction prophet. Something else ticked at the edges of his vision. It appeared in the deeply shadowed counterpoints to the flashing of the lights. When the light hit the space where it seemed to stand, it vanished.

Alex wanted to rise up and go to his wife and daughters, but a fire captain who once had been a paramedic pressed down on his shoulder, keeping pressure on the opened wound and ripped stitches, and unknowingly grinding together the shattered ends of Alex's broken collarbone. So much adrenaline had ebbed and flowed through his body that he probably couldn't have stood up even if it was only Niki holding him down.

He looked at the animated little girl now, her words lost in the wash of sirens and water. Her story was clearly a dramatic one, in contrast to the earnest seriousness of her older sister. Dara, restrained by the man and woman tending to her, pushed strongly against them in an effort to rejoin with her daughters. They were fine.

"You won."

Startled as if he were a ghost he thought no one could see, Alex jumped at the words. His bones grated together like flint and steel and he sank back down as he recognized Inanna standing above him in the hard mist. "You did so much better than we thought you would."

Alex's eyes stayed on his wife. "We?"

Chango stepped out of the darkness. Alex shook his head, resigned to the madness. "I asked my mother about you."

"So, now you know…son."

"Son? Mom can call me that. But you? I could be that. Or just another changeling?"

"Ah. Well, not 'just.' Never 'just.'" Chango smiled at the Workingman. "Good work."

Alex thought of that for a moment and dismissed it. "Well, if that's what I had to do to get balanced..."

Inanna scoffed, surprised. "You? You're not balanced."

Like a child, Alex complained, "But you said—"

"For that, you have work to do, Workingman," Chango announced, gravely.

By way of explanation, Inanna asked, "How's your neck?"

Alex felt his wounds and the strong hands that pressed into his flesh and bones. "Cut up. Hurts like a motherfucker. I don't think it's as bad as it looks."

But Inanna scoffed again. "No, stupid." That drew Alex's eyes to her. She looked deeply into them and asked again. "Your neck?"

Alex quested through his nerves, past the open stab wound and the fresh break, deep into his fibers. He sank a bit. The old ache drilled deep in his shoulder.

Chango nodded, knowing what Alex had found. "The universe got what it needed, but for your own balance... One final task to perform. And it will be the hardest of all."

"Jesus, Chango, now what?"

Instead of telling him, Inanna unfolded a story.

"The hero had lost everything, and that propelled him into his journey. He traveled to places he never thought he'd see, or even existed. He battled monsters and passions and puzzles and traps and escaped even from the other side of death."

Alex tried to interrupt. "I know all this."

Inanna continued, undeterred. "In the end, he met his greatest enemy and defeated it in terrible combat, setting the universe back on its divine fulcrum."

It had been terrible. Though Alex tried to resist, he was drawn into the telling. What came next?

"By the rights of all the myths, all the fairytales and sagas, he should claim his prize. No trophy was beyond his grasp. No reward could be denied him."

The hero's victory sent a surge of electricity washing through Alex. It filled his limbs and energized his body. His legs flexed with new strength and he stood, rising to his full height and making the fire captain take a step back. Alex looked over the chaos of the lot and found his daughters, holding each other in the open door of a police car. From the girls, his eyes moved to find Dara, no longer crying, taking a long draft from her oxygen mask as if drinking from a goblet. She gazed back at him, the most beautiful woman in the world.

One year from now, in a world he's made perfectly plumb, Alex walks through the front door of a condo in the north valley freshly decorated with art made by his daughters, flat-pack furniture, and framed prints of Art Nouveau depictions of ancient gods and goddesses. Though no one is home to see him do it, he flourishes the bouquet of roses he's brought home before setting them on a table by the door.

On his way to the kitchen, the phone in his pocket buzzes at him with the double jangle of an Old-World phone. It reminds him of the throb he once felt in his neck. He checks the screen. It reads, "Mom!" He clicks a virtual button, silencing the digital bells and letting his mother go to voicemail.

Alex snakes a beer from a crisper drawer exactly the right size to hold a twelve-pack. He takes the bottle to the living room, cracking it open as he sinks into the leather couch. He relaxes. His eyes close as he sips the beer and let its coolness wash into him.

He reaches for the remote control on the arm of the couch and snaps the TV on. Scrolling through channels, he lands on the adult-oriented anime he's developed a taste for, just in time to catch a flash of an ahegao face. Drawn into the manic waterfall of light and sound, his mind goes gladly blank. They'll be home any minute.

The front door swings open and Niki and Thea walk in, each with a bag of groceries. He smiles at them and Thea smiles back and Niki waves, silently continuing into the kitchen and not interrupting his show.

Dara appears in the open doorway and Alex can't help admiring the way that top he likes clings to her breasts but then sort of flares out above her waist. The jeans hug her ample bottom, and Alex is pleased to note that though his wife is a mother of two, and not as young as she was, he's still as into her as ever.

Dara spies her husband on the couch over an armful of bags. "Don't get up," she says, meaning it. But Alex rises from his seat and takes the bags from her. There is no stab in his shoulder as he hefts them.

"I'm up," he says. She tries to protest, but he's already taken the bags and headed into the kitchen. That's when she sees the flowers. That means he's in a good mood and not trying to make some kind of point about the bags. Dara lets out a little sigh of relief.

"Good day at work?" she asks, testing the waters.

"Oh. Yeah," he answers dismissively. "I got Sam over a barrel." Alex starts putting groceries away with his daughters. Dara comes into the kitchen with the flowers. She gives him a little kiss as she hunts for a vase. She looks over her tired husband and smiles.

"You've both got homework," she says to the girls. "We'll finish with these. You go get to it."

The girls hesitate and Alex chimes in, "Go. Go. Go." Thea leads Niki dutifully to their rooms.

When they're gone, Dara looks back to her man. "You're still dirty from work."

"Am I?" he asks innocently, knowing the game she is playing.

Dara is smart and learning how to manage her husband's moods. It's very nearly a full-time job. So much the better, now that her viticulture dreams are a thing of the past. She stays out ahead of him, keeps him pleased, and his temper hasn't flared over in weeks. "Take your shirt off."

Obediently, Alex unbuttons his not-actually-dirty shirt and pulls it off. His work-hardened chest sports the freshest of his tattoos: "Dara Forever," right over his heart.

It had all been worth it. A year ago, he'd beaten the universe into balance and then walked across that soaking parking lot to claim his prize. He had saved her, and she knew it. Dara is his because the cosmos wants it that way. She is there to soothe him.

His job was going so well that they'd gotten this new place and Dara could stay at home full time for the girls. That hardly seemed like a curse at all.

But…

CHAPTER 20

Can this be the end for the Workingman?

In a world set one tick out of plumb, Monica Reidy told herself she never wanted to get on a bicycle again. But here she was, peddling away under the unflinching eye of the meanest former football player she had ever met. Of course, she was only pushing four miles per hour, but the pain was greater than anything she remembered from the accident.

Out loud, she called it "the accident," because that word prompted fewer questions and demands to repeat the story of her harrowing encounter with nature at its most basic. In her head, she called it "the Handling," because that's what it had been.

Predators operate in what's known as the "Foraging Cycle," which begins with "Search." At that first stage Monica was on her bike, trying not to think about her master's program studying organic chemistry, and the mountain lion didn't yet know if he would eat that day. Long before Monica knew she wasn't alone, "Detection" occurred—the lion's ears pricked up and his body froze. In an instant, Monica was "Assessed" and determined to be an acceptable risk.

The "Pursuit" stage was incredibly short, just a powerful explosion of the haunches to launch the cat at its target and then the terrible crash that brought Monica to ground and to her last clear memories of the event. In the final stage, before the cycle repeats, the predator "Handles" its quarry, removing the shell or breaking the neck or stripping the quills and then consuming it.

Though the physical therapy was grueling, the hardest part of her recovery was knowing that she had been simply prey.

Her entire gastrocnemius was gone. Eaten. But surgeons laid a lattice of cells harvested from a pig's bladder into the cored-out space of the missing tissue. Muscle fibers stitched and regrew and strengthened, and every agonizing revolution of the pedals on the stationary bike brought her closer to the day she'd have calves the size of cantaloupes.

On that day, she'd swing onto the saddle of her mountain bike and ride it all the way to Africa, into the Masai Mara, to test her mettle taking picture of lionesses twice the size of the cat she'd survived, and black-maned males three times the size of herself. She figured it would take a year. She might have finished her degree by then, but she had been set back by switching her studies to terrestrial ecology.

For the first time in her life, she had a passport. She already booked her ticket.

Bustling with rambunctious chaos, the Califia Youth Club always threatened to overflow its edges, but never did because of the careful attention of and special respect for Mr. Stillman. He walked through the rooms of the community center, ear tuned to the pitch of activities—from dodgeball to bumper pool to hopscotch to a play-fight that could blossom into a real one. He followed that dissonance for a moment, until one of the boys bellowed out a cry that meant he was engaging his superpowers and his next attack would be at Super Saiyan levels.

Satisfied, Stillman continued his unofficial rounds until he identified a curious void in the din. He followed the stillness in the turmoil to a corner of the institution where nine boys and girls stood and sat in captivated silence, watching creation happen.

Cleo was at her easel. She almost danced with it as she made a sweeping stroke with her brush, stepped away to see the effect, and closed back in to deliver follow up feathering. Some hundred years earlier, a German Egyptologist had entered on his official claims form that he was taking a painted plaster bust of a princess back to Berlin. Egyptian authorities had allowed it, but the scientist's personal notes show that he knew exactly what he had: Nefertiti, an African queen even more ancient than Cleopatra. The magnificent bust has been in Berlin ever since, despite the Egyptians demanding her return from the moment her unveiling revealed the true nature of the find. "I will never relinquish the head of the Queen," spoke Adolf Hitler.

Then, some twenty years ago, the Berlin museum allowed a pair of Hungarian artists to place the bust atop a bronze body for a special exhibition. Naked, skinny, and pathetic, the elegant arch of her neck was reinterpreted to be the result of poor posture and a mousey, powerless disposition.

On Cleo's canvas, the four-thousand-year-old pharaoh appeared as a Nubian goddess, taking flight in a swirl of color above the impressionistic Cataracts of the Nile. An explosion of flowers boiled out of her conical crown, trailing behind her like the tail of a marvelous kite, the cobra diadem flared out into wings. Her missing left eye was a window to another world. Cleo painted it with tiny brushes and photorealistic clarity, in subtle contrast to the opulence of the rest of the canvas. If you leaned in close enough to the copper-toned face to look into the eye, you could see the edges of an open door cut into a limestone wall, the other side frustratingly and enticingly out of view.

And the children watching did lean in.

Vernon, California is a little, independent municipality with the lowest population of any city in the state. It's a multibillion-dollar pocket of dirty industry, entirely surrounded by the neighborhoods of East LA. Known for meat packing, steel yards and poisonous slagheaps from battery recycling, it was hardly a hospitable place for a puppy. But the dog had lived off rendering plant slag and sheltered in the lee of a warehouse filled with patch pockets, rivets, and appliques that would one day adorn blue jeans retailing at $400 a pair.

Five and a half miles and months of recovery in a shelter later, the dog discovered that it could run in a tight circle in the front yard, getting perfect traction on the mowed grass. Part rott, part shepherd, and with just enough pit to make his short, stiff coat almost sky blue, his new family named him after the city where he was found. Vernon dashed around the yard and dove through a broken access panel to disappear into the crawlspace under the house. A moment later, he burst out into the backyard through another access, barking a high yip to announce himself. The boy in the backyard screamed with delight, and Vernon ran in another circle around him.

At top speed, Vernon streaked under the house again to yip in the front yard, making the little girl there shriek just like her brother. He was getting tired, but the joy of the figure-eights under and around his new home propelled him to ecstatic exhaustion.

Rodger sat on the porch, reveling in the delight of the three little souls. He hadn't known the access panels were broken, and he'd have to fix them, but for now he was content. At the shelter, they'd speculated that Vernon was cast off by a backyard breeder as a failed fighting dog, which may or may not have been true. But no one suspected—and Vernon would never tell—that he'd once run with The Pack and he'd galloped all the way until dawn to find that warehouse on the night the Leader was taken away.

He remembered those times, but they were like the distant tune of a once-favorite song whose words you no longer know.

Starting with castoffs from the wardrobe departments of multiple studios and rental houses, thrift store after thrift store cropped up on and around Magnolia Boulevard in Burbank. Following the thrift stores, head shops, boutiques, and coffee houses moved in, making the street a destination for the black-clad.

Luna winced as she sat at the glass table with a base made from an M48 practice bomb, painted pink. The pain in her shoulder made her sling her denim jacket like a hussar's, but she wouldn't take it off because of the chills. She wasn't late, but the other three ladies had arrived before her and were already passing back and forth one of their phones, either showing off or appreciating little pictures and video of tweens and teens in a hockey game.

Luna smiled at the presentation and said the complimentary Oohs and things, silently appreciating how much cooler her granddaughters were than all the others. She wasn't the proudest yia-yia at the table, but she deserved to be.

"Luna, are you shivering?" one of them asked.

"I'm fine," she dismissed with a little, regal wave. She sipped her warming tea, but it wasn't the weather that caused her petite tremble. She'd finally had the appointment with her artist.

The long overdue coverup was so fresh you could smell the ink. The eagle-winged black bull had adorned the back of her right shoulder longer than she cared to remember. The blackwork image was bold, and it needed something even bolder to make it disappear. Luna knew exactly what that something should be.

A split-open pomegranate bled red juice down her back. Twin torches of bound rushes crossed the exposed pith and seeds of the glistening fruit, crowning it with an eternal flame that licked her shoulder.

Sara warned her that from across the room it might look like an open wound, and though Luna rather liked the idea her tattoo might cause a little shock, she also knew that no one would ever see this tattoo from across a room. She told Sara, "I will give you credit for your beautiful work, and I will tell them you tried to talk me out of it."

It was perfect. A burning symbol of her power. She also knew, of course, that the eagle-winged bull was still there, invisible to everyone.

The cardboard box landed on the doorstep just loud enough to be heard from inside. Without knocking or ringing the bell, the delivery driver retreated back to his van, following the strict instructions on the invoice not to disturb this client. Irritated by the interruption, Richard Nighton paused his streaming King Crimson channel, rose from his slate-gray-and-white home office, stepped over the fence that kept the dogs out of his workspace, and proceeded to the front door.

On opening the door, Richard was pleased with what he found. He swung the box onto one shoulder.

It was heavy and he carried it into the kitchen like a fresh kill. Setting the box on the polished concrete countertop, he pulled a high-carbon steel santoku from its magnet on the wall. The blade split the packing tape with no effort at all, way too much knife for the job.

The box was beige, the kitchen was white white, and Richard wore muted blue and tan. When the flaps of the carton parted, it introduced a bloom of saturated color into the room. Swirled green Brussels sprouts, blood-red and yolk-yellow tomatoes, and peas as vibrant as jungle frogs topped the box. Richard reached in as if exploring a treasure chest. He uncovered a jar of olives the color of cinnabar and jade, and a spray of spinach as rich and dark as the vintage Jaguar parked outside. Even more prizes lay beneath.

Richard sorted the technicolor cornucopia, silently congratulating himself. He'd joined the CSA years ago, and had always been satisfied, but recently, his supplier had changed to the apparently new "Del Chancho Farms." The produce these people grew was the best he'd ever tasted.

It had been a terrible storm. That night, Bennett found shelter in the narrow, greasy breezeway between a wig shop and a shuttered electronics store. He'd been forced out of his spot under the overpass, and his cardboard lean-to would be useless in that kind of rain. Every surface of the breezeway was running with water, but at least it wasn't pelting down on him. He slept as best he could.

The next morning, he woke to find himself trapped. In the entrance to his little corridor, a six-foot-high mass wedged out the light. Bennet couldn't get around it, but as he searched for some kind of handhold that might help him climb it, he realized the mass had a door. Tentatively, he reached for the European-style handle and turned it. It wasn't locked. The green plastic door swung open.

Inside it was like a tiny room. The first thing he noticed was that if he stretched out diagonally, the space was just big enough that he could lie down and sleep on the floor. Then he saw the tools. The brown plastic side walls had shelves stocked with caulk guns and drill drivers, a circular saw, a hammer, a Sawzall, and more, each secure in their designated slot. On the back wall hung long-handled tools: two shovels, two brooms, a pry bar, a rake, and an electric leaf blower.

Bennet backed out of the shed, used the latch and hinges as rock-climbing holds, and ascended to the slanted roof. He spilled off the other side and found trash and mud pushed up the back of the shed. It had formed a dam and prevented the storm from shooting all this debris through last night's floom of a shelter.

The rain had settled into a cold mist and the morning was just broken, so the street was deserted. Bennett set himself to clearing all the garbage from the back of the shed. When that was done, he gripped the bottom flange of the little structure and tugged. The thing was heavy, but it budged. One shove at a time, some producing no movement at all, Bennet got the shed turned around. Now that it was squared up to the buildings, it looked like it might fit. He forced it back, and back again—sure enough, it slotted into the breezeway with almost no room to spare. When he was done, the shed was set back maybe a foot and a half from the facades of the buildings and looked like it belonged there.

Despite the chill of the morning, Bennet was sweating inside his clothes, but he wasn't finished. He hurried around the corner to his soaked and destroyed lean-to. Many things were gone, washed away, but he retrieved two kitchen-sized garbage bags of his belongings, including a yearbook full of well wishes to somebody else and a soaking wet blanket. He rushed them back to the shed. As he dumped them on the floor, he saw something he'd missed hanging from a hook on a shelf. A key.

Not wanting to hope, but buzzing with sickening anticipation, Bennet tried the key on the door handle. It fit. For the first time in years, Bennet could lock his door.

Two hours later Bee, the wig shop owner, arrived to open up and found that hers was the only store on the street whose front wasn't cluttered with the mud and debris washed down by the storm. Bennet proudly displayed his tools and the work he'd done.

A year after that, he was poaching power from the closed electronics store to plug in his chargers. He knew how to use most of the tools and made enough money sweeping and fixing for the businesses on the block that he could eat two or even three times a day, every day.

And just this morning, Bee asked him if he'd finally made enough to get that little furnished room. He didn't lie when he told her he had. There was enough money for that. But if he implied the had taken the room, that was a lie. He slept stretched out diagonally on the floor of the shed. It fit him perfectly.

Far away from Los Angeles, in Northern California but not quite in the Bay Area, there stand the gray-green and cream buildings of the California Medical Facility. As the name implies, it is a full-service hospital, providing general acute care, elderly care, in-patient and out-patient psychiatric facilities, and even a hospice. What the name does not tell you is that it is a prison.

Since he was in the medium security Level II unit, Baba had a little leeway with his schedule, and he liked to perform his duties for the volunteer program first thing in the morning, when his basso was at its finest. He squared himself in front of the microphone and put his lips directly on the porous surface of the spongy windscreen.

"This dreadful decree of the oracle filled all the people with dismay," spoke Baba. "And her parents abandoned themselves to grief. But Psyche said"—and here Baba modulated his voice just enough to indicate the brave but frightened girl—"'Why, my dear parents, do you now lament me? You should rather have grieved when the people showered upon me undeserved honors, and with one voice called me an Aphrodite.'" Baba tinged his feminine pronunciation with accusatory irony. "'I now perceive that I am a victim to that name. I submit. Lead me to that rock to which my unhappy fate has destined me.'"

Baba paused, allowing the voice of the narrator to break a bit in heartfelt sympathy for the doomed princess. "Accordingly, all things being prepared, the royal maid took her place in the procession, which more resembled a funeral than a nuptial pomp, and with her parents, amid the lamentations of the people, ascended the mountain, on the summit of which they left her alone. With sorrowful hearts, they returned home."

Baba paused again, but this time not to reflect on the abandoned daughter. He was out of breath. His heart still pumped blood to his brain and limbs, but not as well as it used to and maybe never would again. He turned the dial on his rolling oxygen tank and inhaled deeply through the cannula woven through his nostrils. The mustache bristled with annoyance.

Called simply the Blind Project, the prison had started an inmate rehabilitation program to repair and refurbish brailler machines and resurface eyeglasses. This expanded to transcribing audio books into a vast, internationally known talking book library. Baba was a natural, and though he could only record for half the time of other volunteers, between his medical treatments and his general fatigue, he was sought after as a reader and recorder of descriptive video, despite his limitations. Besides, he was getting stronger.

Outside, it was a well- but unfussily-maintained Craftsman Style house on a block of similar homes, all over one hundred years old. Inside, it was clean and decorated with the unchallenging comfort of a budget hotel. There had been additions over the years, and now nine women could live mostly comfortably, though none of their rooms could be called spacious. Two of the women were Administrator Counselors, and the other seven were Residents of the New Century House for Women Veterans.

There was only one Resident home right now, and she took advantage of the solitude to sit on the floor of the room they called the library, relaxing into a trancey playlist and a twenty-minute mindful meditation. She was just coming out of it when Anna, former Resident and current Counselor, popped her head into the room. She waited to be noticed and then announced, "Someone here to see you."

A minute later, a well-dressed woman came into the room. "Candice Moore?" she asked.

"It's just Candy," she answered. "It's not a nickname." Candy moved to one of the comfy chairs and indicated a spot on the sofa. The woman handed Candy a business card and sat down. Candy looked over the card. "Brigid Morrigan – Attorney at Law," and an address in West LA. "I already have a lawyer."

"I know you do," countered Brigid. "That's how I found you."

"Okay," Candy wondered out loud. "Why?"

"Because your parents don't really know where you are."

"So?" Candy's defenses went up, as if someone had shoved her in a club and she wasn't sure yet if it had been an accident.

Brigid paused longer than she should have. She had a plan for this, but it instantly fell apart. She knew she was letting the tension grow, so she retreated back to her last step and repeated it with a slight variation that changed everything. "Because our parents don't really know where you are."

That shove had definitely been on purpose. Candy sprang from the chair to land on the balls of her feet, her hands at low guard. "What the fuck?" She eyed Brigid with feral menace.

Brigid did not exactly remain calm, but she kept herself together, looking up at the dangerous woman. "I'm not saying that we're sisters. Not exactly."

"They may have named me like a stripper, but that doesn't make me stupid."

"No. Maybe it makes them stupid." That didn't make Candy relax her guard, but it did make her wonder.

Brigid went on. "They didn't really give me a name at all, so I found one myself." Now Candy was really curious. "The first thing they told me about you was, 'She just wasn't right. She couldn't be ours.'"

"Sounds like them."

"They were right."

And like parting curtains, Candy saw it. Brigid had the same features, the same eyes and mouth, so close they could be twins—if one had been left out in the sun for a couple decades and the other had been sheltered inside. In a way, that's exactly what had happened. Stunned, Candy lowered her guard.

"If I stand up," Brigid continued, "I'm not coming at you. But this is making me really uncomfortable." Candy looked down on the woman who was not her sister. "Or, you could sit." Candy considered that. She conceded and sat back in the comfortable chair, but now that comfort was in name only. When they were back at eye level, Brigid continued. "Finding our parents reduced me to zero, but there's some power in being a blank slate. I'm building myself from scratch, and I think that's what you're doing too."

Candy knew exactly what she meant, and when Brigid saw that, she continued. "I have a job for you."

"I have a job."

"Why are you the only one home?"

"I'm a model Resident. I have a special curfew."

"Good to hear."

"I run all the tech at a theater in West Hollywood."

"That's mostly at night."

"Right."

"How'd you like to be on days?"

"Doing what?"

"I'm starting a law firm. I want to help people with unique cases like ours."

"If it's unique, there are no other cases like ours."

"'Unique' is the safest word I could use. You'd be surprised what I've seen."

"You'd be surprised what I've seen."

"That's why I'm here. I need an investigator."

"Investigator?"

"And a partner."

Candy grinned, but it wasn't simply joy. It happened the first time she jumped out of a plane, the first time she fired a gun, the first time she snorted speed. It was her reflex reaction to when—good or bad—a change was coming.

In a way, working as a rep was a step down from what she had been doing, but at least it gave her the opportunity to talk about wine, instead of just talking about its waste products. Dara set up her plastic folding table and covered it with white linen. She poured out two different wine tasting flights and began her repeated conversation on sustainability, bouquet, biodynamics, terroir, and pairings. The event was a meet-and-greet marketing mixer thrown by a high-end realtor for her real estate investor clients.

Dara was there representing a new-ish label out of Calabasas, the free tastings being one of the perks for the guests.

At some point, she must have served Mr. Baros, because as she was packing up, his executive assistant came to her table with a business card and printed directions to a vineyard in the Santa Ynez Valley.

So here she was, parked in a newly-paved parking lot, walking up to a barn the size of a small aircraft hangar. The assistant walked out to meet her.

"Ms. Cides, thanks for making the drive." She extended her hand.

"Too intrigued to pass it up," Dara said, as they walked back to the huge, antique structure. "But I did make it clear, I'm not looking to relocate again. Especially not this far."

"Totally understand. You'll find Mr. Baros does too." And with that, she led Dara into the cool dimness of the barn. Inside, light leaked through the old planking and a string of lightbulbs hung like icicles from the loft joists. A giant Easter egg hunt of empty wine barrels lay in random corners, scattered through a space so large it was almost like being outside. In the center of the barn, two rough-edged, heavy cedar planks stretched between two wine barrels to make a high, broad table.

Mr. Baros sat there on a barstool in front of a formal desk blotter, a pen set, notebooks, a laptop, a smart phone, and an old-fashioned desk lamp with a green glass shade. He looked up, saw the women coming and smiled.

Mr. Baros stepped down from the stool and didn't gain an inch of height now that he was on his feet. He came around the desk, repeating, "Welcome, welcome, welcome," in singsong, accented English. Instead of shaking hands, he grasped Dara at arm's length by both shoulders and gave the briefest, gentlest squeeze, in a paternal "welcome home" greeting.

The gesture made Dara freeze with surprise long enough for Mr. Baros to return to his stool. He didn't notice. "Please," he said, indicating the stool his assistant was just putting down opposite him. Dara sat, and the assistant seemed to disappear into the shadows. "Semara already said thank you for driving all this way, I'm sure. But I thank you too."

"It's a pleasure, Mr. Baros."

"But?"

"No 'but.' I just…mentally I brushed up on my Spanish on the drive…"

He smiled, unoffended. "And I disarmed you by being a different shade of brown." Dara shrugged, embarrassed. "I am from Sumatra, but the same mistake happens all the time when I'm in California."

Before Dara could say anything, Mr. Baros reached out and pulled the chain on the brass lamp four times, making it turn off, on, off, on. He chuckled, tickled. "We just had the power put on."

Dara couldn't help but laugh along with him. "Baby steps," she said.

"Quite! That's why you're here."

Dara looked around the dusty space and tried to put this delicately. "It doesn't seem like you're ready for a sales rep."

To punctuate how right she was, he snapped his light off and on one more time. "No. We are not. But," he paused for a little drama, "that's not why you're here."

Dara didn't want to take the bait, but she also didn't want this to be a huge waste of her time. "So, what..."

"Sustainability!" announced Mr. Baros. "Your style was very good at that party. You know what you're talking about, and you're inventive. I looked you up. Recycling." He stopped there, figuring that covered enough of her backstory. "I want this to be the state-of-the-art sustainable winery. Wind, solar, compost tea..."

"Cows," added Dara.

"Yes! See! You will be my consultant."

"That's a huge leap up from my—"

"Never say that in a negotiation." Mr. Barros slowed himself into a storytelling. "I am a serious businessman. Very serious. Very much money. Very dry. I bought this place lock, stock and barrel, pun intended, sight unseen, because I want to make it a completely self-contained... biosystem?"

"Ecosystem."

"Self-contained ecosystem, producing excellent wine. But I don't know how to do it. But you do know how to do it."

Still more than a little blindsided, Dara couldn't stop herself from saying, "I'm a wine rep."

"Do you want to be?" That made Dara stop in her tracks.

"I am very fascinated in the rhythms of the earth, planting by the moon cycles, tapping into the zodiac of the seasons, and also being at the front of science and wine. I can't be here all the time. So I want to surround myself with hungry people of vision. Women, if I can. I have a cellar master from Napa, ready to be a winemaker in her own right. She already knows about you. This place has been growing grapes for years and supplying to other wineries. The vineyard manager happens to already be a woman, which is where I got the idea, but she's no ecodynamics expert."

"Biodynamics," Dara corrected.

Mr. Baros let a wry smirk flash. "You're not so unsure of yourself after all."

Dara's pastoral formative years rolled out behind her eyes, as she considered what Mr. Baros wanted. There were the lessons she learned directly from the old-cowboy-turned-grape-grower, plus what she knew from her hands-on, skinned-knuckles time in the vines, her back-office wrangling, and her on-paper studies and accreditations. If she said yes, she could do the work from her home office, plus frequent trips up the coast. And if she said yes, it would be everything she'd been working toward. Very few things scared Dara anymore, but getting everything she wanted might be one of them.

"Mr. Baros," she said cautiously. He cocked his chin up with anticipation. "My father told me never to work for a man who has electricity in his barn."

"Why not?"

"Because he's gonna have you up working all night."

Mr. Baros' whole face cracked into a broad grin, brightening the barn. "He was right." He stood on the rungs of his stool and offered his hand across the desk. Dara stood and shook it strongly. "Good," said Mr. Baros, straightening with the flick of a finger the already-perfect twin checkmarks of his mustache. "Now, call me Chambu."

Mrs. Smith slowly whisked her roux in a cast iron pan older than she was. When it transitioned from white to cream to amber to the rich, dark loam of cocoa, she halted its progression by adding onions, celery, and—instead of bell peppers—an overflowing handful of stemmed shishitos. Salt and pepper and special herbs dissolved into the stew. While the roux and vegetables slowly simmered together into a rich gravy, she browned the cube steaks. Though this was traditionally a pork chop dish, Mrs. Smith didn't eat swine.

She was happy to take her time for this opulent lunch because her grandson was here, and he had brought his boss. Besides, at her age she couldn't wait for dinner time, and usually had only some raisin toast, or when she was feeling sprightly, a dish of ice cream, before she went to bed.

She joined them in the living room for iced tea while the meat and gravy stewed together. Frankly, she was a little wary of her guest and couldn't devote enough of herself to being a gracious host while also mentally clocking the simmering dish in the other room. With some relief, she announced it was time to check on it.

The tenderized steaks were perfectly ready. Mrs. Smith put one each on three plates preloaded with buttered white rice, and generously ladled gravy over the meat. As a final step, she sprinkled her own secret concoction of spice over everything, dusting the dishes with rose-gold.

At the dining table, her grandson couldn't stop himself from helping distribute the plates of food, despite Mrs. Smith's insistence that he remain seated. She was pleased.

Her guest leaned into the dish and inhaled deeply, with unfeigned appreciation. "Gate," she said, "I haven't eaten a bite and I already know your grandmother is an excellent cook." She turned to her hostess. "Mrs. Smith, this is going to be the best meal I eat all week, isn't it?"

Mrs. Smith couldn't help a bit of a pixy grin. "Oh, I think so."

Good table manners compelled Inanna to slice the steak with her knife, though she could easily have done it with her fork. Mrs. Smith noticed. Just before she put the morsel in her mouth, Inanna observed, "You sprinkled it with allspice and nutmeg. That's for healing and determination and money, plus good luck, clairvoyance, and love."

Mrs. Smith was a little surprised, a little impressed, and a little worried. "Why, yes. Yes, I did."

"A wonderful touch." She chewed and swallowed slowly, so as not to miss a flavor. "I expect that's for your grandson. I can tell you take good care of him."

Mrs. Smith smiled at that, and Gate confirmed it as he ate with pleasure. "She most certainly does. Don't you, Gramma?"

"It also just overpowers the flavor of cherry blossom, so it's not too sweet. Nice and subtle." Inanna continued eating, and so did Gate, but Mrs. Smith froze with her fork halfway to her mouth. "Cherry blossom is for truth telling." She looked Mrs. Smith in the eye. "I expect that's for me."

Mrs. Smith steadily held the gaze and returned her fork to the plate. "Why, yes. Yes, it is," she said, and waited for the priestess's response.

Now Gate was frozen too. He had waited a long time to bring these two women together. He hoped it wasn't a mistake.

Inanna took another bite. "It's so good." When she swallowed, she said, "I bet you could tell me things." Rudely, Inanna's phone rang at that moment. "Oh, I am so sorry."

As Inanna rummaged for the device, Gate told his gramma, "She's sort of on call." Mrs. Smith frowned, conflicted between irritation at the interruption of modern technology she had no time for, and relief at the opportunity to remarshal her wits. She might even have a moment for another concoction.

Inanna looked at her phone and recognized the name of the caller. "Ugh, this guy. He would not be calling me if it wasn't really, really serious." She stood to excuse herself, putting her napkin, folded, by her place setting, not on her chair. "When I'm off, let's finish this wonderful meal." She answered the call, saying, "I'm at an important meeting. Hold a second." She put the phone to her breast and turned back to Mrs. Smith. "You won't need another concoction." Mrs. Smith felt a wave of warm tingles at the easy power of the priestess. "And then...you can ask me anything."

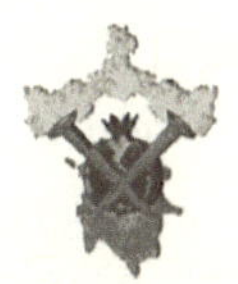

In the clear-skied and chilly mid-afternoon, Thea and Niki walked down the sidewalk, each with a laden plastic shopping bag. Niki swung hers cheerfully. Thea held hers perfectly level, so it hovered over the pavement like an airship. They navigated foot traffic and homeless people, possible delinquents and someone riding a motorized bicycle on the sidewalk. They were aware but not wary, conscious of potential hazards but unafraid. They had seen much worse than these streets had to offer and had survived. They reached a colorful brick building with a Spanish sign and their father's truck waiting outside. They went through the door with a trill from the bell.

Inside, the shelves were repaired and restocked. Even the headless saint stood as a greeter to the girls as they entered. They had tacos, purchased from a semi-permanent stand in the lot of a closed-down gas station.

"We have *al pastor*!" announced Niki.

Alex answered with a distracted, "Okay," and continued to look over a purchase order full of items he didn't recognize. The screws and plates in his collarbone ached, and at the same time throbbed with numbness, but he was finally out of the sling. He thoughtlessly flexed his arm and shoulder as he fretted over the numbers and wondered if he could make this work. The pain there was deep in the fibers of his nerves. He didn't really think about it, the way you don't really notice when your lips aren't chapped.

"Dad," Thea interjected quietly. "Tacos."

Alex nodded again and discarded the spreadsheet. He smiled at the girls. "Best in the city."

They opened the styrofoam containers and let fragrance hit them for a moment before they continued. With neuropathic fingers, Alex squeezed limes over the meat and pineapple, while Niki complained like an informant. "We're reading mythology, but Mrs. Holbrook says they're only stories."

Alex smiled at the girl. "You just let her think that."

Thea had darker thoughts for Mrs. Holbrook, but she kept them to herself.

The old-fashioned phone rang behind the counter and Alex answered it.

"Botanica de Baba." He held the phone closely couched to ear and shoulder when he recognized the voice on the other end, so the girls wouldn't hear. "I've heard of it… Seriously?... Okay, now?... Fine. I know. I know… I'll get it done." The call ended abruptly, and Alex looked to his daughters, about to apologize.

Thea beat him to it. "That was Inanna," she knew.

Niki noisily ate her taco, navigating around the raw onion and not caring at all what was being said around her. Alex considered his growing teen for a moment and decided to just tell her the truth.

"Something about a serpent haunting a Pentecostal congregation." He closed the lid over his food. "Gotta go to work. I'll drop you at your mom's. We can eat these in the truck."

Niki closed up her container and put on her little jacket. Thea looked seriously at her father. "Let me go with you."

Alex leaned in and kissed her on the top of her head, proud of her, and so sorry for disappointing her, again.

Thea knew what that meant. At least she didn't actually have to hear him say no. She handed him his keys. "Set the world on its feet, Dad."

"I do what I can." He led them to the door and flipped the little sign to read, "CERRADA." Alex slapped his thigh. "Yucky!"

The dog appeared in the shadows of the room and ran to catch up with Alex. As he trotted into the light, he vanished. Yucky reappeared as he came into the next shadow and disappeared again before he ran out the door. The dog existed only in shade.

The Workingman headed to his labors and locked the door behind him.

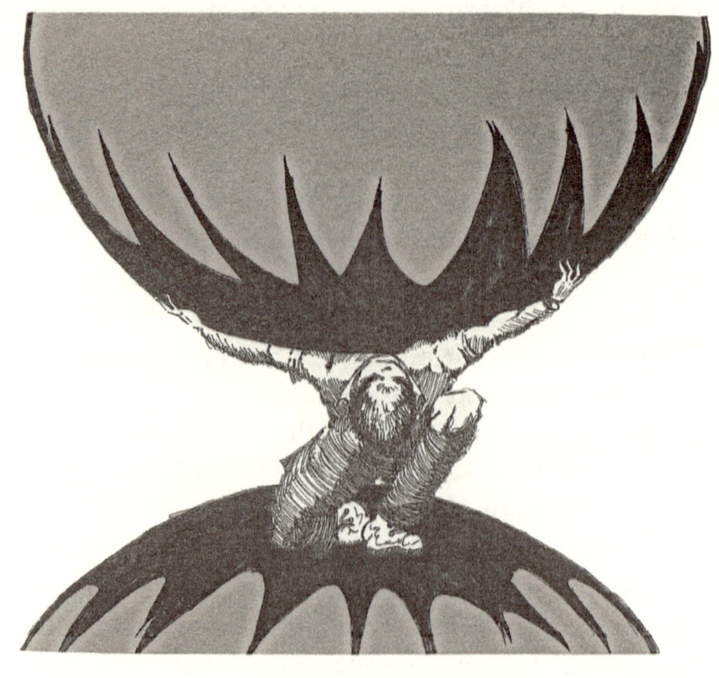

"Set the world on its feet, Dad."

THE END

About the Music

There are no fewer than 19 music references in this story. To hear what was playing in the background or in Alex's head, scan this QR code for the playlist "Overture to the Workingman."

About the Author

Justin DiPego is an author, screenwriter, horseman and artist with a passion for storytelling across multiple genres and media. He lives in a 100-year-old haunted house in South LA and is slowly fixing it up (but not exorcising it) with his wife and their dog.

Also by Justin DiPego:

Seven o'Clock Man

A new breed of homeless is changing the face of LA's Skid Row. Someone is hunting them. Who is the Seven o'Clock Man, and how can one strung out junkie stop him?

Follow for more at DiPegoNow.com